Praise for the Keepsake Cove Mysteries

A Fatal Collection

"Hughes kicks off her new Keepsake Cove series with a charming locale."

—*Kirkus Reviews*

A Vintage Death

— A KEEPSAKE COVE MYSTERY —

MARY ELLEN HUGHES

MIDNIGHT INK
WOODBURY, MINNESOTA

FIRST EDITION
First Printing, 2018

Book format by Bob Gaul
Cover design by Kristi Carlson
Cover Illustration by Mary Ann Lasher-Dodge

Midnight Ink, an imprint of Llewellyn Worldwide Ltd.

Library of Congress Cataloging-in-Publication Data
Names: Hughes, Mary Ellen, author.
Title: A vintage death : a Keepsake Cove mystery / Mary Ellen Hughes.
Description: First edition. | Woodbury, Minnesota : Midnight Ink, an imprint
   of Llewellyn Worldwide Ltd., 2018. | Series: A Keepsake Cove mystery ; # 2
Identifiers: LCCN 2018027586 (print) | LCCN 2018028353 (ebook) | ISBN
   9780738755496 () | ISBN 9780738752273 (alk. paper)
Subjects: | GSAFD: Mystery fiction.
Classification: LCC PS3558.U3745 (ebook) | LCC PS3558.U3745 V56 2018 (print)
   | DDC 813/.54—dc23
LC record available at https://lccn.loc.gov/2018027586

Midnight Ink
Llewellyn Worldwide Ltd.
2143 Wooddale Drive
Woodbury, MN 55125-2989
www.midnightinkbooks.com

Printed in the United States of America

For Madison Hughes, with love.

One

"Ooh, lovely," Dorothy said as she pulled an arrangement of gold and brown leaves dotted with bright red berries out of the large box she'd just opened. "And the perfect size for our lampposts."

Callie smiled, letting out a small sigh of relief. She'd searched long and hard for the right street decorations for Keepsake Cove, the unique section of Mapleton on Maryland's Eastern Shore where she now lived. Filled with every kind of collectible shop anyone could imagine, Keepsake Cove had developed a reputation for stunning seasonal and holiday decorations, which highlighted the Dickensian quaintness of its shops. This, in turn, drew tourists and collectors from far and wide to admire, take photos, and of course shop. In a moment of fearlessness or madness, Callie wasn't sure which, she had volunteered to handle that year's autumn decorations.

It had only seemed right at the time. She'd recently been given so much. First, the collectible music box shop, *House of Melody*, which she'd been shocked to inherit through the untimely death of her Aunt

Melodie. Next, the touching support she'd received from so many Keepsake Cove shop owners once she took over. When the request was thrown out at the association meeting for someone to lead the decorations committee, Callie had raised her hand. It was her turn, she'd decided, and she felt good about it. That is, until her eyes ran down the extensive list of things to do.

But Dorothy Ashby, owner of the vintage sewing shop *Stitches Thru Time*, had volunteered to help, and Pearl Poepelman, of *Pearl's Bangles and Beads*, had offered the unused cottage behind her shop to gather and store the materials. Both offers were extremely welcome—Dorothy's for her experience with the decorations committee, and Pearl's because Callie had visions of boxes piling up ceiling-high in her own tiny cottage.

She absolutely loved the cottage that sat only steps behind *House of Melody*. Her aunt had transformed it into a fairy tale vision with its brightly painted exterior, flower-filled window boxes, and rose-covered trellis arching over the path to the front door. But the little house was not designed for storage, barely offering space for Callie's own belongings. A Cove-full of street decorations would totally overwhelm it.

"I thought these pole banners could hang on the posts at intersections," Callie said, pulling out several rectangular cloth pieces from another box, screen-printed with designs of autumn leaves, corn stalks, or scarecrows. "They're guaranteed for two years, but with luck—and good weather—we might be able to use them longer."

"Love them!" Dorothy declared. "Colorful and tasteful."

"The shop owners will be hanging autumn wreaths on their doors and decorating their own windows, which will add to the scene. And for the big outdoor book event, I've snagged a wagon that we can fill with hay and pumpkins to sit nearby.

"Wonderful! Oh, and a spooky scarecrow and a few floating ghosts would be perfect if you can get them," Dorothy said. "Lyssa Hammond's books are the scary, supernatural kind, you know, which is exactly why we invited her to do an event so close to Halloween."

"Right." Callie's thoughts flew to Grandpa Reed's music box, which might have fit right in with that scene, too, with its disconcerting habit of turning itself on at random times as though commenting or sending a message. But very few people knew that, and Callie intended to keep it that way. "I understand Miss Hammond doesn't live all that far away, in DC, but she'll be staying at a B&B?"

"Yes, that's something she planned long ago. Her house will be going through major renovations. She can't stand the muss and fuss, says she can't possibly write with all that going on around her. So she's taking a room at the Foxwood Inn for the duration."

Callie noticed Dorothy's nose wrinkle slightly at the mention of the inn. "Is that not a good choice?"

"Oh, it's a lovely place. No problem there. It's just the proprietor." Dorothy paused. "My husband." She laughed lightly at Callie's puzzled expression. "You probably thought I was a widow or divorced, right? No, Clifford and I are still married. Legally, that is. We've been estranged for some time."

Callie didn't quite know what to say to that. She *had* assumed the sixty-ish, soft-spoken, gray-haired woman before her was a widow, having heard her addressed as Mrs. Ashby and never having seen or heard of a man in the picture until now. So she settled for "I'm sorry."

"Don't be," Dorothy assured her. "We're both much better off for it. The B&B was Cliff's dream; *Stitches Thru Time* was mine. Despite years of ongoing difficulties between us, I gave the B&B a try when Cliff went ahead and bought it three years ago. We quickly saw it wasn't going to work, so here I am!" Dorothy's smile was so firmly upbeat that Callie had to return it, despite her initial impulse toward sympathy.

Maybe it was the idea that a long-standing marriage deserved to be happier, if only for all the time and effort spent on it? But then Callie thought of her too-long relationship with Hank. She'd been unable to shake herself free of it until her unexpected inheritance offered the opportunity to start anew in Keepsake Cove. She'd dragged along until then, less and less happy but not able to make that final decision until, at twenty-nine, she was suddenly forced to. Callie had to admire Dorothy for apparently taking the reins on her own. At her age, it must not have been easy.

"So," Callie asked, "is Lyssa Hammond likely to enjoy her stay at your husband's B&B?"

"I'm sure she will, once she gets past what I consider Cliff's over-blown greeting. He likes to play the jolly host, welcoming one and all to his home like some kind of B&B Santa Claus." Dorothy's nose wrinkled more firmly this time.

A celebrity author might have to face even more of that jollity, Callie thought. Hopefully she would be able to make it to the peace and solitude of her room, laptop in hand, without too much delay. Callie pictured a bespectacled, hunch-shouldered woman, much more comfortable in the world of her fictional characters than in the real one. Knowing the author had fled her own home to escape the reno-vation noise and fuss, Callie hoped the large crowd expected for the book event wouldn't be too much for her.

"Do you happen to know when she's checking in? I have a Keepsake Cove welcome basket to run over."

"I don't know, exactly," Dorothy said. "But I can find out. I'd offer to take the basket over myself, but I try to keep my visits there to a minimum."

"No problem. I appreciate all the help you've already given me on this committee, believe me."

Dorothy smiled. "Well, let's get the rest of these boxes checked out. Then we can get everything lined up for the volunteers. You do have volunteers, don't you?"

"Oh, yes, several, and we're all meeting here first thing Monday morning, since it's the only day when everyone's shops are closed."

"Sounds like you've got things well in hand, my dear!"

Callie crossed her fingers that the sweet lady before her was right. In her admittedly limited experience, however, it was just when things seemed to be rolling along that bumps in the road suddenly appeared. Sometimes boulders, as had happened on her final visit with Aunt Mel.

But there was no reason whatsoever to think that way, she chided herself. With the current beautiful autumn weather and a crew of great people working together to celebrate it in Keepsake Cove, there was nothing worth worrying about that could possibly go wrong.

⁂

"Lyssa Hammond has arrived at the Foxwood Inn," Dorothy informed her over the phone.

"Great," Callie said. "Thanks. I'll run the welcome basket over as soon as I close up." She was currently on her own at *House of Melody*, as was usual on Sunday afternoons when her part-time assistant, Tabitha, wasn't scheduled to work.

She hung up and glanced around her shop. One customer was browsing through the music boxes Callie considered truly collectible, the ones likely to become family heirlooms. A second person slowly circled the table of musical novelties such as the wind-up, Disney-themed snow globes that were more often chosen by vacationers returning from Maryland's Ocean City.

Callie's favorites, of course, were the collectibles, and she was pleased when the customer in that section finally picked up a lovely box, whose music—*Jesu, Joy of Man's Desiring*—had been listened to more than once. He brought it over to the front counter.

"I'm very fond of that hymn," he said. "And I know my wife will love this inlaid flower design on the lid."

"The mechanism is Swiss," Callie informed him. "But the box itself was made in Italy. It's beautiful, isn't it?"

"I've just started collecting these. I bought my first music box here, a year or so ago." He handed Callie his credit card, and Callie made a note of the name on it, intending to update the list Aunt Mel had kept of regular customers and their preferences. "Another lady was here then," he added. "Older."

"That would have been my aunt, Melodie Reed. She passed away a few months ago."

"I'm sorry. I didn't know."

The man, fifty-ish and tall, looked sincerely sympathetic, and Callie had to swallow the lump that still rose in her throat, especially when the subject came up unexpectedly. She didn't mention the circumstances of Aunt Mel's death—a murder, which Callie herself had uncovered—but simply nodded and turned the discussion back to music boxes.

Her second customer decided to buy a snow globe that played *We Wish You a Merry Christmas*. Inside the globe were two smiling cats wearing Santa hats. Callie remembered having found it at an estate sale during the summer.

"My sister loves cats," the plump woman said. "I'll give this to her as an extra Christmas gift."

"I'm sure she'll like it."

The rest of the afternoon passed with a few more sales, and Callie flipped the Closed sign at five—her Sunday closing time—and headed back to her cottage to take care of Jagger, the large gray cat who'd come as part of her inheritance.

"Would you like a Santa hat?" she playfully asked him as he greeted her at the door, thinking of the snow globe she'd sold. Obviously considering that a silly question, Jagger quickly pivoted toward the kitchen where his food bowl waited. Callie filled it and watched the cat fondly as he dug into it, remembering her first encounter with him and the explanation of his name.

"His previous owner was obviously a Mick Jagger fan," Aunt Mel had said. "I kept the name when I saw how he strutted around the place like a rock star."

Callie sighed softly, leaned over to give Jagger's head a rub, and then turned to get the gift basket from the small kitchen table where she'd left it. There was a variety of wrapped snack bars already in it, a sprinkling of chocolates, Keepsake Cove brochures and coupons for all the shops as well as a map for locating each, and odds and ends of special toiletries. She opened her refrigerator to pull out two perfect apples she'd picked out at a nearby farmers' market and added them to the cache, snuggling them into the plastic grass.

She tore off a sheet of green cellophane and wrapped the entire basket in it, gathering the ends at the top and tying them. She added a pretty bow, then stepped back to scrutinize her work. "Not bad, wouldn't you agree?"

Jagger paused for a millisecond in his gobbling before continuing on.

"I'll take that as a yes." She lifted the basket carefully, grabbed her purse and keys, and, with a promise to be back soon, took off.

Though Callie was becoming more familiar with the area roads, she entered the address of the Foxwood Inn into her GPS just to be safe. But not long after passing the Mapleton town limits, she found that the several signs posted to point the way were all she needed. Within minutes she was pulling up the long gravel driveway.

As the B&B came into view, she took in the charm of its pretty Victorian style, complete with large cupola and veranda. Surrounding gardens were filled with colorful blooming mums, small shrubs, and winding trails, on which at least one guest strolled in the distance.

Callie parked at the side and carried her basket up the steps to the front door, where a sign bid her to enter. Inside sat a hall table with a small brass bell. After waiting a minute or two and seeing no one, she jiggled the bell. As she watched expectantly down the hallway before her, a tall, rotund man suddenly emerged through a door on her left that had been invisibly worked into the wood paneling. It startled her enough to cause her to jump and nearly drop her basket, but he seemed not to notice, only clapping his hands and crying, "Welcome to Foxwood!"

The man's outfit matched the period of the house well: a colorfully embroidered waistcoat and wide tie over a high-necked shirt. From his manner and dress, along with his mop of gray hair, Callie was sure who he was, and she held out her hand. "Mr. Ashby? I'm Callie Reed. I'm here with a welcome gift from the Keepsake Cove Shop Owners' Association for Lyssa Hammond."

"Wonderful!" Ashby smothered her hand in both of his, shaking it and smiling as delightedly as if Callie were a long-lost relative. She feared he might next throw his arms around her in a great hug, but he kept himself in check, only declaring his intention to immediately run up and summon Ms. Hammond for her.

"Please don't interrupt her if she's busy writing," Callie begged. "You could just leave it at her door." But Ashby had already rounded the ornate bannister and was halfway up the stairs.

"Nonsense!" he called down to her. "She'll want to thank you in person, I'm sure." He bounded on up as Callie watched, wavering between a cringe over causing the disturbance and an eagerness to meet someone whose name was on many, many books.

She heard Ashby's energetic knocks on the door and a female voice quietly respond. Soon Ashby trotted back down.

"She'll be down in a minute. Do come into the parlor to wait." He waved with a flourish toward a room stuffed with heavy Victorian furniture but lightened by several tall, lace-curtained windows. Callie admired the numerous perfect details as she crossed the room to one of the velvet-covered sofas, then set her basket carefully on the floor beside her as she sat. Ashby followed behind, clasping his hands and nodding in approval, as though she'd picked the perfect spot.

"So! You're from the Keepsake Cove group. Wonderful event they're setting up for our Ms. Hammond. Not that she needs any help in the publicity department. Oh, no! Her books fly off the shelves." He chuckled delightedly at his own words. "Perfect phrase for her type of books, right?"

Callie smiled politely. "We're honored to have her."

"Good timing, too, with Halloween coming," he said, settling into a curved-leg chair across from her. He launched into a chatter about various subjects that seemed snatched out of the air at random and required nothing from Callie beyond her presence. Her eyes began to glaze over and she thought she could understand Dorothy Ashby's decision to separate from the man, since that was fast becoming her own urgent wish. Much to her relief she heard footsteps on the hall stairs, and Ashby popped up, declaring unnecessarily, "There she comes!"

Callie rose, too, ready to hand over her basket and hurry off. Still holding a certain image in her mind of a reserved and reclusive author, she was surprised when a petite woman of about forty with spiked red hair bounced into the room. Though the horizontal green, red, and black stripes of her tunic emphasized her plumpness, they seemed to be making the statement that color and fun were more important to the wearer. Dark green leggings and ankle boots completed the outfit—an interesting one altogether, Callie thought, for a writer whose work focused on the macabre.

"Hi!" the author cried. "You wanted to see me?"

"Oh! Uh, yes!" Callie stammered, catching herself staring. "How do you do, Miss Hammond." She introduced herself and held out the basket. "From the shop owners of Keepsake Cove."

"Ooh, lovely!" Lyssa Hammond said. She carried her gift over to the sofa, the better to examine it, and patted the cushion next to her for Callie. "And please call me Lyssa."

Ashby settled back into his chair, ready to once again take over the conversation, when a phone rang in another room. He waited, and when it wasn't picked up he rose, looking torn. "Please excuse me, ladies," he apologized, "but duty calls."

Lyssa Hammond flashed a smile but swiftly returned to peering through the green cellophane as he left. "Chocolates!" she cried. "I love chocolates. And apples! Don't they look wonderful. No poison to worry about, I presume?" She asked it in such a serious tone, and with the lift of one eyebrow, that Callie's mouth automatically dropped, which brought a bubbling laugh from Lyssa.

"Sorry. Force of habit. Everything has to have its sinister side when you write what I do, day after day, even thoughtful gifts like these. Thank you so much," Lyssa said. "It's very kind of the shopkeepers to send this. Are you one of them?"

"I am. *House of Melody*. Collectible music boxes."

"Wonderful. Nothing the least bit unsettling or mysterious about music boxes, right? You wind them up; they play."

Oh, you'd be surprised, Callie thought, but she simply smiled.

"I had one when I was a little girl," the author said, looking nostalgic. "I might come by and see what you have."

"Please do. There's brochures for all our shops in your basket if you have a chance to look around. We're very excited about your book signing event."

Lyssa Hammond smiled. "I'm looking forward to it."

Callie got up. "Well, I should let you get back to your work."

Lyssa walked along with Callie, appearing thoughtful, which Callie took to mean she'd mentally returned to her latest work-in-progress. As they reached the door, therefore, Callie offered a quick goodbye, adding only, "It was wonderful to meet you."

Lyssa didn't say anything for a few moments. Then, suddenly digging the toe of her boot like an embarrassed schoolgirl, she asked, "Listen, you wouldn't be free for dinner tonight by any chance, would you?"

When Callie, surprised, didn't instantly respond, Lyssa rushed on. "I know, we've just met. But you seem very nice. I hope nice enough to take pity on a poor author?"

"Oh, of course! It didn't occur to me, but B&B means bed and *breakfast*, not dinner."

"Yes, though they do offer some sort of dinner if you ask ahead. It's just … it probably means dining with … " Lyssa rolled her eyes in the direction that her host had disappeared. "I really don't think I could survive that. Will you help me escape?"

Two

I don't care where we eat, as long as it has a wine list," Lyssa said as she and Callie scurried over the gravel path to their cars, glancing over their shoulders as if expecting Ashby to suddenly appear and halt them. "And my treat, of course, since I roped you into it."

Callie protested, insisting she didn't feel the least bit roped in and was totally happy to dine with their visiting author, but Lyssa remained firm. "Just don't lose me on the highway, please," she begged as she climbed into her shiny red low-slung Corvette. "I can't always see over the big guys in this thing."

Callie promised to keep her in sight and took off, leading the way in her much less exciting and somewhat dusty blue Toyota to Oliver's, a cozy restaurant that was several steps above her more usual haunt of Dino's Diner but not so upscale and popular as to turn away last-minute arrivals. They soon faced each other across the table, Callie struggling to keep her gaze from wandering to the author's spiked red hair.

"You probably think I'm crazy for running out on my first day at the inn," Lyssa said as she pulled off a chunk of the warm bread their waitress had left.

"Actually, I felt much the same after spending just a few minutes in the parlor with Clifford Ashby. But it's a picturesque place, isn't it?"

"The look of it is exactly why I chose it. I could totally see writing a future book around a house like that. Of course, I'd add a dungeon in the basement and maybe a few secret passageways."

The hidden door in the foyer had spooked Callie, but she could understand its appeal to a writer of ghostly tales.

"But then there's Ashby," Lyssa continued. "Always there! It's 'Miss Hammond, would you like ... ' or 'Miss Hammond, can we get you ... ' He would have hovered over us just like that in the parlor if the phone hadn't rung. Hmm." She looked away speculatively. "Maybe I should have the inn's number ready on my cell? To press whenever I see him heading my way?" Her grin quickly faded. "But there's usually staff around to answer, so that wouldn't work."

"Is he like that with the other guests?"

"Not that I've seen."

"So maybe he's impressed with your ..." Callie searched for the right word. "Your celebrity?"

Lyssa's laugh ran up and down the scale at that. "I'm not exactly a Kardashian. Just a wordsmith with a few books out there," she said, which Callie thought was a huge understatement. "But Ashby ..." she went on, more seriously. "There's something just a little creepy about him." She then laughed at herself. "But that's coming from a person who writes 'creepy' all day long, so take it with a grain of salt."

Callie thought she saw a fleeting look of genuine unease on Lyssa's face, though it disappeared so quickly she couldn't be sure. "Can you move to another hotel?" she asked.

"There's not that much choice in the area, unless I want to give up my nice big room. And it's generally quiet there. Too many B&Bs are on busy streets. There's lovely ones in Annapolis, but they tend to be in the bustling historic district. I can't write with a lot of distraction. It's why I left my house." She shrugged. "Small problems, right? As long as I stay in my amazing room, with its wonderful view and four-poster bed, I should be perfectly fine." She took a sip of her wine. "Now tell me about yourself. I know you own a music box shop. What else?"

Callie smiled and began with the bare bones of how she'd moved from West Virginia after inheriting her aunt's shop. She stopped when their food arrived, but after their waitress left, Lyssa encouraged her to go on, seeming genuinely interested. It was flattering, but Callie began to wonder if some of her life might appear in one of Lyssa Hammond's books. When she half-jokingly brought up that possibility, Lyssa's laugh pealed out again.

"Don't worry. If I did, you'd never recognize yourself. I can't help using bits of everyone I meet. Every novelist does it. We're literary Doctor Frankensteins, mixing parts of lots of people together on paper. But what comes out is something totally new. That's not why I'm asking about you, honest. I'd just really like to know."

Pleasantly reassured, Callie continued on but avoided bombarding Lyssa with too many details, skimming over her highlights and slipping in a few minor lowlights, although leaving the main one for a future meeting, maybe.

"So, do you keep in touch with Hank?" Lyssa asked, spearing a green bean from her plate.

"A little, mostly when he calls because he's feeling down and tries to lay a guilt trip on me. It doesn't work."

"Good. He had his chance, right?"

Lyssa then shared a few fun anecdotes from her own life—she was originally from a small town not far from Baltimore and had almost been married twice but decided she preferred singleness—and the dinnertime passed enjoyably. But when they came to their coffee, Lyssa leaned back in her chair to sip. "You know," she said, returning to their earlier subject, "besides his oddness, there's something else about Clifford Ashby that's been niggling at me. I have this feeling I've met him before but can't think of where."

"I've had that feeling, and I hate it," Callie said as she stirred cream into her coffee. "Have you been to Keepsake Cove previously? His wife owns *Stitches Thru Time*. Maybe you ran into him there?"

"No, this is my first visit. Intriguing name for a shop, *Stitches Thru Time*. What does it carry?"

"Vintage sewing things. Collectible thimbles, scissors, needles. Things of that sort."

Lyssa shook her head. "I've never been into sewing, but collectible thimbles sound pretty. I could see a whole shelf decorated with them. So his wife runs it?"

"Well, they're estranged. Dorothy said the B&B was Clifford's dream, not hers. She's a sweet person. Quiet. Very unlike her husband."

"Isn't that interesting." Lyssa took another sip. "But no, I wouldn't have run into Ashby there. Oh, well. It'll come to me if it matters, I suppose."

They moved on to discuss the book event, which was now only nine days away. Callie described the small public park where they planned to hold it, next to the cove that Keepsake Cove itself hugged.

"It's very scenic, especially now with the fall colors. But we'll add as many spooky elements as we can come up with for atmosphere. Our publicity committee has already started spreading the word."

"Fantastic! Fingers crossed that we draw a nice crowd," Lyssa said. She snatched up the bill that had just arrived. "I'm sure this is going to be a great couple of weeks after all. Thanks so much, Callie, for getting it started on the right foot."

She gave Callie a big hug after they both stood, and she promised to come see the music boxes very soon. As they parted outside, Callie looked back as Lyssa climbed into her sports car and started it up. She pictured the author driving up to the big Victorian house whose scenic gardens would now be shrouded in darkness, as night had fallen. The modern lighting indoors, not candles, would certainly help chase the shadows away, but Callie was still happy to be heading to her own cozy cottage. Small though it might be, there were no hidden doors there to startle her. Only a large gray cat who, since he didn't say much, would be definitely preferable to the Foxwood Inn's owner, Clifford Ashby.

❧

Monday morning, Callie was up early to meet with the other shop owners who'd volunteered to help decorate. As she headed out of her cottage lugging a tote filled with odds and ends that she might need, she heard Delia Hamilton hail her from across the greenery dividing their two cottages. Delia, who owned *Shake It Up!*, the collectible salt and pepper shakers shop next to *House of Melody*, was the first friend Callie had made after taking over her aunt's place. Delia was Aunt Mel's best friend, and she'd been extremely helpful to Callie after Mel's death while also dealing with her own loss.

"We'll have a beautiful day for this," Delia said, looking ready for outdoor work. Usually dressed in long skirts that flattered her round shape, Delia currently wore loose cargo cutoffs topped with a purple Ravens sweatshirt. Callie had chosen much the same, though her sweatshirt was a Steelers one that Hank had given her. Though she'd gradually disposed of most of the reminders of their past relationship, a comfy sweatshirt was hard to give up. She hoped she wouldn't get too much flak over the logo.

They headed together toward the meet-up site, Delia carrying a large box of homemade cookies she claimed to have thrown together the night before, "Just to use up some ingredients I had hanging around. I thought I might as well bring them for the group to nibble on." It was the kind of thing Delia always seemed to think of that made her the special person she was.

As they neared Pearl Poepelman's vintage jewelry shop on the other side of Delia's place, they saw Pearl coming down the bordering pathway that led to her unoccupied cottage. The white-haired woman was decked out in a long-sleeved, royal blue dress that flowed over the curves of her short, stout figure. As usual, multiple chains, lockets, and beads from her shop decorated her outfit.

"I just came to unlock the door," Pearl said as she spotted them. "Dorothy's back there already, and the place is all yours. I'd stay, but I'm giving a talk on small business management at our granddaughter's school," she added, which explained her outfit.

"Allowing us the use of your cottage for storage is contribution enough," Callie said.

Pearl wished them a productive day and hurried on her way.

At the cottage, Callie and Delia found Dorothy and another woman peering into the boxes of decorations.

"Good morning!" Dorothy said, looking up with a big smile. "I was just showing my cousin the beautiful things you gathered for us. Jane has delighted me with a surprise visit. It's her first time here in Keepsake Cove." She introduced Callie and Delia to her cousin, who bore a faint resemblance to her but had darker hair. Jane was also a few inches taller, but when she spoke, it was as softly as Dorothy.

"I'm afraid I'm imposing on everyone by being here—Dorothy the most—so I hope you can put me to good use."

"Nonsense, Jane," Dorothy exclaimed. "I'm delighted to have you."

"We can definitely use another pair of hands," Delia assured her.

"Jane drove all the way from Charlotte, North Carolina, on her own," Dorothy said. "I've been begging her to come ever since I opened up *Stitches Thru Time*."

"What finally brought you?" Callie asked, thinking another family event might be occurring in the area. She was surprised when Jane reacted with a deep flush. But was it because the scarecrow-printed pole banner Jane had been holding suddenly slipped out of her hand? The woman swooped down in a fluster to retrieve it, and by the time she'd righted herself, the flush was mostly gone. Dorothy, who'd been standing slightly behind her, probably never saw it.

"Oh, things just worked out at home," Jane said as she placed the banner carefully on top of several others and patted it. "I found I could finally accept Dorothy's standing invitation."

They heard voices of the other volunteers approaching, and the four women quickly became absorbed in the business of the day. Callie glanced at Jane once or twice but saw no signs of further unease. If there was some sort of problem, it was, of course, none of Callie's business. Her business of the moment was getting Keepsake Cove decorated. So she picked up another box, handed it to waiting hands along with the proper directions, and focused on that, straying back to Jane only rarely during the rest of the day.

Three

" $\mathcal{T}$ he Cove looks great!" Tabitha, Callie's part-time assistant, arrived for her late-morning shift, dressed as usual in her own unpredictable style. This time it was a full-skirted cotton dress that reached mid-calf, its dark plaid accented with white cuffs on the short sleeves and a white Peter Pan collar. To top it off, she'd somehow managed to pin her long brown hair into a fairly close semblance of a short 1950s hairstyle. The twenty year-old's spin through the door had lifted her skirt briefly, revealing the stiff crinoline underneath. The entire look brought to mind someone Callie had seen on retro TV.

"Donna Reed?" she ventured.

"Jane Wyatt!" Tabitha corrected in a how-could-you-miss-it tone. "You know, from *Father Knows Best*? I snagged the dress at *Second Thoughts*," she said, referring to her favorite vintage clothing shop.

Tabitha had previously worked for Aunt Mel, and when Callie re-hired her, she'd absorbed all the young woman's extremely useful knowledge about running the music box shop, which Mel hadn't been able to impart. But Tabitha's penchant for creative clothing had taken some getting used to, especially when she combined her outfits with elaborate makeup. That day's makeup was limited to dark red lipstick, which reminded Callie of her grandmother's favorite shade. It looked a lot better on Tabitha.

"Jane Wyatt wore little white gloves, if I remember. And one of those flat-type hats," Callie said.

"I know! I wish they'd had the hat. I have white gloves, somewhere. Just couldn't quite put my finger—ha-ha!—on them. So this is Jane Wyatt at home, not out for the day. Anyway, the decorations look terrific!"

"Do you think so? I worried it might not be enough. Then I worried it might be too much."

"It's perfect," Tabitha said, clicking over to the counter in her high-heeled pumps to drop her vintage purse behind it. "I couldn't have done better myself," she added with a grin. "Which I would have offered to help do, except I had my jewelry to work on." Tabitha had a small, home-based business that sold hand-beaded jewelry, which she was trying to grow. Working part-time at *House of Melody* tided her over financially until such time as it took off.

"We had more than enough help. Laurie and Bill Hart pitched in," Callie said, naming several of the other younger Keepsake Cove shopkeepers. "And Brian, of course."

"Of course." Tabitha smiled but said nothing further. Brian Greer owned the Keepsake Cove Café across the street, and after he'd helped Callie with a few minor incidents, and one particularly dangerous one, during the summer, the two of them had begun spending a lot of time with each other. Callie resisted the term "dating" whenever anyone used it, so Tabitha kept to knowing smiles.

Now Tabitha turned her attention to the music box sitting by itself on the high shelf behind the counter. "Hmm. Looks like I must have skipped that the last time I ran the duster around."

Callie glanced up at the Plexiglas case, complete with lock, that now enclosed Grandpa Reed's music box. It had always been a valued family item, holding fond memories of her grandfather, who had started the original music box collection around which Melodie had built her shop. But having recently learned of the music box's monetary value, Callie had decided to store it more securely. Tabitha had insisted that its habit of turning itself on, on occasion, was Aunt Melodie sending her niece a message; after too many "coincidences," Callie no longer scoffed at the idea, though it still strained all she'd believed up until then. Thankfully, with her aunt's murderer identified and caught, the music box had been relatively quiet, and Callie hoped it would become even more so.

A customer walked in, one that Callie recognized as a regular who had made it onto Aunt Mel's list of serious collectors. The woman studied Tabitha for a moment before asking, "Jane Wyatt?"

Tabitha shot a triumphant look at Callie, who shrugged. The customer, Callie thought, might have had an advantage, being close to her grandmother's generation. Score one for that age group.

❧

After lunchtime, Dorothy Ashby surprised Callie by stopping in. "Jane's watching my shop for a few minutes. I just wanted to tell you that I've been hearing lovely comments on your decorations. You did a wonderful job!"

"It was definitely a group effort," Callie said. "And a lot of fun, wasn't it, with everyone working together yesterday?"

"Oh yes," Dorothy said. "It's what I love about Keepsake Cove. We have our differences now and then, but we pull together when needed. It's what impressed Jane so much."

Callie smiled. "How long will she be staying with you?"

"She hasn't really said. As long as possible, I hope. Jane and I were like sisters growing up. Life separated us, at least geographically, so it's wonderful to spend a good amount of time together."

"You said she drove up from Charlotte. Is her family there?"

"They are. Richard, her husband, passed away some years ago. Much too young. But he and Jane were fortunate to have children, which Clifford and I did not. Her two daughters are married, and her son seems to be heading that way with a wonderful young woman. Jane's very pleased that they're all living nearby."

Callie thought of Jane's flustered reaction to her question on the timing of her visit, at least if she'd read the situation right. Since she was unlikely to ever learn about possible problems in Jane's family, Callie could only hope that whatever appeared to worry the woman would work out okay. Since Dorothy still seemed excited about the unexpected visit, nothing had apparently come up between the cousins.

Dorothy had been wandering casually through Callie's music boxes as she spoke, and she smiled over a tune that played as she lifted one lid. "Jane would love to see these," she said. "She was always the musical one in the family. She plans to browse around the shops this afternoon, so I'll tell her to start in this direction." Dorothy glanced at the clock. "But," she said briskly, "that can't happen until I get back, can it?" She headed for the door and paused before stepping out. "Toodle-oo! Love your dress, by the way, Tabitha."

Tabitha smiled and returned the older woman's wave, but as Dorothy hurried past the front window, Tabitha turned to Callie.

"Toodle-oo?" she asked.

"It probably comes from the time period of the dress," Callie said. "I'd take it as a kind of homage."

Tabitha, looking uncertain, shrugged her plaid-covered shoulders, the white cuffs on her sleeves rising in unison. "Whatever."

When Callie opened up her shop the next morning, she thought about Dorothy's cousin, who hadn't stopped in the previous afternoon after all. Assuming there'd been a change of plans, she wondered if Jane would come by that day. But as she wandered through the tables, realigned a few music boxes, and generally checked on things, she was surprised when instead of Jane, Lyssa Hammond came through her door.

Though the author had promised to stop by the music box shop sometime soon, she didn't appear to be prepared for a day of shopping. Wearing blue jeans and an oversized flannel shirt, she looked like she'd dressed in a hurry. Her red hair flopped limply, as though it had been finger-combed as an afterthought.

"I'm glad I found you," Lyssa said. "I needed to get away from the Foxwood Inn again. This time it's because of something pretty awful."

Callie hurried forward, hoping that this storyteller of the macabre and supernatural was simply being dramatic. The grim set of the author's jaw told her otherwise.

"It's Ashby," Lyssa went on. "They found him dead early this morning. Stabbed. From what I heard, with a pair of vintage scissors."

Four

*L*yssa had been gone for half an hour when Delia rushed into *House of Melody* from her shop next door. "Did you hear?" she asked.

From the distressed look on Delia's face, Callie knew what she was referring to. "Clifford Ashby?"

"Yes. In the park, right where we've been planning to have Lyssa Hammond's book event!"

"She was here earlier," Callie said. "That's how I learned about it. She said the police rousted everyone at the B&B at the crack of dawn after a jogger found the body. The police wanted to know what Ashby was doing in the park, probably very late at night. As far as Lyssa could tell, nobody at the B&B had an answer."

"That's so weird. Do they think it was a mugging? This is Keepsake Cove. We don't draw crime like that here. But I suppose it could happen."

Callie hated what she had to share next. "The murder weapon was a pair of vintage scissors." She paused a moment to let that sink in. "I doubt muggers use weapons of that sort."

Delia stared at Callie incredulously. "Oh, gosh. I don't believe it for a moment, but … oh, poor Dorothy!" They both knew what it meant. Dorothy would be an immediate suspect.

"Let's wait until we learn more," Callie cautioned, and Delia nodded. It made sense and was, in fact, all they *could* do. But it wouldn't keep either of them from worrying.

As Delia returned to her shop, Callie watched through her window, then glanced over at the Keepsake Café across the street, where Lyssa had headed after breaking her news to Callie. Breakfast at the Foxwood Inn was not happening that day, she'd told Callie, as the woman who handled the cooking was too agitated, as well as occupied with talking to the police. Callie would have loved to run over to the café herself to talk with Brian, but the place looked much too busy for any private conversation. Patience would have to be the rule of the day. That, and keeping up a cheery manner for customers who would likely have no idea what had happened and how it was affecting the shopkeepers of Keepsake Cove.

Callie turned from the window to draw comfort from her array of music boxes. She lifted the lid of her newest favorite, a beautiful octagonal wooden jewelry box that played *Clair de Lune,* as soothing a piece of music as existed, Callie felt. As she listened, her gaze wandered toward Grandpa Reed's music box up on its own shelf. It had plagued her with its disconcerting trills from the time of Aunt Mel's death up until her murderer had been caught … What would happen now, with another murder in Keepsake Cove? Would notes of *The Skaters' Waltz* sound out on their own again?

"I love that tune!" an unfamiliar woman cried as she entered the shop, referring, Callie realized after a startled moment, to *Clair de Lune*.

Callie smiled, slipping into shopkeeper mode and to the business at hand. Thoughts of murder and all it entailed would have to wait for a while.

❧

When Tabitha arrived for her shift, it was in a simple dress of soft mauve with matching tights, which told Callie that she'd heard the news.

"I went home to change after I ran into Laurie Hart," Tabitha explained. "I didn't know Clifford Ashby, but I do know Dorothy. Even if I don't see her today, it only seemed right."

Callie smiled at her thoughtfulness. "I'd love to see Dorothy, but I don't think that's going to happen today."

"Laurie said she saw both Dorothy and her cousin being driven off in a police car early this morning," Tabitha said as she rounded the counter. "*Stitches Thru Time* is closed and dark."

Callie found the image of the two women in a police car troubling, which must have shown, since Tabitha added, "It's just routine, I'm sure. Talking to the widow and all, even if the couple has been separated."

"Yes, but I'm afraid there's more." She told Tabitha about the scissors.

"Wow, yeah, that's a lot more. But still," Tabitha said, "even if they're Dorothy's scissors, who's to say who actually used them? I mean, Dorothy's fingerprints should be on her own scissors, right? But maybe they'll find a second person's fingerprints. The actual murderer's!"

"That would be great, and it would end things right there. But if there's no fingerprints ...? Well, as I said to Delia, no use worrying until we have to." Callie dusted her hands together briskly, intending to keep busy and her mind on business.

Unfortunately, as the day wore on, Keepsake Cove shopkeepers kept dropping in, looking for new information or simply rehashing the old, which didn't help Callie's resolve. Occasionally, when someone brought up the possibility of Dorothy being involved, both she and Tabitha argued firmly against that idea. But the more time that passed with no word of Dorothy returning to *Stitches Thru Time*, the more concerned Callie became about her friend.

A few minutes after five, when Tabitha had gone and the shop was still open but quiet, Callie saw Brian step out of his café and lock up. Since the Keepsake Café served only breakfast and lunch, it wasn't unusual for it to close at five. But Brian always had plenty to do after closing to get ready for the next day. His leaving early signaled that something was up.

Callie watched as he walked across the street toward her shop, a light jacket thrown over one of his favorite roll-sleeve plaid shirts that was tucked easily into his slim jeans. Callie was always impressed, and a little jealous, over how Brian managed to stay trim despite being around food all day. Working on his antique car, plus regular bike hikes around the area, a couple of which Callie had joined in on, all helped, she was sure.

As she held the door open for him, he leaned down to give her a quick kiss, but in a distracted way. From his troubled look, she knew he hadn't come about anything good.

"I had the TV news on while I was in the kitchen," he said as he came in.

"Did they report about Clifford Ashby's murder?"

Brian nodded. "And brought up Dorothy."

"In what way?" Callie asked, hoping it was only as the widow.

Brian drew a deep breath. "They didn't actually use the phrase 'person of interest,' but their tone implied it."

"Darn!" Callie had half expected it, but it was still upsetting. "Why does the news have to mention anyone at all unless they're actually charged? It's so unfair when there's no actual evidence!" She paused. "There isn't any—I mean, against Dorothy—is there?"

"The murder weapon belonged to her," Brian said. "That's apparently been verified."

"Is that all? She has a shop full of vintage scissors. Anyone could have bought them or got hold of them somehow?"

"There's the fact that she's still legally married to Ashby, which, I assume, means all his assets would go to her. And with their being estranged, there's always the chance of something having happened between the two of them that we don't know about but the police do."

He looked at Callie grimly. She knew Brian felt at least as bad about it as she did and possibly more so, since he'd known Dorothy much longer. Though she wouldn't call the two close friends, Callie had witnessed an easiness between Brian and Dorothy that came from genuine fondness and trust.

"Is Dorothy home now?" she asked.

Before Brian could answer, two customers walked up to *House of Melody's* window, chatting loudly and pointing as they studied the display Tabitha had set up. When one moved toward the door, Brian said, "I'll head over to her place and see. If I get to talk to her, I'll let you know." He squeezed Callie's hand and stepped aside as the two women entered, then silently lifted a hand in farewell as he slipped out. Callie nodded, then worked at putting on a good face for her customers.

Callie spent a restless night trying to convince herself that no news was good news but not succeeding. At one point she heard the soft thump of Jagger jumping down from the foot of her bed, usually a preferred spot for him, and could imagine his attitude of disgust at her endless tossing and turning. She gave up around six, when it was still chilly and dark outside, and padded down to fix coffee and check the internet for any information on the murder. Unfortunately, crime in Keepsake Cove was edged out by bigger stories in Baltimore and Washington, DC, so she sipped her coffee, ate a piece of toast, and eventually showered and dressed for the day.

Around nine thirty, after having readied her shop, she was surprised to see Lyssa Hammond heading her way once again. Lyssa's bright red hair was back to its carefully spiked mode, and her chunky purple sweater, slim-cut jeans, and boots looked more purposefully chosen than her outfit of the day before. Her walk was brisk and decisive and made Callie, who'd been drooping from lack of sleep, straighten in expectation.

"There you are!" Lyssa cried as she threw open the door to *House of Melody*.

"Yes," Callie answered, wondering where else Lyssa thought she would be. "Is something up?"

"What's up is that a helpless woman in this town is in danger of being railroaded if someone doesn't step in and do something about it quick. I hear you've got experience in this kind of thing, so it should probably be you. But I'm willing to help. Are you up for it?"

Callie gaped in surprise, and in that pause of a few seconds, she heard the notes of *The Skaters' Waltz* sound out from Grandpa Reed's music box.

Five

xperience? Me?" Callie managed to ask.

"Well, yeah," Lyssa countered, not actually saying *duh* but her tone implying it. She didn't appear to have noticed the music box's playing, which had mercifully stopped. "When you told me you'd inherited from your aunt, you conveniently left out the part about her being murdered, so I had to hear that from someone else. With the police calling that death 'accidental,' the murderer would have gotten clean away with it if it weren't for you, right?" Lyssa had her hands on her hips, daring Callie to deny it, which of course she couldn't.

"I, well, yeah. Probably."

"Uh-huh. So you've got the smarts to know when things aren't right. And pinning Clifford Ashby's murder on his wife isn't right. I've just talked to her, and I'm convinced of it."

"You talked to Dorothy? She's home?"

"She's in her shop. But she's a total wreck. Come see for yourself."

Callie only had to think about that for a moment. She was on her own at the shop, with Tabitha not due to arrive for another half hour. But she was eager to see Dorothy and didn't need Aunt Mel's prodding on that score. *House of Melody* would survive being closed for a few unscheduled minutes. She grabbed her keys and followed Lyssa out the door.

"What made you go to *Stitches Thru Time?*" she asked Lyssa as they hurried down the street.

"It was from listening to a lot of talk yesterday during breakfast at the café. I learned a long time ago that if you stay quiet, people tend to forget about you and say a lot of things to each other that can be overheard. I heard plenty of conjecture about Dorothy Ashby and how she might benefit from her husband's murder."

"Oh, gosh."

"I know, and the ones who spoke the loudest and with the most conviction that the police need not look any further had nothing to back it up. So I decided to meet the woman and see for myself. Within two minutes, I couldn't imagine anyone less likely to stab a man to death with a pair of scissors, or with anything else for that matter. But," Lyssa said, looking over at Callie, "I realize that's a quick assumption. You know her better."

"I do, and I agree with you. Brian Greer, who owns the Keepsake Café, feels the same, and he's known Dorothy even longer. Did you talk to him at all yesterday?"

"Nothing beyond giving my food order. He was pretty busy, in and out of his kitchen the whole time I was there." Callie hadn't heard back from Brian the previous evening, so she assumed he hadn't been able to talk to Dorothy, either.

When she and Lyssa arrived at *Stitches Thru Time,* Callie paused to look through the window. Dorothy sat alone behind her counter in an attitude and posture of such abandonment that Callie's heart went out to her. She took a deep breath, then led the way into the shop.

Dorothy brightened a little at sight of them, but her eyes remained sunk in deep shadows. She pulled herself up and came out from behind her counter, and Callie wrapped her in a hug, dismayed to feel trembles in the older woman.

"I'm so sorry, Dorothy," she said, before letting her go.

"Thank you, Callie." Dorothy stepped back, blinking away tears. "It's been a lot to deal with. The love between Cliff and me withered long ago, but still, after so many years together … for something so terrible to take that person … ." Dorothy let out a small sob but drew a deep, controlling breath. "And on top of that, to have to face all those questions from the police. The insinuations."

"But they didn't charge you," Lyssa said, stating what she knew.

"No, and I suppose I should be grateful for that. Jane, of course, assured them I never left the cottage on Tuesday night. Thank heavens she was here! Otherwise there would have been no one to back me up on that. Poor Jane, though. To be dragged into such a horrible situation."

At the sound of her name, Dorothy's cousin emerged from the back office. She had the drawn look of one who hadn't slept much either. Her dark hair, which had been arranged so tidily the day they'd decorated the Cove, appeared to have been merely pushed out of the way. A dab of lipstick, instead of helping, seemed only to accentuate her sallowness, as did the brightly colored cardigan, its cheeriness incongruous to the situation.

"Nobody had to drag me into doing what I could for you, Dorothy." Jane turned to Callie and Lyssa. "I told the police, over and over, how absolutely sure I was that Dorothy never left the cottage all night. I was up, you see, more than once. Sleeping in a strange bed has always been difficult for me. At one point, I even warmed a pan of milk, hoping it would help. I didn't worry about waking you," she said, turning to Dorothy, "because I know how you've always slept like a log. And I could hear you." Jane squeezed her cousin affectionately on the arm. "Not exactly snoring, my dear, but clearly in a deep sleep. I had to repeat that so many times to the police. And in the end, I'm not sure I truly convinced them."

"But you're both back home," Lyssa said. "That's something."

"Yes," Dorothy agreed. "But I feel a huge cloud of suspicion hanging over me. It's awful. Hardly any friends have come by."

"They're probably just learning that you're here," Callie said. "Give them a little time."

"Not a single customer has been in either. They've probably heard my name linked with Cliff's on TV so often that they believe I'm a murderer!"

Callie thought of the wild statements Lyssa had overheard at the café and knew there was truth to that. But the distressed woman in front of her didn't look strong enough at the moment to push through a revolving door, much less stab someone to death. Add to that Dorothy's mild, kindly ways and no one appeared less like a murderer, at least to Callie.

"Dorothy, you're not alone in this," she said. "Lyssa and I believe whole-heartedly that you are innocent."

"Thank you," Dorothy said, her smile quivering.

"And," Lyssa said, "if the police are as bumbleheaded as they seem to be, we're going to do their work for them and find out who actually committed that awful deed. Then everyone else will see you're innocent, too."

"Oh, that would be so wonderful. But how will you do that?"

Good question, Callie thought, but Lyssa, looking filled with confidence, winked. "Don't worry about that," she said. "We have a few tricks up our sleeves. We'll need your help, of course."

"Yes," Callie agreed. "For one thing, what can you tell us about the scissors that the killer used?"

"Oh, those scissors!" Dorothy wailed, shaking her head. "They were a lovely pair, English, made by G. R. Rodgers around 1800."

"Sharp?" Lyssa asked.

"Very. They were patterned on an old Persian design that allowed them to also be used as a dagger. That's exactly what they were called. 'Georgian dagger scissors.'"

Callie winced. "And you told that to the police?"

"I'm afraid so, when they showed them to me in one of those plastic bags. I was only trying to be thorough and helpful at the time. That was before I realized what they were thinking."

"Did you keep those scissors out in the open?" Callie asked.

"Right over here." Dorothy walked over to an area on the wall shelf halfway between her counter and the door. "I showed the police the empty space."

"But they hadn't been sold?"

Dorothy shook her head.

"Anyone could have walked off with them," Jane said. "Dorothy doesn't have security tags on most of her things."

"With the number of items I carry, many quite small, it would be overwhelming and too expensive," Dorothy explained. "I keep the more valuable pieces in the display case. Like that antique sewing box." She gestured toward the wooden item, the size of many of Callie's music boxes and safely inside the under-counter glass case. It had been opened to show a velvet-lined interior in perfect condition, with the usual removable shelf for needles and threads. "That sewing box is worth two hundred dollars. The dagger scissors, old as they were, were priced at only thirty. I made things in the lower price ranges more accessible. People like to pick them up to examine. I've always found my customers to be honest and respectful of my shop. Until now, that is."

"You weren't aware that those scissors had gone missing?" Lyssa asked.

"Not at all. They must have been taken late Tuesday is all I can figure. I was a little busy that afternoon, and with Jane visiting, I closed up in more of a hurry than I usually do. Not your fault at all, Jane," Dorothy assured her cousin, who had winced guiltily.

"It's clear how easily it could happen," Callie said. "With the cooler weather, people are wearing coats or jackets that have pockets. Or an open-topped tote bag could have been used."

"Absolutely. I usually do notice tote bags, particularly on customers unfamiliar to me. But I don't remember seeing any that day."

"Well, however it happened, someone did take them, Dorothy," Jane said.

"And seemed to want to throw suspicion on you by using them as they did," Callie added.

"But who could do such a thing?"

"Exactly," Lyssa said. "Who? You need to think about that."

Callie could tell that the idea of someone perhaps deliberately wanting to implicate Dorothy had further upset the shopkeeper, and she was sorry to see it. But it was an important point. To steal a pair of vintage scissors was one thing. But to steal them in order to murder the husband of the scissors' owner was quite another.

Jane put an arm around her cousin to comfort her, but she looked nearly as rattled herself.

"Perhaps what we should focus on right now," Callie said, "is who would want to kill Clifford?"

Dorothy shook her head helplessly. "He had his shortcomings, definitely, but murder? I can't imagine the monster who'd go that far."

Six

*C*allie would have liked to talk to Dorothy longer, but Pearl Poepelman pushed through the door of the vintage sewing shop, full of commiserations. Laurie Hart could also be seen crossing the street toward the shop, both women likely having just realized that Dorothy had returned. Sure that more shopkeepers would be showing up, Callie cut their visit short and promised Dorothy to return before leaving with Lyssa.

As they walked back to *House of Melody*, Callie said, "Dorothy couldn't come up with anyone who'd have a reason to kill Clifford, but that unfortunately leaves her as the only suspect. If the police don't have any physical evidence other than the dagger scissors, we'll have to dig up a motive for somebody other than Dorothy to want her husband dead. As Dorothy said, he had his shortcomings, but there has to be more. I don't suppose you picked up anything in the short time you've spent at the inn?"

"Other than that Ashby was obnoxiously overbearing? No, I avoided the man as much as possible. But we could talk to the woman who worked for him. I overheard him speak pretty shabbily to her. He wasn't always the jolly Santa Claus figure he tried to present to us."

"Who was that?" Callie asked.

"Paula Something-or-other. She runs the kitchen, and seems to manage the entire B&B from what I can tell. Efficient, but very much a behind-the-scenes kind of person. I don't know what Ashby was ragging on her about, but she was practically cowering, at least before he realized the kitchen door was open and shut it."

"Sounds like someone we should *definitely* talk to."

"I didn't mean that she could be a suspect from that, although if it were me, I'd have definitely thought of murder! But I didn't see enough backbone in the poor thing to believe she'd actually act on it."

"She might be able to tell us a lot about Ashby and his day-to-day dealings. Things Dorothy might not know."

"Right. See, I knew you were the right person to handle this."

Callie didn't feel like she was *handling* anything. Floundering blindly was more like it. But she had to at least try. "Is Paula still at the inn?"

"Yes, for now, at least."

"Good. How about I run over about twelve-ish to talk to her? With you, I mean. Is that a good time?"

"Sure. I'll check that she'll be around as soon I get back, which I need to do right now. I've fallen behind on my book. But I'll be ready for a break around twelve."

Callie's brows went up. "You can actually write during all this?"

"Oh, sure. Once I sit in front of that screen, I turn everything else off and sink into the story. If I waited for the perfect time, I'd never write."

Though still impressed, Callie realized that she did some compartmentalizing herself out of necessity. When dealing with customers, her focus turned to the world of music boxes and away from her personal life. That hadn't always been easy, especially when her grief over Aunt Mel's death was fresh. But somehow she'd managed it.

"That reminds me," Lyssa said. "Is my book event still on?"

"Wow, I haven't even thought of that! But yes, it should be. All the plans have been put in place and the publicity notices sent out. So it's just a matter of last-minute setting up. That shouldn't be a problem."

"As long as there isn't another murder," Lyssa said with a sideways glance and a curl to her lips. Callie knew the author was joking, but she felt a shiver go down her spine all the same.

Was it so unlikely? Maybe not.

❧

Finding two customers waiting at *House of Melody*, Callie hurriedly unlocked the door and waved them in with apologies for the delay. At least news of the murder hadn't totally kept shoppers away from Keepsake Cove. But as the women browsed, they also tossed out questions about the situation, possibly hoping for inside information. Callie deflected the questions politely until finally one of the women purchased a small music box and they both left.

Callie feared that would be the pattern the rest of the day, and she was glad when Tabitha arrived to help. Her assistant had returned to her creative-dressing mode, though toned down a bit. In fact, Callie wasn't a hundred percent sure it *was* creative, at first seeing only that Tabitha's long hair had been parted in the middle, flattened, and tucked unflatteringly behind her ears, and that she wore roundish glasses. Had Tabitha ever worn glasses before?

The clothing was unremarkable to the point of bland: denim skirt, dull-colored vest over a buttoned-up shirt, and dark leggings. Then Tabitha, seeing Callie's puzzlement, hummed a familiar theme song, and Callie caught on.

"Amy! Of *The Big Bang Theory*."

"You got it." Tabitha jiggled her glasses. "Found these buried in a drawer. Clear glass, and left over from some other outfit. When I put them on and looked in the mirror, the rest just fell into place."

Callie was glad that her assistant had come in character, which many of their regular customers had come to expect and enjoyed. Being dressed as someone who was less than obvious that day might keep the questions on that subject and off the murder.

By the time the clock edged closer to twelve, though, Callie had learned that no distraction was going to keep people from discussing the much-more-exciting topic. She was glad, then, to get a break from it all, though aware of the irony that it was in order to pose her own questions to the Foxwood Inn employee. Her own motives, she hoped, were loftier—to help a friend rather than out of idle curiosity. What her inquiry would produce, though, was yet to be determined.

When she drove up the inn's driveway, she saw Lyssa standing at the top, waiting for her. "Paula's in the kitchen," Lyssa said when Callie climbed out of her car.

"Have you talked to her yet?" Callie asked.

"Not about Ashby. Her last name is Shull, by the way." Lyssa spoke over her shoulder as she led the way into the inn, then nearly bumped into an older man in a dark suit who'd just come down the stairs.

"Excuse me, Miss Hammond," the man apologized.

"My fault, George, and please call me Lyssa. Heading out?"

"Yes, for a quick lunch before my meeting."

"I can recommend the Keepsake Café. They're quick and *much* better than the burger chains. It's right across from my friend's music box shop," Lyssa said, introducing Callie to George Cole.

"A music box shop?" Cole asked Callie, adding politely, "How interesting," though his tone hinted that he was not a keepsake collector. "Are your shop and the café anywhere near Mrs. Ashby's sewing shop?"

"About half a block away," Callie said, hoping she wasn't in for more of the gossipy-type questions she'd just escaped from.

But Cole simply nodded and said to Lyssa, "Thank you for the recommendation. I've definitely had my fill of burgers and fries."

Before he made it out the door, Lyssa asked, "Will you be staying on?"

"Possibly," he said, turning. "It depends on a few things, including, of course, Miss Shull's willingness to keep the place going."

"Yes, well, we'll hope for the best."

He bid them a good day and left, Lyssa looking after him thoughtfully. "Cole makes a good point about our stay here being iffy," she said. "I want to hang on, but I'd be happier not to be the lone guest. Most of the others have taken off. Well, one more thing to bring up with Ms. Shull."

They headed toward the partially closed door at the far end of the hall, and Lyssa leaned into the room, asking, "Paula, got a minute?" Without waiting for an answer, she led the way into a large, beautifully updated kitchen with stainless steel appliances and loads of butcher block counter space. The Victorian theme, Callie thought, had been halted at the hall. A second doorway opened into the dining room.

"Paula, this is Callie Reed. She's a friend of Dorothy Ashby."

Paula was leaning over a mound of bread dough, which she'd been punching and kneading. Flour covered her board as well as dotted areas of her face and dark hair. Some, Callie thought, even floated in the air. Though they were not obviously muscular, Callie saw that the woman's hands manipulated the thick dough with ease, probably from much practice, she thought.

"Glad to meet you," Paula said, glancing up quickly, "but I can't stop right now. Please excuse the mess."

"I'd be very suspicious of a kitchen that wasn't messy," Lyssa assured her. "Love that yeasty smell, don't you, Callie? Is it for tomorrow's breakfast, I hope?"

Paula nodded. "Brown bread, made with oats and molasses. It was my mother's recipe."

"My grandmother made something like that, too," Callie said. "We loved it when she brought some with her. She said it was a lot of work."

"It is," Paula agreed, keeping her eyes on her task as she folded and kneaded. "But I like to keep busy, especially after what's happened. This helps keep my mind off of it."

"I hope that also means you'll keep the inn running," Lyssa said.

"I'm willing, but it might not be up to me. Mrs. Ashby owns it now."

"If that's the case," Callie said, "Dorothy will probably be grateful to leave it in your hands for the time being. She's dealing with quite a lot at the moment."

"I'm sorry about what happened to her husband," Paula said. She transferred her smoothly rounded mound into a large greased bowl, turned it over once, and covered it lightly with a towel. She set the bowl in a sunny window, then turned away from Callie and Lyssa to wash her hands at the sink. "I should tell Mrs. Ashby that," she added.

"She'd appreciate it, I know," Callie said, moving to the counter beside the sink. "You might be able to help in another way. Dorothy's under a lot of pressure right now because of the police. It was her scissors, you know, that killed Cliff Ashby."

"Yes, I heard that," Paula said, scrubbing sticky dough and flour from her hands.

"So, you see," Callie said, "it puts Dorothy in a tricky situation. She has a lot to gain, financially, from her husband's death, and the murder weapon belonged to her. On top of that, her alibi—that she was home, sleeping—comes from her cousin. Given their close relationship, the police might be skeptical."

"Oh! I didn't realize that." Paula looked over to Callie. "I'm sorry to hear it, but I'm not sure what you think I can do. Isn't it all up to the police?"

"Only if we let it be," Lyssa said, sliding onto a nearby stool. "We want to make sure they look beyond Dorothy, but we'll need to have something to point them to. You've been working around Ashby probably daily. You must have picked up things about him, right? People he met with? Or maybe certain phone conversations? Anything sinister about them?"

"Sinister!" Paula seemed shocked by the word. She reached for a towel and clutched it to her.

"'Unusual' might be a better word," Callie suggested soothingly. "Anything that seemed off or puzzling. Somebody murdered Cliff Ashby deliberately, not randomly, so there was something going on in his life that brought it on. I only spent minutes with the man, so I need your help to know him. What was he like, generally? Did you like him?"

"Like him?" Paula was less shocked but still seemed surprised, as if the idea had never occurred to her. "He was my boss. I did my job, and he paid me. I needed the job, so I was grateful."

"But he wasn't always pleasant, was he?" Lyssa asked. "I did overhear him raise his voice to you once."

Paula's eyes darted to Lyssa. "That must have been when I didn't call the people to pick up the leaves soon enough. Mr. Ashby wanted things done when *he* wanted them done."

"Was that part of your job?" Callie asked. "Not just looking after the food, but arranging grounds maintenance?"

"I started out just handling the kitchen. But I took care of more things, little by little."

"And wonderfully," Lyssa said, earning her a grateful smile. "So you rose in the ranks, so to speak. That must have been great for your paycheck."

"Well..." Paula hesitated. "We hadn't actually worked that out yet."

She looked so uncomfortable that Callie shifted the subject. Ashby had clearly been taking advantage of his employee, but that wasn't their focus at the moment. "We know Ashby acted as the host, here at the inn. But how else did he fill his time?"

Paula thought a bit. "He spent a lot of time in his office, on the phone."

"Oh? Handling inn business like ordering supplies or booking reservations?"

"No, I did all that. Calls for reservations came in on that line." Paula pointed to a phone at a small desk. "He used his cell phone, mostly, and kept the door closed."

Callie grimaced, thinking *no help there*. Then Paula said, "But once a call came for him on the inn's line. I answered but said that Mr. Ashby was out. I took a message, and it was an odd one."

Callie perked up, and Lyssa sat a little straighter.

"The caller was Karl Eggers, the owner of one of the shops in Keepsake Cove. He said, 'Tell that crook Ashby he can bad-mouth me all he wants. I'm not coughing up.'"

Seven

Karl Eggers?" Lyssa asked.

"My next-door neighbor," Callie said. "He owns *Car-lectibles.*"

When Lyssa waited, wanting more, Callie added, "Karl can be blunt to the point of offensive, though it's generally more bark than bite." She asked Paula, "How did Ashby react when you passed that message on?"

"He laughed."

"Laughed?" Lyssa asked. "He's been called a crook and he laughs? Did he say anything?"

"Maybe something like 'We'll see,' but I'm not sure. Whatever it was, he wasn't upset. That I remember."

Callie met Lyssa's eyes.

The desk phone rang and Paula hurried over to answer it. "Foxwood Inn. Oh, hi, Jackie. Yes, please do come in for your shift. We still have guests whose rooms need doing." She hung up, but when the phone rang again almost immediately, she turned to Callie and Lyssa.

"I really can't talk anymore," she said before picking up. "Foxwood Inn. Yes, we are open. Our website has photos of all the rooms, but if you'd prefer a brochure ... "

The two women left her to her work and headed down the hall. Callie was saying she would talk to Karl Eggers about the message he'd left when she suddenly stopped.

"There's a door here, somewhere," she said. "Ashby popped out of it when I came here that first time and nearly gave me a heart attack." She scanned the wood paneling. "But where is it?"

"A door?" Lyssa asked. "Really? I never saw that." She moved closer to examine the intricately carved and trimmed woodwork, nearly pressing her nose against it. Then she cried, "Aha! Here it is. See the crack?"

Callie leaned in and did see it. "Wow! It blends into the shading of the wood and becomes nearly invisible. Amazing. I wonder where the door leads to?"

"Well, it obviously can't be opened from this side. Maybe Ashby's office is on the other side? I'll ask Paula. Or one of the cleaning ladies might know. I love the idea of a hidden passage in an old house. If it leads to a dungeon, even better! But I can't see it having a bearing on the murder, can you? Since Ashby wasn't murdered here, I mean."

"Maybe not, but anything connected to Ashby, especially if it's mysterious, is worth examining." Callie glanced at her watch. "I'd better get back to my shop," she said, "and drop in on Karl Eggers." The thought didn't thrill her, but it needed to be done. She took off, each woman promising to update the other on what they learned, if anything.

On the drive back, Callie reflected on the difference between looking into Ashby's murder and the search for answers she'd made some months ago after Aunt Mel's death. When she'd lost her aunt, she felt on her own and unsure of her suspicions, which had ended up putting her in great danger. It was good to have Lyssa to work with, as well as to have someone who'd watch her back. Though surely there was no danger to worry about in this case. They were just looking for anything to help Dorothy, and when they found it they'd turn it over to the police. End of story. Callie ignored the tiny uneasiness that niggled at her deep inside, which could surely only be her concern that they'd actually find something helpful.

❧

She had barely opened the door of the collectible model cars shop when Karl Eggers barked, "I won't chip in for funeral flowers, if that's why you're here." Fortunately there were no customers in the shop, which was what Callie had watched for, though she suspected Eggers's regulars were accustomed to his brusqueness and not generally startled by it.

"I'm not collecting," she said to her burly, dark-bearded neighbor.

"Good, 'cause I'm not pitching a penny toward anything for Ashby."

"You obviously didn't like him."

Eggers blew a noise of disgust.

"Would you tell me why?" When Eggers glared, she added, "The woman at the Foxwood Inn took your message about not coughing up. Coughing up for what? What was Ashby up to?"

Eggers glared some more, but Callie ignored it and waited, having learned that Eggers's seeming hatred of all mankind was not necessarily accurate. Though she doubted she and her neighbor would ever chat amicably over coffee, they had progressed to polite, acknowledging nods. All things considered, that was huge.

"Looking to squeeze money out of what he had no business doing," Eggers finally said.

"Such as..."

Callie waited again. *Talk about squeezing! Getting anything out of Eggers is like wringing blood out of—*

"The brochures," he grumbled.

"Yes?"

"He expected me to pay him for carrying my shop brochures at his inn." Eggers harrumphed. "No respectable hotel does that. They're glad to hand out our material. Just as we do with theirs. Tit for tat."

Callie knew that was how it usually worked. She was surprised at Ashby's action. Then she remembered the second part of Eggers's phone message. "You said something about his bad-mouthing you. What was that about?"

"Phhtt! He claimed the rest of the Keepsake Cove shops were going along with his payment plan, and if I didn't, his guests might—" Eggers paused. Not one for air quotes, he made a disgusted waggle of his head. "They might get a *negative* impression of my place."

"Really! He threatened that?" Not putting out someone's brochures in a neighborly way was one thing. Actively backstabbing was another.

"Not in a way that would stand up in court, but I got the gist. He would steer anyone he could away from my place unless I coughed up. He came to the wrong man." With an air of having said all that needed to be said on the subject, Eggers picked up a model car that had been on his counter to examine it before returning it to its box.

Callie watched as he did so. "That makes me think of Nancy Drew's roadster," she said, nodding toward the model.

Eggers's expression asked *who?*, but his anger cooled half a degree as he turned the car over in his hands. "Mercedes Benz 1936, 500K

Special Roadster. Doors open, wheels steer, 1:18 scale. Made by Maisto."

He might not know Nancy Drew, but he knew his collectible cars.

Callie nodded respectfully. "One more question about Ashby, if you don't mind," she said. "He never approached me about that kind of payment for displaying brochures. Do you know who he did ask, besides you?"

Eggers thought about it. "He threw out *Christmas Collectibles* and *The Collectible Cook* as examples. Could be more. Or he mighta just got started."

"Right." Callie decided to ask around. "Thanks, uh, Karl." They had tentatively advanced to first names some time ago, but it still felt awkward to her. She was grateful that they'd also made it to a calm exchange of information. Compared to how they'd started off, that was monumental.

Leaving *Car-lectibles*, Callie longed to immediately head over to the two shops Karl had named, but she still had a business to run, which might be a good idea to check in on. After passing the privacy fence that Aunt Mel had put up between her property and Eggers's when things were prickly between them, Callie peered into *House of Melody*. Tabitha was helping one customer while another waited. She hurried inside.

The waiting customer, it turned out, had chosen a unique and quite charming mini sewing machine music box. Complete with treadle and tiny drawers that opened, it wound up by a key on its side and played when its top was tilted back.

"I love it," the woman buying it said, and Callie did, too, though the sight of the miniature scissors glued next to the machine gave her a twinge. She wrapped it carefully and rang up the sale.

Once the shop had cleared, she asked Tabitha about *The Collectible Cook*, one of the few Cove shops she hadn't yet visited, though that number was shrinking.

Tabitha shook her head. Normally a font of information on all things Cove-related, this was a rare time she couldn't help. "I'm not much of a cook," she admitted, "so I've never stopped in there. Sorry."

"No problem. I'll be going there myself sometime. Just hoped to get a heads-up on the proprietors. Delia will probably know them." She told Tabitha what Karl Eggers had said.

Tabitha's eyes widened. "Sounds nasty. Do you think there's a motive for murder there?"

"No, but it says something about Ashby, doesn't it? If he was someone who thought and acted along those lines, did he stop there?"

"Yeah. Sounds like Karl Eggers put a fast stop to things. But if Ashby pushed others harder and got more—I'm talking extortion, here—nobody's going to want to talk about it, are they? I mean, it would put them in an iffy spot, right?"

"It would. But sometimes you can learn a lot from what people don't say, or their reactions. Or other issues come up. I think it's worth a try." Callie paused. "Ashby approached Karl, who's right next door to me, but not me. I wonder why not?"

Tabitha thought for a minute before grinning. "He went to *Car-lectibles, Christmas Collectibles,* and *The Collectible Cook.* He was working it alphabetically!"

Callie laughed, picturing the man making tick marks on his list. "If so, Delia's *Shake It Up!* didn't hear from him. But I'll check with her when I can."

"Why not go now? And to the other shops, too. I'll be fine."

They heard a small trill coming from Grandpa Reed's music box, up on its shelf. A nudge or a slip in the mechanism? Who knew? Callie smiled. "I guess I will. Call if you need me," she said and slipped the light jacket she'd worn earlier back on. Though sunny, it was still October, and she buttoned it up against the slight chill in the air before stepping out. A glance through the *Shake It Up!* window showed Delia occupied with customers, so Callie crossed the street to *Christmas Collectibles*.

When she'd first arrived, in early summer, it seemed odd to see Christmas decorations blinking brightly in its windows. But according to Delia, some shoppers couldn't get enough of the holiday and loved to add to their collections. The colors of the Christmas shop's window displays did clash somewhat with the fall decorations that Callie and her crew had spread over Keepsake Cove, but the proprietors had gamely hung an autumn-leafed wreath of golds and browns on the door, which Callie appreciated.

A peek through the window showed Howard Graham alone in his shop, so Callie went in to be instantly met with a tinkly version of Jingle Bells and a mechanical Santa Claus calling, "Ho, ho, ho, Merry Christmas!" Though she'd heard it before, it still startled her, and she wondered how Howard managed to keep his sanity with that greeting going off every time someone walked into the shop. Howard's expression, as he looked up, appeared reasonably stable, so apparently it wasn't a problem.

The first time Callie met Howard, she'd wondered why thoughts of her childhood pet gerbil, Mr. Nibs, kept popping up. Then it clicked how mouse-like the man was, both in personality and appearance. He often dressed in a combination of grays and browns, which echoed his drab hair and complexion, and he'd done so that day, too. Howard stood out in his shop only because of the contrast to his brightly colored ornaments, figurines, and centerpieces. If he sold something monochromatic, things like hardware, Callie thought, he might totally disappear.

"How nice to see you, Ms. Reed. How can I help you?" Howard asked it so nicely that Callie felt instantly bad about her musings and banished them. The small desk he'd risen from was piled with paperwork, so Callie decided to get right to the point.

"I just learned about the arrangement Clifford Ashby was trying to set up with Keepsake Cove shopkeepers. Did he approach you about it?"

"You mean about the brochures?" Howard asked, suddenly looking nervous.

"Yes. Did he want you to pay for him to display them?"

"Didn't you pay? He told me all the Keepsake Cove shopkeepers were going along with it."

"I didn't find out about it until today."

"Oh!"

"But there was more to it, wasn't there? I mean, it wasn't just about handling the shop brochures."

Howard turned even paler than his usual color, which Callie wouldn't have thought possible, and he'd started wringing his hands. "He didn't precisely spell it all out."

"Would you tell me what he implied, then? Please? It's important, Howard, or I wouldn't ask."

The shopkeeper looked toward his windows as if hoping someone would come and rescue him from an uncomfortable conversation. Callie checked, too, and had an urge to flip the Closed sign on Howard's door and turn the lock. But she feared the man might then run out his back door. Better to keep things calm. She smiled encouragingly.

"He ... he talked about all the connections he had, people who wrote about collectibles on blogs or newsletters, and about those review sites that come up when you do a search on a business. He said business reputations could be destroyed with a few well-placed words!"

"Wow." Callie could see the possibilities. Perhaps not from one or two review sites. But if a flood of negativity appeared online, it could be devastating. "So you paid what he asked?"

Howard nodded. "He called it a monthly service charge for handling my advertising materials at his inn." He named a sum that, while modest, would add up nicely for Ashby if many of the Keepsake Cove shops kicked in. "He never actually said he'd cause anything bad to happen online or wherever, but I couldn't take the chance. Our busy season is coming up! We depend on it to carry us during the slower times." He looked at Callie miserably.

"I understand," she said soothingly. "Was that all he proposed?"

Howard nodded vigorously. "It wasn't so much, when you think about it," he said defensively. "And Ashby did say, well, not in so many words, I guess, but I got the definite impression that he would put up some positive reviews on those sites. And that'd be a good thing."

So Howard had managed to put a positive spin on the whole disagreeable business.

Callie glanced back, and seeing a customer heading their way, knew their discussion was over. "Thank you for telling me this," she said and turned to go.

As she put her hand on the doorknob, Howard asked, "You won't mention this to my wife, will you? I mean, I never entered anything in the books. She wouldn't be happy about it."

Too bad Ashby hadn't talked first to Mrs. Graham, Callie thought. She'd never actually met the woman, who seemed to be perpetually out of the shop for one reason or another, but if Howard's anxiety over her learning about what he did was any indication, his wife might have reacted much as Karl Eggers had.

"No, Howard, I won't say anything to her," Callie promised and left. The police, on the other hand, might be another matter.

Eight

Callie checked the time, then hurried down the street toward *The Collectible Cook*. It was at the far end of Keepsake Cove, but if she was in luck and the shop wasn't flooded with customers, she'd have just enough time to talk with the Moores, who owned it. Tabitha hadn't been able to tell her anything about them, and all Callie had been able to dig up was their names—Jerry and Renata Moore—as listed on the Keepsake Cove Shop Owners' Association list.

She slowed down to glance into *Kids at Heart*, Laurie and Bill Hart's vintage toy shop, thinking she'd like to pop in and pick their brains about the couple she was going to meet. But she saw Bill busy ringing up a sale and Laurie on the phone, so Callie resumed her pace. She glanced across the street at *Stitches Thru Time*, which appeared to be open but quiet, though it was hard to tell from that distance. She'd stop in on her way back if she could.

Callie found *The Collectible Cook* just to the left off the main street, where she could see a few browsing customers inside. She waited, studying the shop's collection in its window. She realized she'd expected to find antique kitchen items, things like brass kettles or cast-iron skillets that she remembered seeing on a long-ago visit to Colonial Williamsburg. What she found instead were pieces she recognized from Grandma Reed's kitchen and even her mother's, things like stainless steel tea kettles, ceramic cookie jars, and aged *Better Homes and Gardens* cookbooks with faded red plaid covers. There were even a few Corningware dishes with the familiar blue flowers.

Overall, it had a cozy feel, bringing back pleasant childhood memories, and the couple she saw inside waiting on their customers added to the impression with their matching *Collectible Cook* aprons tied around plump middles and their solicitous air. From Callie's viewpoint, they looked like the genial aunt and uncle who'd ply you with tasty homemade food the minute you stepped through their door.

The customers gradually drifted out with their bulging bags. The last one held the door for Callie, which kept the bell from signaling her entrance to the Moores, who had gone to their back room. Unaware that someone was there to overhear, they'd started snapping at each other, their voices carrying to Callie at the front of the shop.

"Why did you have to point out that chip on one of those Pyrex bowls?" the woman's shrill voice demanded. "She wouldn't have noticed!"

"Not notice? The woman wasn't blind, Renata. Do you think I'm stupid?"

"Well, genius, you lost us the big difference in the tag price and the discount she insisted on."

"So you'd rather deal with her showing up to demand her money back? And never coming back? Who's the stupid one now?"

Appalled, Callie tip-toed to the door and opened it, its *ding* bringing immediate silence in the back.

Renata Moore slid out from the back room, a super-sweet and genial smile on her face, tucking a stray hair into her gray-streaked bun before folding her hands serenely over her ample waist. "Welcome to *The Collectible Cook*, my dear. How can I help you?"

You could help me understand how you managed that instant Jekyll and Hyde switch, Callie wanted to say. Instead, she introduced herself, also naming her shop.

"Oh yes!" Renata cried. "Melodie Reed's place. Jerry!" she called. "Come meet our newest Cove shopkeeper!"

Jerry Moore stepped out, not quite as warmly as his wife but courteously enough.

"Well, well," he said. "Mel's niece, right?" He held out his hand. "We heard that you'd taken over, there. Meant to stop in and say hello, but things have been super busy lately, haven't they, Renata?"

Too busy to have made it to Aunt Mel's funeral as well, Callie guessed, since shopkeepers usually mentioned that they'd first met her that day, understanding the difficulty she'd have remembering all their names and faces. What this meant, if anything, she'd think about later. She knew she hadn't seen the two at any association meetings, either.

Renata Moore nodded vigorously. "Crazy busy. We did a total redo of the shop over the summer. I mean *total*! New shelving and paint, which meant shifting the stock constantly."

"Which fell onto me, of course, since *somebody's* back was acting up like it always seems to at certain times." Jerry grinned lopsidedly, apparently trying for humor but failing.

Renata shot him a look. "Well!" she said, turning back to Callie. "Looking for something for your kitchen? Or just out for a little stroll?"

"Neither, actually," Callie replied. "I mean, I love your shop, especially that Kit Kat clock I saw in the window. I remember seeing one of those on a neighbor's wall when I was a kid and being fascinated with the eyes and tail moving in tandem. I'll definitely have to come back. But right now I'm looking for information."

Renata and Jerry, who had been nodding contentedly at her praise, suddenly stiffened. Callie quickly explained. "It's to help Dorothy Ashby. The police seem to be focusing totally on *her* regarding her husband's murder."

"Oh, the poor thing! How awful it must all be for her." Renata's hands flew to her face. She rocked her head back and forth, displaying all the proper elements of distress and sympathy. But after what she'd heard earlier, Callie wondered if that was all it was—a display.

"One of the things I've learned," Callie continued, "is that Clifford Ashby was pressing Keepsake Cove shopkeepers for payment in order to protect their shop's reputation. Apparently there were subtle implied threats involved. I've already spoken with two other shops that Ashby approached. *The Collectible Cook* was mentioned as another. Did he come here?"

"Oooh, yes, he tried that little arm-twisting thing on us," Jerry Moore said. "We told him in no uncertain terms what he could do with it."

Renata nodded, pursing her lips virtuously. "I was shocked that he'd come up with that sort of scheme. And to think that we'd fall for it! We saw through it in an instant, didn't we, Jerry?"

"In an instant. We would have reported it to the police, but it was probably just short of illegal, so why bother?"

They might have reported it to the Keepsake Cove Shop Owners' Association, Callie thought, and saved Howard Graham and possibly a few others some anguish and money. But Karl Eggers hadn't reported it either. Maybe that was another way Ashby picked his shopkeepers—choosing ones he figured would either go along with it or do nothing?

"So how is this helping Dorothy?" Renata asked.

"At this point, it's simply learning about Clifford's activities once he came to this area and opened his inn. Somebody lured him to the park and murdered him. They knew Clifford and Dorothy well enough to use her vintage scissors and throw suspicion on her. The more we can find out about him, the closer we might get to a motive for his murder, and to his killer."

"Yes, I see," Renata said, though looking a bit doubtful. "Unfortunately, we can't help much. That was the only time we spoke to the man. Wasn't it, Jerry?"

"Practically threw him out before he could finish." Jerry looked as though he relished the image.

"So it breaks my heart that we can't do a thing for my dear friend. How is Dorothy holding up?"

If you'd visit your dear friend you'd know. "Fortunately, she has her cousin with her, for now. But it's been hard on both."

"Oh, I'm sure. Terrible times, terrible times. Please give them my love, will you? Jerry, why don't you fix up a nice pot of stew to take over?"

"Oh, really?" Jerry's look was to kill. "Better yet, why don't *you* just whip up a nice casserole, since you're the one with all the free time, or how about—"

"I'd better run," Callie said, quickly interrupting. "Thank you, both, for your help."

"Absolutely!" Renata cried, the super-sweet look back on her face. "Anything we can do. Please stop by again."

Callie nodded, but gave a sigh of relief as she left the shop.

She checked her watch and saw that it was time for Tabitha's shift to be over, so she hurried on back to *House of Melody*, weaving rapidly between shoppers, just short of a trot.

"Sorry to hold you up," she apologized as she rushed in and whipped off her jacket.

"No problem," Tabitha assured her. She grabbed her purse from its spot under the counter. "But I do have to dash. There's a lady coming pretty soon to pick up the necklace I made for her. Had a couple of nice sales here while you were gone," she added as she headed for the door. "And a question about one of our orders. It's there in the message box." She waved toward the cash register. "See you tomorrow!" And she was off, leaving Callie catching her breath but grateful that she had someone as efficient as Tabitha to entrust her business to.

By the end of the day, after having dealt with several customers, a few calls, and one return from a woman who'd already brought back her purchase two other times, apparently having trouble settling on the "perfect" music box, Callie was more than ready to close up. She had just taken two steps toward the door when her phone rang.

"*House of Melody*," she announced as she picked up, trying to inject life into her tone.

"Hey!"

Callie paused, taken aback. Then it clicked. "Hank?"

"How's it going down there?"

Hank was calling, she knew, from Morgantown, West Virginia—not exactly the North Pole, though it had felt like that sometimes when the wind blew on frigid winter days. But Hank was aware, or should be, that Maryland's Eastern Shore was only a few hours' drive away. Happily for Callie, he'd never made the drive.

"It's fine," she answered him. *Other than for a recent murder.* "But I don't have time to chat right now, Hank. Why are you calling?"

"Right down to business, huh? That's good. I don't mind. Our good times are in the past, I know. I get it."

60

Pile it on, Hank, Callie thought, having heard it all before. "Really, I've got to go, soon. What's up?"

"I got this overdue bill," he said. "For the boots."

"Boots?"

"The snakeskin ones. You know, the ones you thought were so great and said I needed to get? You said every good Country Western performer needs to dress right for the part."

Did she? Callie thought she remembered the boots but not the rest of it. "And?"

"And now the bill is gone overdue. Those things weren't cheap. I gotta have the money, now."

"What, you want me to pay for them?"

"*You* told me I had to have them."

"If I did, I don't exactly remember forcing you at gunpoint," Callie said, feeling her blood pressure rise.

"Heck, no. But all the same—"

Did he really think she was going to cover the bill for those things? In the old days, when she was so young and naïve, it might have worked—when she had been so convinced he was the next Johnny Cash or Garth Brooks. Unfortunately, she hadn't realized that it took a lot more than a good voice and an engaging smile. It took discipline and hard work, two things Hank was short on. Knowing him, he'd probably blown his latest gig money on something stupid.

"It was your own decision, and they're your own boots. Pay for them with your own money. I'm going now, Hank. 'Bye." Callie hung up, restraining herself, for the sake of the phone, from slamming it, and stomped over to the door. She expected to hear the phone ring again but instead heard a soft trill come from Grandpa Reed's music box. It felt like an encouraging pat on the back, as though Aunt Mel were saying to her, "Good girl." Callie smiled and felt herself calm down, which was a good thing for her door shade, which might have been yanked off its holder otherwise. It was also a good thing for Brian, who she saw heading across the street toward her shop, and who now wouldn't have to face a snarled greeting.

"Hi," she called pleasantly as she opened her door. "What's up?"

Brian waited for a bicyclist to roll on by before answering. "Feel like a fish dinner tonight?"

"Uh, sure! Are you offering?"

He stepped up on the curb. "I am. Well, actually, Annie is. Mike caught some nice bluefish. They're cooking them up tonight and need someone to help eat them."

"I could be talked into helping," Callie said with a grin. "It sounds great. Can I bring something?" Her mind ran over the contents of her kitchen and quickly noted she'd have to run out for anything beyond microwave popcorn. Fortunately, Brian shook his head.

"I've got plenty of fresh veggies at the café. We can throw together a stir-fry while Mike grills the fish."

There were definite perks to seeing a café owner, besides his being a great all-around guy—who didn't wear snakeskin boots. Callie was about to ask how soon she should be ready when the sound of a car pulling up to the curb caused Brian to turn. She saw his jaw drop, and it wasn't because of the attractive woman with spiked red hair sitting behind the wheel. It could have been Taylor Swift in the driver's seat, but Brian, car aficionado that he was, would have seen only the Corvette.

"Hey! Glad I caught you," Lyssa called. "I've got some interesting info for you."

Nine

*A*s Lyssa climbed up and out of her low-slung car, Callie saw that she'd changed from the comfortable writing clothes of stretchy fleece she'd worn earlier to a chunky, cream-colored sweater over dark-wash jeans.

"I was talking to George Cole after he came back from his meeting." Lyssa turned to Brian. "I sent him to your café, by the way. He loved his lunch!"

"Good to hear. Thanks," Brian said, his gaze moving between Lyssa and her Corvette, lingering longer on the car.

"Anyway, George was in a chatty mood. I'm guessing his meeting ended with a trip to the bar. So I turned the conversation to what we each said to the police the morning after the murder. Guess what I found out."

"What?" Callie asked, not up for guessing.

"Dorothy's cousin, Jane, was at the inn Tuesday afternoon, talking to Ashby."

"Really! She never mentioned that. Did Cole hear the conversation?"

Lyssa shook her head. "No luck. He only saw them from his window." She grinned. "After he said it, he nearly clapped a hand over his mouth, like he'd violated an oath or something. I told him it was all fine. It wasn't like we were on a jury. He didn't know who she was, of course, but he has pretty sharp eyes. Once he described her—with a little prompting—I knew it was cousin Jane."

She paused, looking from Callie to Brian as though something had just clicked. "Hey, I'm holding you guys up, right? I can update you on the rest later, no problem."

Callie looked over at Brian, but he was on the same wavelength. "We're just heading over to my sister's for a fish cookout," he said. "Why don't you join us? There'll be plenty of food."

Seeing Lyssa's hesitation, Callie added, "It's very last-minute and casual. Annie and Mike would love to have you, I'm sure."

"Hmm. Clear it with her first," Lyssa said.

Brian pulled out his cell phone and after a brief chat turned back to Lyssa. "She says please come. She'll throw another potato in the pot."

Lyssa laughed. "Okay then. Just show me the way!"

Callie begged for a minute to freshen up, change, and feed her cat, and Brian needed to pack up his veggies at the café.

"Meet you both back here in fifteen?" he asked.

"Perfect. I have a little stop to make first," Lyssa said.

They took off in separate directions, Callie dashing through her shop to the cottage, where she ran through her tasks in record time. When she returned to the sidewalk out front, zipping up the navy hoodie she'd thrown on against the evening chill, Brian was just driving up in his beloved 1967 red-and-black Impala. In a minute, Lyssa pulled up behind him.

"Want to ride with us?" Callie asked, but Lyssa shook her head.

"I'll follow. Just don't lose me!"

Callie thought it'd be hard for either of them to lose sight of such a distinctive vehicle. She only hoped Brian could keep his eyes away from his rear-view mirror long enough to drive safely. She climbed into the Impala and buckled up.

"Nice of you to invite Lyssa along," she said as he slowly pulled away.

He nodded, eyes flicking, as Callie expected, between mirror and road. "Always room for one more at Annie's," he said.

"Especially if a Corvette comes with her, right?"

He grinned. "I'd love to get a look under that hood."

"And if she invites you to take it for a spin?"

"I'll be cool about it... until I collapsed in a puddle of ecstasy."

Callie laughed. "Let's hope Mike and the boys can contain themselves."

❧

When they came to a stop on Mike and Annie Barbario's driveway and opened their doors, Callie caught a whiff of burning charcoal. It brought a pleasant memory flash of childhood picnics in Grandpa and Grandma Reed's big backyard. "Smells like the grill is ready."

The red Corvette pulled up behind them, and Lyssa climbed out just in time to meet all the Barbarios coming toward them. Callie smiled to herself as she saw Mike, his perpetual five o'clock shadow in place, try to cover his awed reaction, identical to Brian's, over Lyssa's car as they gathered around. The boys, Justin and Ben, at ten and eight respectively had no such inhibitions and let it all out.

"Wow! Wow, wow, wow!" they said in unison, the football they'd been tossing instantly dropped and forgotten, as was Lyssa as they rushed past her to examine the Corvette.

"Boys, mind your manners," Annie admonished, bringing up the rear, her dark pony tail swinging. She had thrown on her husband's gray windbreaker, which engulfed her trim frame. "I apologize for my cavemen brood," she said, welcoming Lyssa.

"No problem. Hey, you have a great place here! And look at that vegetable garden! Bet you guys ate like royalty all summer, right?"

Callie saw Annie beam, and knew that Lyssa had touched on Brian's sister's pride and joy, second only to her family. Annie urged them to come on back, but Lyssa turned to reach into her car first.

"I took a chance that somebody here might like beer," she said, lifting out the heavy carton. Mike immediately stepped up to relieve her of it.

"No risk there," he said, laughing. "Hey! Craft beers! Nice and cold, too."

"They put together a mix for me," Lyssa said. "From local microbreweries. It's a little quirk of mine, trying different things. Hope that's okay?"

"I think we'll do justice to them. Thanks!" Mike led the way around the house to where a blazing fire pit warmed the back patio.

"How perfect," Lyssa exclaimed, going closer to warm her hands.

"We use it a lot," Annie said. "Even in warm weather. Brian, want to tell me what to do with those veggies of yours?"

"I'll take care of it," he offered, though Annie followed close behind as he headed to her kitchen.

"He'll rearrange my whole kitchen if I'm not there," she stage-whispered to Lyssa and Callie, at the same time declining their offers of help. "Mike will put the fish on the grill in a minute, and the rest is done. Help yourself to one of the beers, or there's sodas and other stuff in the cooler."

Ben and Justin resumed tossing their football a little distance from the patio, and Mike tinkered with his grill. Left alone for the moment, Callie asked Lyssa, "So, what else did you find out?"

Lyssa, who had leaned back into a lounge chair, sat forward. "I asked Paula about that hidden door. She said it only leads to Ashby's office."

Callie was aware of some disappointment, though not sure what she'd expected. "Does it connect directly to it?"

"I don't know. She wouldn't let me see. Said as the person in charge for the time being, she wasn't going to allow guests into private areas. She did say the police had been all over the place, and that should be enough."

"Did they know about the door?"

"Paula says yes, but I'd still like to get a look at it myself, on the other side. For one thing, George said he thinks he heard noises coming from behind his wall when Ashby was still around."

"George's room is on the second floor?"

"Right. All the guest rooms are. His is two rooms down and across from mine."

"It's an old house. I've lived in a few older places that had squirrels in the attic. Could it have been that?"

"I asked that, too. He said the noises didn't seem to be overhead but more like on the other side of the wall," Lyssa said.

"Had you heard anything?"

"Nope." Lyssa grinned. "But I don't hear a lot. When I'm writing, I wear earplugs so I can concentrate. And once I'm in bed, I'm out like a light. It'd take a pretty loud fire alarm to wake me up."

Callie wasn't sure what to make of George's noises, but she thought of something else. "You said George described Jane well enough that you recognized her?"

"Yes! Remember that gorgeous cardigan she had on this morning? All those colors swirling around? I remember thinking how cheery it was but way out of sync from her mood. But if it was all she'd packed, she could have been wearing it on Tuesday, too. George described that sweater, along with basics like hair color and such. It was her."

"Did you ask Paula if she'd seen her?"

"I did, and she hadn't. Tuesday was her afternoon off."

Callie told Lyssa about her talks with Karl Eggers, Howard Graham, and the Moores. By the time they'd hashed it over, Mike was calling out that the fish was ready, and Brian and Annie were carrying out bowls of stir-fry and potato salad. Callie and Lyssa jumped up to help bring out plates and silverware, and soon everyone was digging into the food that had been laid out buffet-style.

They all pulled chairs around the fire pit to eat, and after a few bites Annie asked Lyssa about her books. "I'm afraid I haven't read any," she admitted. "Will they all be available at the big event?"

Lyssa laughed. "Let's hope it's big," she said. "Yes, the bookstore people promised to bring copies of everything of mine still in print. God bless them. It's a lot to handle."

"Copies of how many books?" Mike asked after taking a swig of his beer.

Lyssa paused to think. "Nineteen. I think."

"Nineteen!" Justin shouted. "You *wrote* nineteen? Who-ee! I haven't even *read* that many."

"Of course you have," Annie said. "If you count all the Dr. Suesses. And look how many Harry Potters you've read."

"Oh, yeah. And those were big!"

"I love Harry Potter," Lyssa said. "Which one's your favorite?"

Justin frowned, considering, and finally came up with *The Chamber of Secrets*.

"I liked that too," his younger brother chimed in.

"You never read it," Justin said accusingly. "You only saw the movie!"

Annie calmed the argument that ensued and turned back to Lyssa.

"With nineteen books under your belt, you must have started early. Or did you work at something else first? I've heard of authors wanting to get *life experience*." Annie made air quotes on those last words.

Callie glanced at Lyssa, interested in her answer. Did one start making a living as an author immediately, or was it like it was with actors, who paid their bills by waiting tables until the breaks came? She'd heard of overnight successes in publishing, but there seemed to be more stories of long struggles. What was Lyssa's story?

Surprisingly, Lyssa, who hadn't struck Callie as one to hold back, appeared unwilling to share much about her beginnings. "Oh, I've always had stories running around in my head," she said. "And I type fast," she added, laughing. When she saw several pairs of eyes locked on her as the adults waited for more, she flapped a hand. "Trust me, it's never as exciting as people imagine. What I'd like to hear, and haven't yet, is what you two do," she said, waving her fork between Annie and Mike.

Annie laughed. "I take care of these guys, mostly. And I help Brian at the café once in a while."

Lyssa looking genuinely interested. "And grow your garden," she added, which brought a smile from Annie. Lyssa then turned expectantly to Mike.

"Construction inspector," he said. "Keeps me traveling around a bit, but it gives me a day off now and then, for fishing!" He grinned.

Lyssa asked a few questions about his work, which Mike was happy to answer, including that the job used his engineering experience and degree, something Callie hadn't fully understood and was interested to know. Lyssa, she saw, was quite good at getting people talking. Good, too, at holding on to her own privacy. Maybe that came from years of giving publicity interviews?

The conversation moved on, and Callie scraped up the last of her meal and sipped her craft beer, feeling nicely relaxed. When the boys had run off again and it was just the adults left around the fire pit, Annie asked after Dorothy.

"I've heard she's not doing well," she said, explaining that a friend of hers had relayed this after stopping in at *Stitches Thru Time*.

"We saw her this morning," Callie said. "She was upset and worn out but hanging in there."

"Well, Rose must have stopped by after that. She said Dorothy's cousin was handling the shop because Dorothy had taken to her bed."

Callie and Lyssa exchanged glances. "Sorry to hear that," Lyssa said. "We'll check on her tomorrow."

"I can do that," Brian said. "I was going to take a dish over in the morning. The Keepsake Café meatloaf and sides combo she's always liked."

"I'd like to talk to Jane, actually," Callie said. "How about I deliver it? I'll make sure they know it's from you," she added with a grin. "Not that anyone would mistake my cooking from yours."

Brian began to protest the cooking part, but Annie cut him off. "Brian garnered most of the culinary genes in the family, that's for sure. Why you didn't go to that Culinary Institute instead of studying something that ended up putting you at the Airport Authority, I'll never know."

Callie remembered Annie's explanation of how Brian had ended up in Keepsake Cove as a café owner. It seemed he'd suppressed his true calling until the café opportunity in Keepsake Cove arose just as dislike for his government job reached its peak. Lucky for the Cove.

"If I'd gone to the Culinary Institute," Brian said, "I might be stuck in some five star restaurant in New York instead of here, where I make one third as much money while working longer hours."

"Yeah," Annie said. "You're right. Good call." She said it jokingly, but Callie knew that deep down, Annie was happy her brother was nearby and close to her family. Callie was finding it very pleasant as well, though she'd vowed to take things slowly between them. After her serious misjudgment of Hank, even given her immaturity at the time, she didn't fully trust herself to commit to another relationship. Not just yet.

Since it was a school night, it wasn't long after the food was cleared that Annie sent her boys indoors to get ready for bed. That reminded the rest of the group that the next day was a work day. Still, they lingered a bit longer to watch the fire die down, conversation fading comfortably along with it, until Lyssa made the first move.

"It's been great, but I'd better get on back," she said.

Thanks were made all around as chairs were moved back into place. As they returned to their cars, Lyssa stopped at Brian's antique Impala and peered in.

"My dad had one of these," she said. "I never got to drive it. But I always wanted to."

Callie looked over at Brian, guessing what Lyssa was leading up to but also aware of what the car that Brian had spent many hours restoring meant to him. Could he bear to put it in someone else's hands for a few miles?"

"If you wouldn't mind driving mine back to Keepsake Cove," Lyssa continued, "I'd be so delighted to take yours there. What do you say?"

To Callie's amusement, Brian didn't hesitate. "Drive yours? Sure!" He dug out his keys and tossed them to her. "No problem."

Lyssa passed him her keys with a small smile. "You go first. Meet you in front of *House of Melody*."

Callie had planned to update Brian on what Lyssa had shared with her but saw that anything she said from then on would be so much wasted breath. She took her place beside him in the amazing Corvette, buckled up, and enjoyed the motor-purring, super-cushioned ride. There'd be time for murder later.

Ten

That night, before turning out her light and as she waited for Jagger to settle down at his end of the bed, Callie did some browsing on her phone. Lyssa's non-answer about the beginnings of her writing career had made her curious.

She typed *Lyssa Hammond* in the search box and groaned as several pages of results appeared. She sifted through them to find Lyssa's website. There, Callie found plenty of information about Lyssa's books, but very little about the author herself. The *About Me* page was minimal, basically saying she had grown up and currently lived in the Washington, DC, area, which Callie knew covered at least two states as well as the District. It also said she'd traveled extensively, her favorite explorations being old castles in Europe. Lyssa loved meeting her fans and invited them to come see her at various appearances, which were listed on the Events page. Callie went to that page and saw the upcoming Keepsake Cove event, *Meet Lyssa Hammond*, featured prominently, along with directions for getting there.

She left that website and browsed some more, but found very little of a personal nature on Lyssa. Everything online concerned her books and what various critics said about them. Callie gave up and closed her phone. Either Lyssa hadn't drawn enough attention from the media to have her personal life looked into and picked apart, or they'd looked into it and decided it was too boring to report on. Lyssa's claim that it wouldn't be as exciting as anyone imagined was probably all there was to it. Callie reached over to her lamp and turned it off.

In the shop the next day, Callie glanced at the clock often, looking forward to Tabitha's arrival so that she could head over to *Stitches Thru Time*. With few customers to distract her, the time passed slowly, and by the time her assistant walked in, she had dusted and polished every music box in the shop to a gleam.

"Thank goodness," Callie said, dropping her dust cloth behind the counter. "If you'd been late, my arm might have fallen off." She studied Tabitha's outfit of the day. With its fringed shirt and bell-bottomed pants, it was similar to the '60s clothing Tabitha had been wearing when Callie first met and hired her. But the strings of beads woven through her chestnut hair took things to a new level, one that Callie couldn't quite nail.

"Give me a hint," she said.

Tabitha began to sing. When the lyrics reached "the age of Aquarius," Callie got it.

"Somebody from *Hair*?"

"Right! Sheila. I heard they're putting the show on at the high school this year, and that inspired me."

"The high school! I'm guessing with a few adjustments?"

"Adjustments? Why?" Tabitha put on a blank face before breaking into a laugh. "We'll find out." She glanced around. "Why the burst of cleaning? I thought everything was in pretty good shape when I left yesterday."

"It was. I just couldn't sit still. I'm going to run over to *Stitches Thru Time*, for a couple of reasons." She caught Tabitha up quickly on what Lyssa had learned, then reached for her jacket. "I should be back in a few minutes."

As she pulled the door closed behind her, she could hear Tabitha singing another tune from *Hair*. Her assistant had an enviable knack for compartmentalizing and could apparently put worrisome thoughts aside easily, until needed. Callie wished she could do the same. But then, her music boxes might not be quite as shiny.

She crossed over to the Keepsake Café to pick up Brian's dish for Dorothy. As she walked in, she saw the place was filled with the lunchtime crowd. Though space at the café was limited, Brian had managed to squeeze in enough square laminate-and-chrome-topped tables to minimize wait times, though chairs might bump if patrons didn't slide in or out carefully. Brian had just delivered two sandwich platters to a table when he saw her.

"It's ready in the back," he said. "I'll just slide it into a bag."

As she waited at the counter, Callie picked up bits of conversations from the tables—mostly occupied by shoppers, some of whom she recognized as having been to *House of Melody*. Her ears perked up when she heard *Stitches Thru Time* mentioned.

"It was her *husband!*" a sharp-faced woman wearing a jack-o'-lantern-embroidered sweater said to her companion, whose eyes widened in excitement. "Probably did it for money, or, who knows, maybe he was two-timing her! I don't see her there anymore. She's probably been arrested, though they're not saying anything yet."

Callie half-slid off her stool, wanting badly to correct that statement, but stopped when she felt a hand close over hers. Brian shook his head as she turned. "It doesn't help," he said quietly. "I've tried." He held the bagged meal out to her. "There's directions inside on how to heat it. Let me know how she's doing, okay?"

Callie nodded and squeezed his hand in thanks—both for the dinner and for stopping her from wasting her breath. She left, feeling angry with people who jumped to hurtful conclusions. How many customers had Dorothy lost because of it? What was it doing to her health? The truth had to be discovered, and soon, before damage to the poor woman became irreversible.

Callie had come within half a block of *Stitches Thru Time* when she saw a man exiting the shop. Her first thought was *Good, Dorothy's had a customer*. Her second was *That's George Cole!*

He was dressed differently than when Lyssa had first introduced him at the Foxwood Inn. Instead of a suit, he now wore a casual windbreaker over khakis. But his glance in Callie's direction as he checked traffic gave her a good look at his face. He crossed the street before she could catch his eye, and, walking rapidly, soon distanced himself. Had he bought something? Callie didn't think she'd seen a package.

She soon entered the sewing shop herself, spotting Jane standing with her back to her. Jane took a moment before turning, and when she did it was with a flushed face, though she smiled when she recognized Callie.

"Are you okay?" Callie asked.

Jane waved a hand in front of her face with some embarrassment as she nodded. "There was a gentleman just in who said some very nice things. About Dorothy, I mean, and how he hoped things would straighten out for her soon. It just caught me by surprise. It was so nice of him."

"I saw who you mean. George Cole has been staying at the Fox-wood Inn." Callie paused. "In fact, he mentioned that he'd seen you there on the afternoon before Clifford Ashby was murdered."

Jane was quiet for a moment before saying, "Yes, I was there. I went as a favor to Dorothy. She needed some papers she'd left behind. She'd called Clifford and asked for them many times, but he was ignoring her. Dorothy disliked going to see him, face-to-face, so I offered to do it."

"I see. Were you successful?"

Jane sighed. "Clifford made it as uncomfortable as he could, I suppose because he enjoyed it. But eventually he got the papers for me." She paused. "I did tell this to the police."

Callie was glad to hear that, as well as the simple explanation for Jane's being at the inn. "How is Dorothy?" she asked. "I heard she might be unwell."

Jane shook her head. "It's the stress. Her arthritic psoriasis has flared up because of it. I told her to rest and I'd look after the shop. The only thing that will help," she added, her voice rising in anger, "is to have this horrible mess over and done with. I blame it all on her miserable excuse for a husband! If he'd been a halfway decent person to begin with, none of this would have happened."

Callie felt she had a point, though Ashby obviously didn't choose to be murdered in order to aggravate his wife. There were plenty of things to think about when picking a life partner, Callie knew. If only people actually thought of them.

"What was he like when they first met?" she asked. "How *did* they meet?"

"They were both working in the Maryland court system, in Annapolis. He seemed fine, then. Very personable. No one would have guessed…" Jane flushed again. "Sorry. I just feel so bad for Dorothy. That things turned out so terribly for her."

"I understand. Dorothy said you two were like sisters growing up. And still are, obviously, since you're so willing to help when she needs it." Callie looked down at the bag she held. "Oh, I almost forgot! This is from Brian Greer. It's one of Dorothy's favorites from his café menu. It feels heavy enough to be more than a couple of meals for you two."

"How very kind!" Jane said, taking it. "Let me run this back to the cottage and put it in the refrigerator. Would you mind staying for just a minute?"

"Not at all. Give my best to Dorothy. Oh, and would you ask her if I could have her permission about something?" She explained about Paula's refusal to allow Lyssa to explore behind the hidden door at the inn. "Just a note or a call to Paula saying it's okay is all we need."

Jane promised to do so and took off. Left alone, Callie gazed idly around the shop. She wandered over to a shelf filled with small items. One intriguing piece caught her eye: an oval, wooden sewing case, barely two inches long, whose ends had been pulled apart to show a small spool of thread, a thimble, and a paper of needles and pins. The wooden edges of the spool looked darkened and dry from age, though the case itself was well polished. Callie smiled, imagining the woman from another era who would have carried and used such an item.

The rows of thimbles nearby were beautiful, many of them ceramic and colorfully decorated. Dorothy had been right to point out that the size and number of much of her stock made it impossible to protect them with security tags. Anyone so inclined could easily walk off with most of the merchandise, including the scissors that had murdered Ashby.

Callie browsed some more, but her thoughts went back to Jane and the woman's emotional reactions to so much of what had come up, most recently George Cole's kind visit. Perhaps the stress was getting to her, too? But then she remembered their first meeting, on the day of the Keepsake Cove fall decorating, before the upsetting events had begun. Jane had flushed when she'd asked after the reason for her sudden visit. With Dorothy so delighted to have her cousin there, it had seemed a surprising reaction, though it could mean nothing. Jane might be one of those unfortunate people whose feelings tend to inconveniently display themselves whether happy, sad, or somewhere in between. It also implied a tender heart, which was exactly what Dorothy needed at the moment.

"Dorothy was so pleased with the dinner," Jane said, returning from the cottage. "Please give Mr. Greer her warmest thanks. And she will call Paula about allowing you to look around, though she says she never came upon anything particularly odd at the inn during her brief time there."

"That's good to know, and we might not find anything of interest, but—" Callie stopped as she realized that Jane's attention was caught by something, and she turned to see what was going on. An elderly woman had reached for the shop's doorknob but a younger woman came up to stop her. She whispered something in the older woman's ear and steered her firmly away from *Stitches Thru Time*.

Callie winced. "Don't let it bother you too much," she said to Jane. "Once the truth comes out, things will get better."

When she left a few minutes later, she wished she'd been able to do more than offer a platitude with very little to back it up. It was time, she told herself, to come up with something concrete.

Eleven

When she got back to the shop, Callie phoned Lyssa and told her about Dorothy's permission to look around at the inn. They agreed to do so together, after Callie had closed the shop. She had just hung up when Delia walked in and raised a subject that had temporarily slipped off her radar.

"We should review preparations for Lyssa Hammond's book event. It's only four days away, you know."

Callie winced. "You're right. Dorothy was going to handle some of the last-minute things. That's out of the question now."

"The entire park is available again, now that the police have finished with the crime scene. Thank goodness, at least, that it didn't happen close to the bandstand area where we'll be. And I've been checking the weather forecast. No rain predicted … so far."

Callie didn't like the "so far" part. "Tell me again why we decided to have it outdoors?"

"Because we wanted room for lots and lots of people. People who would leave the event in a happy mood and head for our shops. Remember? Keepsake Cove shops will remain open extra late that day."

"Oh, yeah. We probably decided all that back in August when there hadn't been a drop of rain the whole month, right?"

"Probably." Delia grinned. "But we did arrange for a tent, which I can call to double check on, as well as the people bringing chairs. Is Brian handling concessions?"

"He is, and I'll check to see if he needs helpers. I arranged for a hay wagon to be there, and I have volunteers to add pumpkins and ghostly decorations."

"You know what would be great?" Delia asked. "Spooky music playing as people arrive. And maybe as background when Lyssa is reading from one of her books. What do you think?"

"I like it, but how do we get it? Know anyone who can set up a sound system for that? Someone we can afford?"

Delia screwed up her face. "Not offhand. Maybe Tabitha would know?"

"Possibly. Let me start writing this all down. With murder on my mind—past tense only, of course—almost everything else has been pushed out. Poor Jagger is lucky if he gets fed on time anymore. Though he does make sure I hear about that."

"I know what you mean. Just the other day, I—oh! I just had a thought. Jerry Moore might be able to do the sound system. I remember their grand opening. He had music playing through a loud speaker with regular announcements about the specials going on at *The Collectible Cook*. Some of his immediate neighbors weren't too thrilled with it, but it was effective. I'm pretty sure he set it up himself."

"I'll check on the tent and chairs if you'll take on talking to Moore. I was just there yesterday, and that was enough for a while for me."

Delia nodded knowingly. "Will do. He might insist on payment, even though this is supposed to be a volunteer effort by the association. I'll see if I can convince him that it's his civic duty."

"Hope that works. Oh, before you go, there's another thing I wanted to check with you." Callie explained about Ashby's shady payment pressure on certain shopkeepers. "Did he approach you?"

"No, he didn't," Delia said, looking astonished.

"Me neither. It worked with Howard Graham, unfortunately, but not Karl or the Moores. I guess you haven't heard about this happening to anyone else?"

"Not a word. I can ask around, though."

"Karl thought Ashby might have just got started, and Tabitha thought he was doing it alphabetically, which might be why you and I didn't get the pitch. Who would be next after *The Collectible Cook*?"

Delia thought. "There's *Dave's Disney Collectibles*. I can't think of any E's. I'll need to look at the association list. But I can stop in at Dave's and ask when I talk to Jerry Moore."

"That'd be great. And good luck with Jerry."

Delia held up crossed fingers and took off, Callie once again grateful to her helpful neighbor. She made her call about the chairs and tent and checked with her volunteers between customers, and things seemed to be pretty well in hand. The only item she couldn't put a nice, big, satisfying check mark next to was the weather, but she wasn't going to worry about it then. She'd think about that tomorrow.

Callie was in the shop's back office when she heard the front door open. She'd been looking into an order, which appeared to be in transit, so she put her laptop into sleep mode and went out. To her surprise, she found George Cole waiting.

"Nice to see you, again," she said. She remembered Lyssa mentioning *House of Melody* to Cole, but he hadn't seemed terribly interested at the time. Perhaps he'd come about something else? "What can I help you with?"

"I wondered…" Cole paused, gazing about the shop a bit uncomfortably. "That is, do your music boxes come with all kinds of tunes?"

"They do. We have many choices here in the shop, but I can also track down and order specific tunes. What were you looking for?"

"*The Surrey with the Fringe on Top*. That song from *Oklahoma*? It's old, I know. Any chance you'd have it?"

"I'm afraid that's not in our current stock." Callie pulled a large catalogue up from behind her counter. "But let's see what I can find."

She asked a few more questions about the style of box and price range, but Cole seemed much less concerned about that than the music itself, so she pointed out a few boxes in the catalogue that could be ordered with a choice of tunes, including *Surrey*, and let him study them. After a few minutes he pointed to a very pretty rosewood jewelry box.

As Callie wrote up the order, Cole seemed to feel he should explain. "It was one of my late wife's favorite songs. I thought my daughter would like it. Her birthday is coming up."

"What a nice idea. I'm sure she'll love it."

Cole looked a bit uncomfortable again, and Callie assumed it was from thinking about his late wife. She was about to lead the conversation toward more upbeat thoughts of daughters and birthdays when he brought up his wife again.

"Margaret was a good singer."

Callie smiled and nodded.

"Not professional," he added. "But she enjoyed it." He paused. "We came here a few years ago, you know, before she got sick. This area, I mean."

"Oh, really?"

"Stayed at the Foxwood Inn then, too. Previous owner at that time, not Ashby. It's the reason I arranged to stay on after my business was done. Kind of a sentimental journey."

Callie was used to customers sharing stories behind their music box collecting, so she wasn't too surprised to hear Cole ramble on, though it wasn't strictly about music boxes. When he seemed to have come to an end, she brought up a related topic.

"Lyssa told me about the strange noises you heard during this recent stay at the inn. Had you heard anything like that during your first visit?"

"Not at all. Well, the usual groans you'll get from an old structure. But what I heard this time was different."

"From the other side of the wall?"

"It seemed like that. Like the creak of a floorboard. Something you might hear outside your door when someone walks by. But this was solid wall, not a doorway."

"The wall between your room and the next?"

"No, the back wall of my closet. An outside wall."

"Could something have been scraping it on the outside? A tree branch, perhaps?"

"There is a tree there, so it could be that, I suppose. It just didn't sound like a branch to me."

Callie handed Cole his copy of the order. "I'll be at the inn tonight. Lyssa and I have permission from the owner to look around. Would you mind if we checked your closet?"

"Be my guest. But I can't guarantee you'll hear anything."

"Have the strange noises stopped since Ashby was murdered?"

Cole paused, thinking. "For the most part," he said. "I can't be one hundred percent sure." He made a rueful laugh. "But then, who knows? Maybe I've imagined it all!"

Callie had to agree that it could be the case. A single noise heard when half asleep could certainly lead a person to thinking they'd heard more, or believing they'd heard something very different. But she still wanted to see—or listen—for herself.

After Cole left, she began to close up, having seen few shoppers lingering out on the sidewalks. She was interrupted by a call from Delia.

"Good news," Delia said. "Jerry Moore will set up his sound system for the book event."

"Yay!"

"And," Delia added, "at no cost to the association."

"Great! How did you manage that?"

"With surprisingly little effort. Renata jumped in first to fuss about the time, trouble, and possible expense involved, but after letting her rag on, Jerry just said, 'I'll do it. No problem.'"

"Wow. Maybe I've misjudged him."

"Maybe," Delia agreed, though doubtfully. "He is, on the other hand, married to Renata. I could have smacked her at one point."

"Delia!" Callie knew her sweet-natured neighbor would never do any such thing, but it was still shocking to hear her say it. "What about?"

"She was bad-mouthing Dorothy terribly."

"Wow. When I was there, it was all 'my *dear* friend' and 'please give her my love.' What did she say to you?"

"Utter nonsense. Claiming she'd known Dorothy for years and had always been aware of her bad side."

"Oh! How awful. Is it true? I mean about having known Dorothy a long time? I thought they just met here at the Cove."

"I don't know. I didn't have time to stop at *Stitches Thru Time*. One of us should ask her about it."

Callie heard Grandpa Reed's music box ding behind her. Encouragement? Or a simple slip caused by vibrations from a passing truck? Either way, she knew she'd look into it. Statements as vicious as Renata Moore's could not be left unchallenged.

After she finished closing up her shop, Callie went back to her cottage, feeling sorry for Dorothy but also energized to work harder at resolving her terrible situation. Lyssa had requested dinner at the inn, so Callie filled Jagger's bowl, then popped a block of frozen leftover stew into the microwave before stretching out on her sofa. In a minute or so, Jagger joined her, and she relished the downtime as she stroked his furry body and scratched behind his ears.

"Are we on the right track?" she asked as the cat shifted to make himself comfortable while emitting loud purrs. "We've stirred up a lot of questions, but are we getting any closer to finding the answers?"

Jagger nudged her hand, which had paused in its petting.

"Who killed Clifford Ashby and why? It was such a bizarre way to kill him, with a pair of old but very sharp scissors. Did somebody plan it that way in order to implicate Dorothy? How did they get Ashby to the park late at night? And what, if anything, does it have to do with hidden doors and strange noises at the inn?"

She glanced at Jagger, as if for a response, but all she heard was the ping of her microwave. At least she had an answer for her growling stomach. That, Callie thought as she gently eased the cat off of her lap, would have to do. At least, she amended, for now.

Twelve

*L*yssa was waiting, once again, on the graveled driveway as Callie arrived at the Foxwood Inn. The wind had picked up and the spikes of the author's red hair stood up straighter than usual from the gusts. She hugged her cotton jacket tightly to herself.

Callie was glad to have thrown on a warm hoodie, and she pulled the hood up after climbing out of the car. "Is Paula here?" she asked as she scurried over.

"Cleaning up in the kitchen."

"And she got the word from Dorothy?"

"Yup. We have the run of the place." Lyssa turned away from the latest gust. "Let's get inside before I blow away."

They dashed inside, several leaves blowing in with them, and Callie instinctively bent down to grab them.

"I'll get those. Don't worry," a broad-faced woman called as she came down the stairway. "I left the extra blanket you asked for in your room," she told Lyssa.

"Thanks, Jackie. Shift over?" Lyssa asked.

"More than over. Kelsey's quit, so I'm doing it all myself. Those young ones come and go a lot. Don't mind the extra hours, though. Extra time means extra pay, which I can always use."

"Have you been working here a long time?"

Jackie put her hand on her hip and blew a strand of hair off her face. "Thirty years, I guess. And my mother before me."

"Really!" Callie said. "So you must know every inch of the place."

"I ought to," Jackie said, laughing. "Probably cleaned every inch a few hundred times."

"Have you heard any strange noises?" Callie asked. "I mean, noises that seem to be coming from behind the walls?"

Jackie tilted her head, a small smile curling her lips. "You mean, like, ghost noises? No ghosts here, at least none that I ever saw. You'd think there would be, a place this old."

"How old?" Callie asked.

"Built before the Civil War. Or the War Between the States, as some call it. Early 1850s, I'm sure."

"That's old all right," Lyssa said. "Anyone famous live here?"

"No presidents or ones like that. I heard a Quaker family owned it first, but I don't know the name. But now you're here, Ms. Hammond, they can say someone famous stayed here!"

Lyssa laughed. "And have to hear 'Who?' every time? That's great, though, that the house has lasted so long. So many were just torn down."

"Or burned down," Jackie added. "Lots of candles and kerosene lamps around in those days. It's a wonder anyone lived through it. Well, I'm off. Have a good night!"

"You too."

They waited until Jackie had pulled the door closed behind her. Then Lyssa said, "If George Cole has heard odd noises, you'd think someone working here would have, too."

"You'd think. But Jackie isn't here twenty-four seven."

"True. Well, let's get a look at what's behind that invisible door." Lyssa led the way into the kitchen, where they found Paula wiping down her work counter. Pots and pans had been washed, and the stove gleamed. She glanced up as they walked in, not looking all that pleased to see them, Callie thought. Perhaps she was ready to leave, too, and they were holding her up? Callie realized she didn't know if Paula lived on the premises.

"All done?" Lyssa asked. "That poached salmon was amazing tonight," she said, coaxing a smile from Paula. "So, is Ashby's office locked or what?"

Paula left her cloth on the counter and moved to the stove, where she pulled a set of keys off a hook on the wall. "It's through here." She led them down a short hallway that ended at the underside of the hall stairs Jackie had just come down. On each side of the passage was a door.

"This is the one that goes out to the front hall," she said, indicating the door on the left. "The one you don't notice from out there." She pushed it partly open, giving Callie and Lyssa a glimpse into the area of the house they'd just passed through. "And this is the office door." Paula tapped the one opposite. She slid a key into its lock and turned it.

The door swung open to reveal a windowless room with a desk, two chairs, and a large file cabinet. A printer sat on a low table in the corner, against the back wall, with an overly large framed print looming above it. The walls were paneled in dark wood.

Lyssa grunted. "Ugh! What a dungeon. I can't imagine being holed up in here for any length of time."

Paula switched on the overhead lights, which brightened the room.

Callie stepped in, noting that the air was fairly fresh. Ceiling vents apparently kept the warm or cool air circulating as needed. "Did Ashby spend a lot of time here?" she asked Paula.

"I guess. I didn't really pay attention. I had my own work to do. He didn't always leave through the kitchen, either. Sometimes I'd go back to ask him something and found he'd left by that hall door."

"Handy," Lyssa said. She stepped out to try the hall door herself. It opened easily and silently.

Callie circled the possibly twelve-by-twelve room, not knowing exactly what she was looking for but trying to take everything in. "Is this an outside wall?" she asked, tapping on the wall directly opposite the door. The paneling, she noted, was elaborate, with molding that framed large squares from floor to ceiling.

Paula shook her head. "There's a storeroom on the other side, half pantry, half catch-all. That room has the outside wall and a window. You get to it from the kitchen."

"So it seems like this room was blocked off to make the office and the narrow passage with access to the hallway," Callie said. "The first time I was here I rang a small brass bell that was on the hall table. Cliff Ashby popped out through that invisible door within a minute. Could he hear the bell through these two doors?"

"I doubt it," Paula said. "The bell was there to alert me if he wasn't around. He thought it added a Victorian touch. But he had a security camera connected to his computer. Without any windows, he could still see who was coming in."

"Where is his computer?" Lyssa asked. "Oh, wait. The police probably carried it off, right?"

Paula nodded. "And things from his desk and the file cabinet over there."

Callie glanced at the file cabinet, perhaps five feet tall, then gazed around the room one more time. There wasn't very much to see. She moved closer to a framed photo on the wall. It was of Clifford Ashby's retirement party, the clue coming from an overhead banner, and she remembered Jane saying he had worked in the court system in Annapolis. She scoured the faces and finally spotted Dorothy some distance from Clifford and not appearing to be having a good time, despite the corsage pinned to her dress and the drink in her hand.

Callie slid open the desk drawers, one by one, but all that was left were basic supplies such as notepads, staplers, and paper clips. She left the office and turned to her right, taking three or four steps down the short passageway to where it ended beneath the hall stairs. The area there was dark and shadowy, so she pulled out her cell phone and switched on the flashlight app. All it illuminated were dust and cobwebs that obviously hadn't been disturbed for some time.

She went back to the office. Lyssa had opened the file cabinet drawers. "Nothing interesting," she pronounced. "Shall we move on?"

"Sure. Is George Cole in his room?"

"You want to see Mr. Cole's room!" Paula asked, surprised. "I can't let you in without his permission."

"It's okay. He told me he wouldn't mind," Callie said, heading back to the kitchen.

"And he's in there," Lyssa said.

"But what do you think you'd find there?" Paula asked.

"We won't know until we find it," Lyssa said with a grin. "Probably nothing."

"Seems like a waste of time, then," Paula said, not returning the grin.

Paula was obviously growing annoyed, so Callie asked if they were keeping her from heading on home.

"No," she said, shoving her hands into her deep apron pockets. "I've been staying here at the inn since the murder, in one of the smaller rooms. We had cancellations, so there was space available."

"That's very thoughtful of you," Callie said. "Dorothy Ashby will appreciate that, I'm sure."

Paula nodded with a small smile. "I can't do it too long. She'll have to decide what she wants to do with the inn. Keep it or sell it. I know there's someone who's interested in buying."

"Is there?" Lyssa asked. "Who's that?"

"Vernon Parks. I think he was a friend of Clifford Ashby."

"So Dorothy would know about this?"

Paula shrugged. "You'd have to ask her."

"Well, I want to head upstairs," Lyssa said. "Ready?"

Callie nodded and began to turn toward the kitchen until Lyssa stopped her.

"Might as well take the short cut through the hidden door."

"Oh, right!" Callie placed her hand on the door and pushed it open, feeling like she was part of a magic act as she stepped through to the hall. Ashby must have loved springing that surprise on people. With anyone else, Callie would have taken it as childish fun. With Ashby, though, it had a sinister tinge.

The door closed silently behind them, disappearing into the wood paneling. Paula had gone directly to the kitchen, so Callie headed over to the stairway, stepping aside to let Lyssa lead the way to George Cole's room, which she did with energy.

"We're here, George," she cried, giving two sharp raps to his door.

Cole opened it quickly. He had a paperback book in one hand, one finger marking the page he'd been reading.

"Are we interrupting?" Lyssa asked, nodding toward the book.

"Not at all. Just passing the time, but in a good way." He held it up. "It's one of yours."

Lyssa laughed. "You've found the way to my heart, George Cole, you devil, you." Cole laughed, too, but Callie noticed a blush creep into his cheeks. "So, where's that ghost closet of yours?" Lyssa asked.

Cole led them across the room, whose decor was in keeping with the Victorian style of the inn with flowered wallpaper and heavy curtains over the window. A comfy-looking chair still rocked slightly from its recent occupant. The closet was at the far right-hand corner, adjacent to the bathroom, whose door was partly open. Cole slid the closet door open to reveal a dark suit hanging beside two shirts, khaki pants, and a windbreaker. The long back of the closet was against the wall that separated Cole's room from the next one. He pushed aside the suit and rapped at the closet's short end on the left.

"That's where the creaky noise I heard seemed to come from." He stepped aside to let them see.

Lyssa tapped several times at the panel. "It doesn't sound solid, does it?"

Callie had been eying the room's outside wall and comparing it to the closet's inside length. "The closet doesn't extend all the way to the outside wall, although it appears to with the door closed.

Lyssa stepped out to see. "You're right. The closet is shorter inside than it looks from out here. By about two, maybe three feet, I'd say."

"Wide enough for someone to stand in?" Callie asked.

"Maybe," Cole said. "But how would they get there? Perhaps it's just a heating duct, or space for pipes?"

"That's one possibility." Lyssa pressed an ear against the narrow end. "No sound of anything: running water, rushing air, or creaks. We should look at the room next door. It's empty, right?"

When Cole nodded, Lyssa said, "Good. I've got Paula's keys."

She led the way out to the next door, unlocking it quickly. They all marched in and over to the closet in the left hand corner, against the dividing wall from Cole's room. A quick examination showed it to be identical to George Cole's closet, with its shorter inside length and hollow-sounding end panel.

"Hmm," Lyssa said. "Now I've got to check my own closet."

Lyssa's room was on the opposite side of the hall. It was larger than Cole's, with a four-poster bed and broader view of the landscape. Her closet was also larger and crammed with many more clothes.

"No secret compartment as far as I can tell," she said, after struggling through hanging tops, pants, and jackets to reach all the closet walls. "Mine is against the hallway wall, so that's the difference. We should probably look at the rest of the rooms on George's side."

They went into the two remaining rooms on Cole's side of the hallway. Both had the same arrangement as his, with closets hugging the outside wall and mysterious end panels.

"Okay," Lyssa said, hands on her hips. "So what does that tell us?"

"That something is behind the wall of Mr. Cole's closet and possibly the other closets on his side of the inn. But we don't know what."

"It's a pretty narrow space," Cole reminded her. "I think it's for utilities, myself, though not being much into building construction I couldn't say exactly what."

"So, what do we attribute the creaking noises you heard to?" Lyssa asked. "Water pipes or heating ducts?"

Cole shrugged. "Wood shrinkage or expansion?"

"Ghosts?" Lyssa said it with a combination of humor and wishfulness.

"The major question is what it has to do with Clifford Ashby's murder," Callie pointed out. "Right now, I don't see any connection, but it's still an unanswered question which I'd like the answer to. Remember how Mike, Brian's brother-in-law, said he's a construction inspector?" she asked Lyssa. "Maybe he can help us."

"Great idea! Call and get him over here."

"It's a little late for that," Callie said, smiling. "But I'll see if I can get him soon."

They all agreed that would be their next step. As they said good-bye, George Cole asked about Lyssa's book event.

"It's Tuesday evening. At the park, right?" Lyssa turned to Callie for confirmation.

"Right." *Which gives me four more days to get everything ready*, Callie thought with a slight feeling of panic. But she smiled confidently at the guest and star of the event, who shouldn't have to worry about any behind-the-scenes hassles. "It'll be a terrific night!" she added. *Assuming it doesn't storm, that people actually show up, that the sound system is in place, and, and, and…*

Thirteen

The next morning, Callie was finishing her breakfast when she heard a tap at the cottage door. Glancing out the living room window, she was surprised to see Brian on the doorstep.

"Hi!" she cried, pulling open the door. "What's up?"

"Sorry to come by this early. But I wanted to tell you something before I opened the café."

Callie waved him in. She was holding her mug of coffee but didn't bother to offer Brian a cup. Besides making superior coffee himself at his café, his body language fairly shouted *not much time!*

"My car club met last night," he said, referring to the club for antique car enthusiasts that Callie had heard him mention occasionally. "After the meeting, a few of us went out for beer. One of the guys is a deputy with our local police."

"Oh!"

Brian dropped onto the sofa, apparently not noticing Jagger, who'd been cleaning himself nearby and leapt away with jack-in-the-box swiftness. Callie sank onto a chair.

"Clifford Ashby's murder case has been turned over to the state police, so this guy, Jason, isn't involved anymore, though maybe he still shouldn't be saying anything about it. But after a couple of beers, he let slip something that came up early on in the case."

Callie was all ears. "Yes?"

"A friend of Clifford Ashby's pointed the finger at Dorothy almost immediately after the murder was discovered. A guy name Vernon Parks."

"Vernon Parks!"

"You know him?"

"I heard his name just last night. Paula, the woman who's been keeping the inn going, told us Vernon Parks has an eye on buying the place."

"Well, that's interesting."

"Isn't it? He'd have a motive for having Dorothy charged with murder. But does he have a motive for murder?"

Brian shook his head. "He has the perfect alibi. Apparently he's a friend of our police chief, and they were both out of town that night at a golf tournament. The chief hurried back when the murder was discovered the next morning, and Parks came with him. He had the chief's ear with his opinion of Dorothy."

"But the chief isn't in charge of the case anymore."

"No. But we have to assume that everything was passed on to the state police."

"I imagine so," Callie said. "Did Jason indicate they were following any other leads?"

Brian shook his head. "That's all he said about it."

"Hmm. How good of a friend are you with him? "

Brian smiled. "He was looking for someone to help him with a job on his '58 Ford. I could volunteer."

"That would be very generous of you. And maybe take along a few beers? You know, in case you and he get thirsty."

"I just might," Brian said, grinning wider. He glanced at the clock. "Gotta go," he said, popping up from the couch.

"Thanks for the info," Callie said. "I'll see if I can talk to Dorothy about Vernon Parks."

Brian nodded and dashed out the door. Callie's thoughts churned as she stood in her open doorway, still holding her coffee mug, until she shook herself to get started on her own day. She longed to get on her laptop and run a search on Vernon Parks, but that would have to wait. First she had to open up *House of Melody*. Saturdays were often her busiest day of the week, but she hoped to catch a moment to investigate.

The moment came after several browsing customers left her shop later that morning, one clutching a purchase of a favorite of Callie's: an angel figure outlined in crystals, which rotated on its base as the music played, casting rainbow colors as it caught the light. When the shop door had closed behind them, Callie hurried back to the office and opened her laptop.

Typing Vernon Parks's name and "Maryland" into the search box brought up plenty of hits. After rejecting several that were obviously not right (assuming Parks was not ninety-nine years old nor a retired clown of Barnum and Bailey's), she zeroed in on the correct man.

Parks, she discovered, had owned a brunch-and-lunch place in Annapolis, as the caption of a newspaper photo of him stated. It was a place apparently frequented by many state and city employees as well as passing tourists. So that might be a connection to Clifford and Dorothy Ashby, who had worked in Annapolis. She also found his name mentioned in golf articles, which gave his current place of residence as Mapleton. That probably explained his friendship with Mapleton's chief of police. But there was nothing that offered a clue as to why Vernon Parks would be so quick to point a finger at Dorothy in her husband's murder. She would have to find that out from Dorothy herself.

As she waited for Tabitha to arrive, Callie placed a call to the Barbarios, hoping to catch Mike at home. Annie answered, and Callie explained why she hoped to get her husband over to the Foxwood Inn.

"I'm sure he'd do it if he were in town," Annie said. "But Mike is off on one of his work trips. He won't be back until late Monday."

"Darn! Lyssa's book event is Tuesday, which will be a super busy day. So we'll have to put off any inspection of the inn until after that."

"I'll tell him what you need the next time he calls," Annie said. "He'll work something out."

"Thanks, Annie." Callie hung up, disappointed at the delay. But a call concerning the book event came soon after and perked her up.

"Miz Reed? Del Hodges here." Callie recognized the name of the farmer she'd contacted about the hay wagon and held her breath until he added, "The wagon's set, so's I can bring it just about any time. When do you want it?"

She thought about that. The weather prediction was frustratingly iffy. "Will the hay go bad if it gets rained on?"

Hodges chuckled. "Don't worry about that. We'll tie a tarp over the bales. You can pull it off anytime, no problem."

"Great! Then bring the wagon whenever it works for you between now and, say, Tuesday morning."

"Will do."

Callie hung up just as Tabitha walked in. So focused was she on the many things she needed to do that she barely registered what her assistant was wearing that day. Or perhaps Tabitha's creative attire had become the expected unexpected, barely triggering a reaction any-more? Whichever it was, Callie was happy to see her.

"I need to run over to *Stitches Thru Time* for a minute," she said, grabbing her cell phone and waving it to show she would, as always, be reachable. "I'll catch you up on things when I get back, okay?"

"Sure, no problem," Tabitha said cheerily.

Callie held the door for two arriving customers before taking off, knowing they'd be in good hands while she was gone. She had thought of simply calling Dorothy, but she'd decided that seeing the woman's reaction was important. After all, she had leaped into this investigation on pure faith and conviction that her older friend could never be capable of the awful crime she was suspected of. That faith needed to be bolstered once in a while with face-to-face, look-in-the-eye conversations. If Jane protested that her cousin must not be disturbed, Callie would apologize but insist.

Happily, that wasn't necessary. Jane, who was once again minding the vintage sewing shop, gave no argument. "Just let me give her a head's up," she said. She called the cottage, spoke briefly, then nodded to Callie. "Go on back. She's glad to see you."

Callie walked through the shop and out the back to Dorothy's cottage, an arrangement that was very similar to her own shop and home. Dorothy's place, however, while perfectly nice, couldn't come close to her own; all credit, of course, being due to Aunt Mel, whose decorative renovations had turned her little house as near to a fairy tale cottage as anyone could come without a magic wand. Callie mentally thanked her aunt once again for the gift while hating how it had come about. She lifted her hand to knock, but the door opened before she could.

"Come in, dear," Dorothy said with a smile, though she looked tired.

"I'm sorry to disturb you," Callie said. "Something new has come up that I have to talk to you about." She waved away an offer of coffee or tea and waited until Dorothy had settled in a comfortable chair before taking another.

"What can you tell me about Vernon Parks?" she asked, plunging right in and watching Dorothy's face closely.

"Vernon Parks!" Dorothy's expression flew from surprise to disgust in a flash. "I hope you don't have dealings with him. He's a most unpleasant man."

"How do you know him?"

"Cliff and I knew him from way back. We used to stop in his lunch place in Annapolis. Vernon owned it, but the only work he seemed to do was watch his employees like a hawk and fuss over anyone important who happened to stop in. Situated in the state capital as it was, quite a few did. He and Cliff hit it off, but I never liked the man."

"Why?" Callie asked.

Dorothy drew in a deep breath. "I never trusted him. I thought he was two-faced." She grimaced. "Which must be why he and Cliff got along, though I didn't realize that at the time. They might have seen elements of themselves in each other, elements that they both admired."

"Did Parks know what you thought of him?"

"I'm sure he did! I caused him a good amount of trouble."

"Really? In what way?"

Dorothy shifted a pillow behind her back with a slight wince. "Eating at his place as often as we did, I saw a lot of what was going on. I looked the other way with most of it. But then I reached my limit."

She starting coughing and turned toward an end table. Callie saw the glass there was empty and jumped up to refill it for her.

"Thank you, dear," Dorothy said after a few sips. She cleared her throat. "Allergies," she said, adding with a wry smile, "on top of everything else." She set her glass down and resumed her story.

"Vernon Parks had bought the place just a year earlier from a lovely couple who had built up its reputation but were ready to retire. They asked that Vernon retain their employees, one of whom was a very sweet and efficient lady in her fifties. Over the next few months I noticed new workers appearing but didn't think about it too much. Restaurant people tend to move around, and maybe some found better opportunities.

"But then one day, when I was there without Cliff, Francine, the sweet woman who'd waited on us so often, told me it was her last day there. She had tears in her eyes, so with a little pressing I learned that it wasn't her choice to leave. Vernon Parks apparently wanted younger, prettier waitresses and had been systematically replacing those who didn't measure up to his standards. I saw red when she told me that, and I advised her that it was discrimination and she could sue. I even gave her the name of a lawyer who would take her case."

"Good for you. But Parks knew what you'd done?"

"He did, and I didn't care. I had to find another place for my lunch, but it was a small price to pay."

"I think Vernon Parks saw to it that you paid a much higher price."

"What do you mean?"

Callie told her what the Mapleton police deputy had shared with Brian. "Also, Parks wants to buy the Foxwood Inn, according to Paula. I think he saw a double opportunity when Cliff was murdered: to get revenge on you, and also to put you in a position to have to sell the inn in a hurry at a bargain price."

"That horrible man!" Dorothy's hands curled into fists against her lap. "Could he have murdered Cliff as well? With my scissors?"

"He has a good alibi, so unfortunately, no. But at least you see what's been working against you."

"Yes, but what do I do about it?"

That question, Callie had to admit, she couldn't answer.

Fourteen

Callie was about to leave when she remembered what else she'd meant to run by Dorothy: Renata Moore's disparaging remarks. "One more thing," she said. "If you're not too tired?"

"I'll be less tired after a few sips of the raspberry iced tea that I just remembered Jane's set in the refrigerator," Dorothy said, a twinkle appearing in her eye. "And pour yourself some, too," she added as Callie got up.

The tea was bracing and very tasty, Callie found, and she watched Dorothy enjoy it for a few moments before launching into her next query.

"Renata Moore has implied that she's known you a long time. Is that true?"

Dorothy closed her eyes briefly and sighed. "And what has she been saying about me?"

"Something about having always known there was a bad side to you." Callie winced as she said it. "I'm sorry."

"No, don't be. I'm not the least surprised. Or offended anymore. We both were appalled to find ourselves in the same location again. Renata has disliked me for years."

"What, you set a lawsuit on her, too?"

Dorothy laughed. But the laugh started a fresh fit of coughing that even her iced tea couldn't help. When she could speak, she said, "Jane can tell you about it." She began to cough again.

"Of course," Callie said, getting up. "I hope you feel better."

Dorothy lifted one hand in acknowledgment as her other hand tried valiantly to muffle her coughs. "I'll be fine," she managed to gasp.

Callie returned to the vintage sewing shop, knocking twice as she walked in to alert Dorothy's cousin.

"Did you get what you needed?" Jane asked, looking up from where she sat behind the counter. An opened magazine lay in front of her, indicating that business was still painfully slow.

"Not everything. Dorothy needed a break, but she suggested you could tell me about her relationship with Renata Moore."

"Oh, Renata!" Jane said, wrinkling her nose in distaste as she shook her head. "I didn't recognize the woman at first. She's gained a lot of weight over the years. She was Renata Gunderson when I knew her."

"When was that?"

"Years ago. We were all in school together, though I was a year behind Renata and Dorothy."

"And they didn't get along?"

"It was much more than that. Renata was horrible, and the funny thing was she didn't need to be. She had a lot of advantages, if she'd only recognized them." Jane sighed. "It's a long story."

"I have time," Callie said. Her cell phone hadn't dinged with any texts from Tabitha. "And it doesn't look like we'll be interrupted by customers."

"No, it doesn't, does it?" Jane agreed wryly. "Well, all right." She shifted in her chair. "Pull up a stool and get comfortable."

With a final glance toward the door, Jane began. "Renata's father headed the bank in our little town. Dorothy's father—my Uncle John—owned a modest but very nice shoe store. The bank held mortgages on that as well as their house, and my uncle, I was told, paid what was due faithfully each month. One year, unusually heavy rains caused a dam to break up river—a very freakish thing—and the low part of town was flooded. Uncle John's shoe store was hit hard. His insurance didn't cover that kind of damage, and the financial loss was devastating. He fell behind on his mortgage payments, and the bank foreclosed immediately."

Jane heaved a long sigh. "My uncle's health declined, partly from the stress, I'm sure, and the family struggled but somehow kept going, though it was tough. We were all in high school by this time. Renata surely knew all of this, but she still felt a need to make nasty remarks about Dorothy's drab secondhand clothes or the fact that she wasn't participating in certain costly school events. She'd say it as if Dorothy was doing it all on purpose, as some sort of disrespect for the school."

"Wow! Why would she do that?"

Jane shrugged. "Who knows? As I said, Renata had her advantages coming from her well-off family, and she did okay in school as far as I knew. But Dorothy, for all her struggles, managed to do a little better. She won scholastic prizes and she was well-liked just for herself. Perhaps Renata thought she deserved to have it all and couldn't stand that she didn't? Anyway, Renata tried to put down Dorothy every chance she got."

"And how did Dorothy deal with it?"

"Well, she hated it, of course. She told me once that the only thing that kept her from slapping Renata outright was that she couldn't bear to add more stress to her parents by causing trouble."

"So she swallowed it?"

Jane nodded.

"Tough on a teenager," Callie said.

"And maybe a bad habit to get into—not standing up for yourself, I mean. I sometimes wondered if it was why she put up with Cliff as long as she did."

Callie raised an eyebrow. "Good point," she said. "You're a very wise woman."

Jane flushed at that. "I don't know about that. What wisdom I might have was a long time in coming. What's that saying? Old too soon and smart too late?"

Callie smiled. "Probably true of a lot of people." Had she, for one, grown smart too late regarding Hank? She wasn't exactly old, but... her phone dinged and she saw that Tabitha had sent a message. There was a call from a supplier that she needed to deal with quickly. "I'd better go. Thank you for sharing this."

Jane nodded.

"How long are you planning to stay, by the way?" Callie asked as she returned her stool to its original place. "Your plan had been for a short visit, I think, wasn't it?"

"It was. But I can easily stay as long as Dorothy needs me. I'm a widow, you know, and my children are grown. They're the dearest thing in the world to me, but they have their own lives now, so my time is my own."

Callie remembered Dorothy telling her that Jane's two daughters and son lived close to her. But it also seemed as though Jane had made her unannounced visit because of some sort of problem at home. Or perhaps that was just an impression from when she'd first met her? Since Jane had offered no subsequent hint of this, Callie could only suppose that the problem, if there was one, had been either minor or resolved. She thanked Jane again and headed back to the music box shop to deal with whatever problem awaited her there, hopefully one that was very, *very* minor.

❦

Callie was mulling over the Vernon Parks situation later that afternoon, during a quiet time at the shop, when her phone rang. It was Laurie Hart, one of her volunteers for the book event. From the tone of Laurie's voice, Callie knew something was wrong and braced herself.

"I called the bookstore," Laurie said. "Just to double check that we were all on the same page? Well, guess what? They canceled their huge order of Lyssa Hammond's books!"

"What!" Callie had to sit down. "Why?"

"They said you called and told them Lyssa was sick and that the event was called off."

"What are they talking about? I never called to say any such thing. We have to have those books! Did you tell them to reorder?"

"I did. But they say it's too late to get them in time. What are we going to do?"

Callie groaned. All the arrangements had been made, including ads in the papers, shops staying open extra hours, decorations, refreshments, music, and plenty of people planning to show up who would not be happy, to say the least. "Let me call them."

"Good luck," Laurie said, though the way she said it made it sound highly unlikely.

Callie quickly got the bookstore manager on the line.

"I'm so sorry if there was a misunderstanding," the woman said, sincerely. "But when you called to tell us the book event couldn't happen, we had to cancel the books. We just couldn't afford such a large order without the guaranteed sales."

"But I didn't call, and Lyssa isn't sick!"

"Oh, dear. I didn't take the call myself, but my clerk seemed convinced it was you. Or maybe she said it was someone representing you. I'm not sure. But I'm really, really sorry. If I could get that many books in such a short time, I would. It's just impossible."

Callie groaned again, but this time silently. It wasn't the bookstore's fault. Someone had sabotaged them both. Who that was, she intended to find out. But not just now. First she had to tell Lyssa.

Lyssa picked up, sounding in her usual good spirits, and Callie took a deep breath, knowing what she had to say would change that.

"We've got a problem," she said, and explained.

She was met with deep silence from the other end. After a few moments, she rushed into an apology. "I'm so sorry, I should have—"

"No, no," Lyssa said, stopping her. "I was just trying to remember where my boxes of books were right now. Things have been shifted around so much with the remodeling going on at the house."

"You have books?"

"Of course I have books!" Lyssa said with a quick laugh. "I just don't carry them around with me. And I'm not sure how many copies I have of each book. I might have to scramble a bit. Let me think. Maybe my publisher could send some directly? If only it wasn't a weekend. I'm not sure there'll be time. Other bookstores, maybe? But I'll check at home first. Give me this bookstore's number. I'll need to talk to them before I take off."

Callie's spirits started to lift. She recited the number.

"Got it. Don't worry. We'll work something out, even if it's having to give out vouchers. But we have to figure out who made that phony phone call."

"Right. Whoever it is has put you to a lot of trouble. But that wouldn't have been the motive," Callie said.

"Exactly. Someone wants to pull us away from looking into Ashby's murder."

Callie heard Grandpa Reed's music box give a trill behind her. This time she didn't think twice about the reason. Things were getting dicey if a murderer was aware of her actions and moving to put a stop to them. *I'll be careful, Aunt Mel,* she promised. *But if you could give me a hint about what to look out for, it'd be very helpful.*

"I'll call you when I know more," Lyssa promised.

"Yes," Callie said. "And I'll do the same. Stay safe," she added, but Lyssa had already clicked off.

Fifteen

As she prepared to close the shop for the day, Callie spotted a small pile of mail that must have arrived while she'd been at *Stitches Thru Time*. Tabitha apparently had sorted out the junk and left the rest on the back office desk as usual, though the events of the afternoon had kept Callie from noticing. She flipped through the pile.

Among the various invoices and catalogues, one hand-addressed envelope stood out. The sloppy printing would have been enough for her to identify the sender, but the return address sticker (with an incongruous teddy bear decoration) confirmed it. Something from Hank.

Callie sighed and reached for her letter opener. Inside was a single sheet of paper—a bill. It was for Hank's snakeskin boots. *Gotta take care of this soon*! he'd scribbled on a Post-it note stuck at the top.

"Then do it!" Callie cried out to the walls. What next? A bill from Hank's barber because she'd once said that he needed a decent cut before performing? Or from the grocer because she'd once suggested that choices beyond his steady diet of pizza and chicken wings would be good for his voice?

Callie knew Hank was having a hard time getting past their break-up. It had caught him unawares, probably because he was unaware of almost anything beyond his band and video games. But she doubted that she'd actually broken his heart, as he liked to claim. What she'd mainly upset was the routine he'd grown comfortable with and expected to continue with little effort on his part. He didn't like that change. And this was his way of getting back at her, she supposed. Well, good luck with that.

She crumpled the bill and dropped it in her wastebasket. Then she picked up the phone and pressed a number on her speed dial.

"Hi," she said when Brian answered. "Feel like doing something tonight? My treat."

❧

As they drove into Mapleton, Callie suggested Sullivan's just because she knew Brian liked its pub food, but he shook his head, saying, "Not tonight. How about a place where we can actually hear each other?"

Had he sensed her need to talk? There were men who actually picked up signals from the woman they were with? Amazing. They ended up at a new place that had yet to be discovered and so had tables available. The soft music piped in was another draw, and they settled comfortably into a quiet booth. When she opened her menu, Callie found enticing choices, and the basket of crispy, seasoned flatbread raised high hopes for what was ahead.

The only downside was their highly solicitous waiter—usually a good thing, but not when you want to discuss a subject like murder. "More water?" he asked after they'd barely taken sips. He hovered anxiously once their entrees had been served, eager to address the slightest request. Finally Brian got the message across that they could safely be left alone with a firm "We're fine. Thanks." He waited until the man had withdrawn to the other side of the room with more than one backward glance, then looked over to Callie. "So, what's been happening?"

Callie set down her fork and drew a deep breath. "A lot."

She described her visit to the Foxwood Inn, checking out Clifford Ashby's office and the rooms with oddly shortened closets. She took a bite of her seafood platter, which was delicious, then told about her conversations with Dorothy and Jane. Another bite prefaced her appalling news about the book order cancellation and Lyssa's jump into action to salvage the book event. She considered mentioning Hank's dunning letter but took a long sip of her water instead.

"Wow," Brian said. "You've been busy."

"A bit," she agreed. "So, what do you think of Dorothy's explanation?"

"About Vernon Parks? It makes sense, and, knowing Dorothy, it's totally credible. I've seen her stand up for people like she did for Parks's employee."

"You have?"

"Uh-huh. At association meetings, before you came here. Not on the scale of getting someone slapped with a lawsuit, but I felt it revealed her character. One situation involved a shop owner who'd been putting up sidewalk-sale stands that spread farther and farther onto his neighbor's sidewalk. With the crowds that gathered to pick through the items, access to the next-door shop was blocked. When his neighbor spoke up meekly, the space hog took no action until Dorothy stepped in."

"Good for her. I gather she developed that kind of assertiveness relatively late. Jane blames Dorothy's bad marriage in part on her habit of swallowing Renata's harassment in school."

"Could be," Brian said. "But let's hope Jane didn't say that to the police. I can imagine it being interpreted as pent-up anger leading to murder."

"I thought of that, too, but only later, and it was disturbing. I just wish the police, if they do think that way, would know Dorothy as we do, and not pick out negative-sounding things that could help their case."

"Well, it's their job. And they're human. For pretty much anyone who's already leaning a certain way, something that supports that lean is likely to be believed. It happened to me once, though in a different kind of situation."

"Oh?"

Brian paused, as though weighing if he wanted to talk about it, then said, "It was back when I was engaged."

That was news to Callie, who hadn't heard about any engagement. She waited.

"We'd met in college, and everything was good while we were there and away from her family. But once we graduated and moved back home, Jessica's sister started working on her."

Had Annie ever mentioned a Jessica, Callie wondered? She didn't think so.

"Her sister," Brian said, "had just had a bad break-up with a boyfriend who'd cheated on her. So, to her mind, every guy was a potential cheater. She put Jessica on edge believing I shouldn't be trusted, which I'd never given her reason to doubt before." He grimaced. "Maybe I should be glad that it showed up before we got married. But we had a great relationship before, and if we'd had time, without interference, to mature a little, things might have actually worked out. Anyway, my new job called for working closely with a girl who was fairly attractive—also good at her job, but that didn't seem to matter to Jessica. Her sister's constant dire predictions had wormed their way into her head, and when I refused to withdraw from a work-related trip that included this coworker—and a bunch of other people, I might add—Jessica took that as confirmation of her worst fears and broke the engagement."

"I'm sorry."

Brian smiled. "No need. It's all in the past."

Was it, or was that smile forced?

"And I certainly didn't have anything like Dorothy's situation to deal with. But I think it kind of shows how confirmation can be found for any preconceived conclusion if you try hard enough."

"It does," Callie agreed, though she wondered if that had been Brian's primary intention in telling her that story. Was it, perhaps, something deeply personal he wanted her to know? She hadn't said much about Hank, partly because it was embarrassing to admit that she'd been that naïve for so long. But perhaps it was time?

"How're you doing here?" their ever-helpful waiter asked, having silently slipped over. "Ready for dessert?" He held out two dessert menus to them, which Brian automatically took but Callie waved off.

"Just coffee for me," she said.

"Yeah, same here," Brian said, handing the menu back.

That seemed simple enough, but their server then launched into a mind-boggling number of choices, including flavored coffees, espressos, lattes, café macchiato, and a latte macchiato. As the list went on, Brian caught Callie's eye with a look of mock horror, and she had to struggle to keep a straight face. They eventually were able to request, or beg for, two plain black coffees, to the obvious disappointment of the waiter, who returned within moments with their coffees as well as a small pitcher of cream, "Just in case."

The moment for sharing confidences had passed, along with the mood, as they joked about if and when they'd be allowed to actually leave the restaurant and whether or not Brian was being remiss in his attention to his café customers.

When they eventually did leave—with multiple thanks and expressions of hope for their swift return—Callie breathed a sigh of relief, then inhaled the crisp, autumn air. She was glad Brian had had to park a distance away, which let them enjoy a stroll.

Before they'd gone more than a block, she spotted a familiar face heading toward them. Orlena Martin, proprietor of *Treasured Boxes*, a shop not far from the Keepsake Café, was out with her husband. Dressed as usual in colorful garb that included more than one flowing scarf, her broad, dark face lit up as she recognized the two.

"How wonderful to *see* you!" she cried as though it had been weeks instead of days since they'd talked, quickly engulfing each of them in hugs. Orlena's husband, Randal, while of similar imposing size and stature, was his wife's opposite in temperament and simply gave Callie and Brian a quiet nod and smile.

"We have had the most wonderful day," Orlena said, launching into a detailed description of the dinner they'd just enjoyed. "But before that, a visit to the Harriet Tubman Museum!"

"Not the museum," Randal gently corrected. "We went to the Harriet Tubman Underground Railroad Visitor Center."

"Yes, but that is such a mouthful, is it not?" Orlena said, laughing. "'Museum' is easier. Whatever you want to call it, you should go to see it."

"Where is it?" Callie asked. She'd only managed to explore the Eastern Shore in short bursts since taking possession of *House of Melody*.

"Cambridge, isn't it?" Brian asked.

"Yes, Cambridge. Exactly."

Randal shook his head. "The Tubman *Museum* and Educational Center is in Cambridge. The Tubman Visitor Center is at the Blackwater Wildlife Refuge outside of Cambridge."

"Well, they are not far from each other," Orlena insisted. "Go to see both. We intend to do an Underground Railroad driving tour. Randal has promised me."

"How interesting!" Callie said. "On the Eastern Shore?"

"All through the Eastern Shore, wherever runaways knew they would find refuge on their way north. Harriet Tubman was born in Dorchester County, did you know? It was all farms and plantations then. And no Bay Bridge in those days!" Orlena said it lightly, but Callie saw the gravity behind her comment. Traveling long distances on foot in the nineteenth century was no easy task.

"I'd like to see that museum, um, visitor center," Brian said, correcting himself with a glance at Randal. "We could take bikes with us and ride through the wildlife refuge, too. What do you think?" he asked Callie.

"Definitely. After things get settled," she added.

"Oh, yes," Orlena said. "The book event will be soon, of course. But there is that terrible mess still circling around Dorothy. Renata Moore does her best—I should say her *worst*—to keep it spinning."

"So you've heard that?"

"I hear it from customers who come to my place after shopping at *The Collectible Cook*. I try my best to show what they tell me for what it is, baseless, malicious gossip. But Renata has convincing ways about her, does she not? The stories, I fear, have grown and spread ."

Seeing Callie's troubled look, Orlena reached for her hand, covering it with both of hers. "It will end," she said with grave seriousness.

"Do not worry too much. I am very good at feeling what is to come, as you know. I cannot always say how, and that is the way it is with me now. But I am very sure that this terrible talk will end."

Randal cleared his throat. "We should go, sugar," he said quietly.

Callie saw the intensity leave Orlena's face as she looked over at her husband. "Yes, it is time." She turned back to Callie and Brian and smiled with the same cheerful delight she'd first greeted them with. "Good night, my dear ones!" She adjusted the scarf at her neck, took her husband's arm, and walked off, leaving her younger friends to stare after her.

"Wow," Brian said. "What was that?"

"That," Callie began, then stopped. She searched for any sort of explanation and finally gave up. "That," she said, "was Orlena."

Sixteen

Sunday morning, Callie's phone rang as she was cleaning up her breakfast dishes. It was Lyssa.

"We're good to go," she said. "I think. My publisher will FedEx books. Don't ask how I managed to reach someone on the weekend. These are people who disappear from the face of the earth at five o'clock on Fridays. But they promised to have the books at Keepsake Cove by Tuesday afternoon, at the latest."

"Wonderful!"

"I'm bringing back the ones I have at my house, too, just in case. And I can't wait to get away from here. The mess from the remodeling is horrendous. It's total luck that I found my book boxes buried behind it all."

Callie wished her safe driving, relieved that one crisis had passed. She looked out her window to see a mild sunny day and prayed it would continue that way until Tuesday night. Gazebos and tents were fine, as far as they went. But lightning and driving rain could destroy an outdoor event pretty fast. She'd been checking the weather predictions online regularly. So far so good, but she didn't totally believe the forecasts, remembering countless outdoor plans that had been ruined when a sunny day had been predicted.

To take her mind off such concerns, she stepped out into her little yard for some fresh air, grabbing a sweater from the front closet on the way. Aunt Mel's mums graced each side of her door in beautiful golds and ambers, though the summer blossoms had long since faded. Callie remembered her first encounter with Karl, at the time those flowers were in full bloom. How different things had been then.

She heard scratching noises coming from Delia's side of the shrubbery and strolled over to peek through an opening in the branches. Delia had been raking leaves and now stood upright, rake in hand, beside a small mound, catching her breath.

"Need a second pair of hands?" Callie called.

Delia's head swiveled toward her. "I do! Come on over and hold this leaf bag for me, if you will."

Callie pushed through the greenery and picked up the environmentally friendly paper leaf bag that Cove residents put out at the curb for pickup. She'd already cleaned up her own leaves, the few that settled in her small yard having mostly blown over from trees at the back of the cottage, which Aunt Mel had left uncultivated. Callie liked the slightly wild look in that area as well and was happy to leave it that way. Delia, on the other hand, in addition to having trees behind her cottage, had one spreading oak in her front yard, which provided her with lovely shade during the summer and piles of leaves in autumn. Callie held the leaf bag open for her as she scooped her latest bunch into it.

"Thanks!" Delia said. She looked around her yard. "That'll do it for now. Come in for coffee?"

Callie shook her head, suspecting Delia could use a bit of rest before opening *Shake It Up!* at the standard Sunday start time of noon. "Thanks, but I just finished a big breakfast. How's Pete doing?" she asked, noting that Delia had moved her parakeet's Victorian-style cage outside.

"Sassy as ever," Delia said, strolling over to slip a finger fondly between the wires. She turned to Callie. "Oh, I forgot to mention that I checked with Dave about Ashby's pay-to-promote-or-else scheme, and he said that Ashby hadn't approached his shop."

"Good to know, thanks." Callie smiled as Pete hopped over to nuzzle Delia's fingertip.

"I ran into Jane last evening, by the way," Delia said.

"Oh? Where?"

"At the supermarket. Dorothy is so fortunate to have her. There was someone with her, a man I didn't recognize."

"You didn't get to speak with them?"

"No, she was checking out as I walked in, and the place was pretty busy. I just waved."

"You're sure this man was with her, not just in line?"

"Yes, they were unloading from the same basket. Definitely together. A man about her age, slim, gray-haired, wearing a blue windbreaker."

"That sounds like George Cole." Seeing Delia's puzzled look, Callie explained about the other current guest at the Foxwood Inn besides Lyssa. "Jane told me he stopped in at *Stitches Thru Time* the other day to say how sorry he was about Dorothy's situation. I thought it was very nice of him, and she obviously thought so too."

"Well, he seems to have started offering more than just moral support. What do you know about him? Is he trustworthy? I'd hate to see either Jane or Dorothy taken in by a con man during a vulnerable time."

Callie's brows shot up at the startling thought. She'd never thought to question Cole's motives. He'd always been perfectly nice and polite. But he would be, wouldn't he, if he'd had some sort of personal gain in mind?

"He told me he was a widower when he came into my shop to order a music box."

"Are you on Facebook?" Delia asked.

"Um, yes. Why?"

"Ever get one of those fake friend requests? They're always widowed. Or divorced. And have an adorable little daughter."

"George was buying the music box for his daughter."

"Uh-oh."

"That doesn't prove anything! It could just be coincidence."

Delia gave her a stern look. "I think we should keep a sharp eye on Mr. Cole." She glanced at her watch. "Oops. But first I'd better get this little guy back in the house and get myself cleaned up."

Callie held her friend's door as she carried Pete's cage into the cottage, then headed back over to her own place. Could George Cole not be who and what he had presented himself to be? It was hard to believe, with his mild, ever-courteous manner. But all they really knew about him was what he'd told them. It would be a good idea—and she scolded herself for not thinking of it earlier—to see what she could find out about him from more neutral sources.

Callie got her chance that afternoon, after happily seeing off her latest customers. The family had walked in with small children who were promptly set free to wander throughout the shop, opening each and every music box they could get their little hands on as the parents dithered over what to buy for a mother-in-law. The quiet once the family left—sans purchase—was wonderful, along with the relief that nothing had been damaged, though the *you break it, you bought it* rule would have been enforced. After a quick glance outdoors to reassure herself that they weren't returning, Callie went into the office and opened up her laptop.

An online search for George Cole, she soon found, wasn't going to be easy. All she had was the name, without even a middle initial to narrow the field, along with an approximate age of sixty. She didn't remember him mentioning his home town or even a state, which meant having to scroll though endless George Coles who lived all over.

Had he mentioned his wife's name? Callie thought hard until it came to her: Margaret! Typing that in, however, didn't prove any more useful. He'd said he was in the area for business meetings, and the suit he'd worn that first day jibed with that. But she was sure he hadn't given any details on the type of business.

Had he told Lyssa at some point? Callie knew they'd shared at least one dinner together at the Foxwood Inn and possibly several break-fasts. Surely the topic would have come up? She could wait to ask Lyssa until she got back. Or she could call Paula. Paula might have information on Cole, taken when he checked in. But Callie hesitated to approach her. Paula had been reluctant to share information about anything that she or Lyssa had asked her about. Callie could imagine her refusing to talk about George Cole on some sort of hotel confidentiality grounds. Plus, there was the possibility of Cole overhearing the conversation. She would wait to speak to Lyssa.

"No, George didn't give me any details about his work or his location," Lyssa said when Callie reached her later that evening. "At least not that I remember. Seems to me we mostly talked about my books." She laughed. "No surprise there, since it's my favorite subject! Want me to probe? Too late to do it now. Got held up trying to reach my contractor. Harder to do than finding an editor on a Sunday. Turns out Saffron Spice is *not* a paint color I can live with in my master bath. It has to go, and I needed to tell him before he moves the new vanity in tomorrow. Creamy Latte is the color I can deal with before coffee. Who comes up with these names? Anyway, I'm sure I'll see George in the morning."

"Yes, please see what you can get out of him, discreetly, of course. I think we need to understand exactly who he is, since he seems to be getting close to Jane and possibly Dorothy."

"Consider it done. Now I've got to crash. It's been a long day."

Callie thought about heading to bed herself. Jagger obviously was leaning that way, as he'd begun following her about the cottage with significant glances toward the stairs. The hour was right, but Callie's body didn't agree, as agitation from all the thoughts running through her head kept her keyed up. Would reading something totally off-topic do the trick?

She was scouring through Aunt Mel's bookshelves in the guest bedroom when she heard the sirens. The sound was unusual in Keepsake Cove and caught her attention. She listened closely to try to pinpoint the location. Where were they headed? Away from *House of Melody*, she could tell, as the sound gradually faded. But how far?

It worried her enough for her to trot downstairs and step outside. The sirens had stopped. But where?

Callie hurried down the path along the side of her shop to get to the front sidewalk, where she saw Karl Eggers staring down the street in the direction of *Stitches Thru Time*. "Fire truck," he said, and Callie's heart jumped.

"One of the shops?" she asked.

Karl shook his head. "Don't know. Might have gone farther down. Maybe the park."

Callie couldn't just stand there, wondering, so she took off, not caring that she'd left her cottage unlocked or that she was jogging in a pair of fuzzy pink slippers, which required regular stops and adjustments. The farther she ran, the more smoke she saw, rising above the roofs of shops and cottages. She passed *Stitches Thru Time*, relieved to see it was okay, and made it to the edge of the park. She slowed as flashing lights and shouts of firefighters assailed her. With no way to move closer, she looked around at the crowd that had gathered and spotted Bill Hart, Laurie's husband, across the street. She hurried over to him.

"What is it?" she asked, struggling to catch her breath and get the words out.

"It's the hay wagon Del Hodges brought over for the book event," Bill said. "It's gone up in flames."

Seventeen

Callie watched from the edge of the park along with the other spectators until the smoke finally thinned. When the firefighters started wrapping up their hoses, she knew the fire had been successfully put out, though the word spread that Del Hodges's wagon was a total loss. Luckily it had been isolated enough that the flames were contained. Dejected, Callie headed home along with dozens of others.

As she drew closer to her shop, she spotted Delia standing in front of *Shake It Up!* in a blue robe and matching slippers. Her long hair, normally tied up in a bun, hung over her shoulders. Callie told her what had happened.

"Poor Del!" Delia said. "How did this happen?"

"On a clear night like this, that fire wasn't caused by something like a lightning strike," Callie said. "Somebody must have started it."

"Who? And why?"

"I don't know, but I hope the police can find out." Callie looked down at her slippers. The cottony material wasn't designed for outdoors, not to mention jogging. She could feel the cold pavement through significant rips in the soles. "Thank goodness the wagon was a couple hundred yards from the gazebo, and the fire didn't spread. A passerby spotted the smoke and called 911 before that could happen. We have tomorrow to clean up leftover debris in the park and the gazebo area and to set up the tents. Assuming they allow us in, that is."

Delia shook her head. Whether it was distress over the fire or over the major set-back to their event preparations, Callie didn't know. But as she rubbed at the goose bumps on her arms, she envied her friend her warm-looking robe and particularly the slippers. With the level of protection her own currently offered, her feet might as well have been bare. She glanced at the nearby trash can and considered peeling her slippers off and dropping them in, but then decided something was better than nothing.

She noticed a familiar figure heading their way after separating from a small group amidst muted good nights. Callie realized it was Brian. Had he been in the milling crowd? How had she missed him?

"The fire chief said they found evidence of an accelerant," he said as he came up to them. "They'll have to do more testing, but they're leaning pretty heavily toward arson."

"Could it have been kids playing a malicious prank?" Delia asked.

Callie shook her head. "I think someone wanted to stop the book event. Coming on the heels of that fake cancellation message at the book store, it must have been the next attempt. The only question is why. What's so threatening about an author event?"

Delia looked blank, and Brian said, "Beats me. Somebody with an agenda against Lyssa, maybe because of the subject of her books—

vampires and witches? A few people have very strong opinions against what they consider to be glorifying evil."

"But why not just petition for another author?" Callie asked. "We picked her exactly *because* of her stories, because Halloween is coming up. Has anyone around here ever protested celebrating Halloween?"

Both her companions shook their heads. "Might someone have wanted to hurt the Keepsake Cove Shop Owners' Association?" Delia asked. "This whole thing, after all, was to benefit the shops."

Callie shrugged. She couldn't see that. But none of it made sense. Probably the most they could hope for was that the culprit would be caught. She had a sudden thought. "What about the tents? We need to set them up tomorrow. The same person could come back and burn them down tomorrow night!"

"I'll see about getting a police guard," Brian said. "After this fire, I can't believe they'd refuse, but if they do, I'll organize volunteers to keep watch."

"Thanks, Brian. I'll willingly sign up for a shift if we have to go that way."

"Me too," Delia said.

"But now," Callie said, rubbing vigorously at her arms, "I need to get indoors. I'm freezing! See you tomorrow," she called as she hurried off, picturing the hot shower she intended to hop into as quickly as possible.

❧

Up early Monday morning, Callie threw a warm but ratty sweatshirt on over an old pair of jeans. Who knew how much of a mess they might be faced with in the park? Boots would also be a good idea, she figured, what with the amount of water she'd seen spray from the fire hoses. She was dumping coffee grounds into her trash when her phone rang. It was Lyssa.

"I just had breakfast at the inn with George. Hah! Sounds like that musical: *Sunday in the Park with George*! No singing, though. Just me trying to worm things out of the man. Jeez! You'd think I was trying to get his bank account numbers, the work I had to put in. But I got a couple of things, like where he grew up. It's a small town in southern Virginia called Greenock." She spelled it.

Callie grabbed a pencil and wrote it down. "Anything else?"

"Just that he left Virginia after college and has moved around a lot ever since for his work. He told me his wife died a few years ago, but you heard that already."

"Right. I tried to find him on the internet, but there's a million George Coles. Did you get anything about who he works for? That might help."

"Nope. That was it. I brought up Jane's name, prattled on about her and about Dorothy, but he never took the bait. Sorry."

"It's a good start."

"Yeah. I'll see if I can get more later. Can't be too obvious, obviously, hah! Hey, what's happened at the park? I heard there was a fire."

Callie told her everything, including Brian's thoughts on why it might have happened.

"Well, I've heard from a few disgruntled readers about the subject matter of my books, but I've never had any threats, thank goodness. Funny thing, though. The complainers always have finished the entire book. I know because they can quote from beginning to end. Bet they went on to buy the next one so they could write another *oh, how awful!* review somewhere." Lyssa chuckled. "Can things still go on tomorrow night? We have a lot of books being trucked in."

"Absolutely. There's plenty of your fans who'd be devastated if we canceled. But we're also taking precautions that nothing more happens. Everything should be set up by tonight."

Lyssa made an offer to come help, but not a particularly strong one. Callie guessed she was already composing the next scene in her head and eager to tap it into her laptop. She assured Lyssa that she had plenty of volunteers, who were probably already gathering at the park. They wished each other a successful day and rang off.

❧

When Callie arrived, along with a few members of her crew, she saw Del Hodges standing at the edge of a scorched circle of grass, hands on hips as he stared at the remains of his wagon. The others quickly scattered, leaving Callie to deal with him. She approached tentatively. His posture and the expression on that sun-bronzed, leathery face strongly suggested he was ready to spit nails.

"Mr. Hodges?" she said.

He turned to pierce her with steely eyes. Then they softened, and his shoulders relaxed. "Miz Reed. Heck of a thing to happen, isn't it?"

"It is. I'm so sorry."

"Not your fault. Some fool took it in his head to cause a whole lot of trouble for everyone. Not for the first time, I'd say. I've had crops damaged by dirt bikes, and cows let out of their pens to go wandering down the roads. Kids' idea of fun. *Some* kids, that is. This is probably the work of one of them."

Callie disagreed but held her tongue.

"I can call around," Hodges said. "See if we can get you another hay wagon by tomorrow night."

"Really? That would be great. But after what happened, would anyone want to risk it?"

Hodges chuckled. "You're new here, aren't you? We help each other out. When one of us runs into a jam, we pull together to get them out of it. We might even catch the guy who did this, just to make sure nobody else goes through it."

Can you catch the guy who murdered Clifford Ashby while you're at it? Callie wanted to ask. But she thanked the farmer profusely before moving on to catch up with the others.

Laurie Hart was already sweeping the gazebo, and Bill had started hanging the Halloween decorations that Callie had ordered: skeletons, bats, and huge lifelike spiders. Too lifelike. Callie gave one a wide berth as she stepped up and into the gazebo.

"We're lucky," Laurie said. "None of the water reached this far, so no mud to deal with."

"Thank goodness," Callie replied, to which Laurie vigorously nodded agreement.

"Ready for the throne?" Delia called out. She'd driven over with one of her dark wicker chairs for Lyssa to sit in as she read from her newest book. At the end of her presentation, the chair would be moved to a nearby table that would be piled high with books Lyssa would sign for her fans. If, that is, all went well and the books arrived in time.

"Sure," Laurie said. "Bill, want to help Delia bring the chair in?"

"I'll do it." Callie heard Randal Martin's deep voice, and she waved to him.

"Thanks, Randal," Bill called. "I'll keep working on the decorations here."

Callie saw Krystal Cobb, the Keepsake Cove association's president, arrive, but from Krystal's garb—a houndstooth blazer over dark trousers—it was clear that she wasn't there to work.

"How does it look?" Krystal asked. "Can you get everything ready by tomorrow night?"

"I'm sure we can. We might even get a replacement for the hay wagon."

"Wonderful. How about the tents?"

"Arriving any minute, along with the rental chairs."

Krystal looked around at Callie's volunteers busily tidying the area. "That's a big relief. When I heard about the fire I feared we were done for. Thank you, Callie, for stepping up and taking on this big job. There's a lot of your Aunt Melodie in you, I can see."

Callie smiled. There was no higher praise, to her mind. However, her job was still far from done. "You'll be introducing Lyssa tomorrow night?"

"Absolutely. Looking forward to it!"

"The tents are here!" someone shouted from a distance, and people scurried to make way as the truck pulled slowly in.

Callie was fascinated at how organized the tent crew was, unloading and laying out their equipment in choreographed precision. They pounded stakes into the ground, spread out the huge canopy for the main tent, and in an impressively short time raised and secured it on center and side poles. The smaller tent for concessions was then set up at the same time the chairs were unloaded. Callie had ordered side walls as protection in case of rain, and she talked with the tent crew manager about whether or not to attach them.

"Your call," the man in hard hat and coveralls said. "But I haven't seen any rain in the forecast."

"Laurie? Bill?" Callie asked. "What do you think?"

Between them, they decided to risk it and leave the sides open. "Much easier for people to come and go," they all agreed.

The manager picked a spot to leave the folded side walls in case the weather changed and gave directions on how they should be attached—information that Callie devoutly hoped not to need.

The tent truck drove off, and Callie was admiring the look of it all when she saw Jerry Moore walking up but with empty hands. "Have you brought your sound system?" she asked.

"No way!" he barked, and Callie's heart sank. "I'll set it up tomorrow. I'd be out of my mind to leave my equipment here overnight. It's weatherproof but not theft-proof. I came to look things over and figure out where to put things."

"Thank you so much," Callie said while shaking her head. Of course he wouldn't put his expensive equipment at risk. What was she thinking? "Do you need outlets?"

"Nah, my stuff's wireless. Top of the line. She's going to be in there?" he asked, tilting his head toward the gazebo.

"Right. The two-step rise should make Lyssa visible to everyone seated in the tent."

Moore studied the layout. "You want the spooky music playing beforehand, right?"

"Yes, as people are gathering. Can you also keep it on while she's reading, but on low?"

"Sure. Want some sound effects while she's reading, too?"

"That sounds like fun. But you'd better coordinate that with Lyssa." Callie dug a piece of paper out of her tote, wrote down Lyssa's number, and handed it to him. "Thank you so much, Mr. Moore, for doing this."

"Jerry," he said. "Mr. Moore's my father." He laughed. "And it's no problem. Hey, it's a group effort, right? For all of us Keepsake Cove people. Um…" He dropped his voice and moved closer. "Is Dorothy Ashby going to be here?"

"I don't know," Callie said, surprised at the question.

"It's just that, well, Renata got a pretty angry call from her. Seems Dorothy didn't like some of the things she was told Renata said about her. Really lit into her."

"That sounds unlike Dorothy, though I've heard a few things Renata said, and they weren't, uh, very nice. The problems between them go way back?"

"Yeah, they definitely locked horns when they were kids. I tell Renata it's time to grow up and move on, but she can't let things go. Has to show she's right no matter what. 'Course, Dorothy's got her temper, too. I mean, I could hear her screaming through the phone from halfway across the room. That's why I was hoping she wouldn't be here tomorrow. It could get nasty."

Screaming? That was a side of Dorothy that Callie hadn't seen. Was the pressure getting to her? "I doubt that she'll come," she said. "But Renata could also stay home to avoid any problem."

Jerry rolled his eyes in a look of extreme skepticism and left it at that, returning to his search for spots for his speakers. He wandered off toward a tree with low-hanging branches.

"I don't blame Dorothy for being furious."

Callie turned to see Laurie Hart a few feet behind her. "You heard?"

"Yup. And I've heard what Renata's been spreading around. Nasty stuff."

"They have a history," Callie said.

"Oh?"

"Dorothy has had to deal with Renata's ragging since their school days."

"Good gosh! Well, it sounds like she's finally had it. Maybe not the best time, though, what with all the unresolved suspicions swirling around."

"I'll see if I can talk to her," Callie said.

Just then Annie showed up with questions about the concessions stand she'd be helping Brian handle at the event, and a volunteer ran over with a question about the parking area. Callie put her plan to talk to Dorothy on her mental to-do list, below a dozen other things. She took a deep breath and hoped all the items would have a thick black line through them by the time she got to it.

Eighteen

The morning of the book event, Callie called Lyssa from the shop to check that she hadn't come down with laryngitis or broken out in hives. The author chuckled merrily at the thought.

"A tiny bit nervous, are we? All is well, I promise. Not even a hint of a cough. Don't worry. I've done so many of these that I think I could carry one off through double pneumonia and tornado threats. The books have made it as far as York, Pennsylvania, by the way, so I think we're good on that score."

"Great," Callie said, though a bit weakly. She'd prefer to hear that the books had actually arrived.

"Did I mention I'll be showing up in a hearse?"

"What? Really?"

"Too much?"

"No, it's fantastic. The crowd will love it."

"I got the idea Sunday, on my drive back. Called around and found one that was, well, I can't say it was free, but it was at least unoccupied." Lyssa's laugh rang out again.

Callie grinned, finding her nerves settling during the conversation. A grand entrance like that was going to be so much fun. "Have the driver wait for my call. Once everyone's settled, I'll make sure he can pull right up. "

Right after she disconnected, the phone immediately rang. "Is that Lyssa Hammond thing tonight?" the caller asked.

It wasn't the first such call she'd received, and she expected it wouldn't be the last. She wished she'd set up a recording on another number with the event information, but it was too late now.

She was relieved to see Tabitha walk into the shop, and not surprised that her assistant's costume of the day was a black dress and pointy witch's hat.

"In honor of Lyssa Hammond, of course," Tabitha said. When Callie told her about Lyssa's plan to arrive in a hearse, Tabitha clapped her hands. "Love it! This is going to be so great! Think it'll translate into sales here afterward? I mean, people don't normally associate ghosts with music boxes."

"Or with salt and pepper shakers or collectible cars. We're hoping that everyone who shows up will be in such a good mood that they won't want the evening to end and will hang around and shop."

"Then again," Tabitha said, rolling back one long black sleeve, "if they knew about Aunt Mel and Grandpa Reed's music box ... " She flicked her eyes toward the music box in question, sitting in its Plexiglas case on the shelf behind the counter.

"And they won't know, right? Because *we* don't really know that Aunt Mel is communicating. It could all be coincidence."

Tabitha shot her a knowing look but said nothing, and the music box remained mercifully silent as well. After a long pause, the phone suddenly rang, causing Callie to jump. Tabitha reached for it and calmly recited *"House of Melody"* along with a greeting. She listened for a moment, then gave directions to the Keepsake Cove Park for the evening's event.

"They've been calling all morning," Callie said when she hung up.

"Good. That means a great turnout."

"Hope so. The books are getting closer and nothing has caught fire in the last twenty-four hours. So far, so good."

She left Tabitha in charge of the phone and went back to her office, thinking she'd take a moment to search online again for George Cole using Lyssa's latest info.

She typed in his name, along with Greenock, Virginia, and then sat back and waited. It didn't take long. A few lines of an article in the *Greenock Gazette* showed up with George Cole's name, but it was in the paper's archives. In order to access it fully, she needed to subscribe to the newspaper, which she quickly decided was worth it. After a few minutes of tapping in the required information, including her credit card number, the door to the archives opened, and she was in.

The article turned out to have been published thirty-eight years ago. It was a "local boy makes good" story, talking about how George Cole, after graduating from James Barbour High School, had gone on to excel at the University of Virginia, earning a degree in economics, and had taken a job as a business analyst with Liberty Mutual Surety. He would be working in the company's Richmond offices. Well, that sounded positive. It was, however, thirty-eight years ago, and a lot could have changed in the local boy since then.

Curious about the size of Greenock itself, Callie left the newspaper site. From Wikipedia she learned that the population of the town was currently 6,541. Forty-some years ago it likely had been smaller, which explained an article like the one on George Cole appearing in the newspaper.

She went back to the newspaper archives to look for more. After refining her search, she found a mention of George in the guest list of a local wedding. His name was buried among many others, and Callie was on the verge of clicking away when she thought to scroll upward to check the names of the bride and groom: Dorothy L. Jenkins and Clifford F. Ashby. The bride was attended by her cousin, Jane A. Jenkins.

Callie sat back in astonishment. George Cole had attended Dorothy and Clifford's wedding, which took place in Greenock, Virginia, some four decades ago. Since weddings were usually held in the bride's home town, the news story on it was likely because of a connection that Dorothy, and possibly Jane, had to Greenock. Clifford, so far, was up for grabs. But George hadn't said a word about all this to Lyssa or Callie. Nor had Jane. What did that mean?

Callie didn't have time to mull it over, since she could hear Tabitha dealing with a customer as the shop door opened for another. She went out to lend a hand, though she ended up answering more questions about that evening's book event than about her music boxes. Her customer did buy a small musical globe before leaving, and Tabitha made a sale on a vintage rotary telephone music box.

As both customers walked out, a third walked in, and Tabitha stepped up to greet her. Callie hurried back to the office to make a quick call to Lyssa.

"Sorry to interrupt whatever you're doing," she said, "but I just learned something I thought couldn't wait." She gave Lyssa the details of her online search.

"That devil! He never said a word about knowing those two. And remember when he told me about seeing Jane from the window of his room, talking to Cliff Ashby the afternoon of the murder? He said it as if he didn't know who she was. I only guessed it was Jane because of the sweater he described."

"I also remember you said it seemed to have just slipped out. You said he looked like he wished he could take it back."

"That's right. But what does it mean?"

"I don't know. But George hasn't been totally open with us," Callie said. "I thought you should keep that in mind when you're talking with him from now on."

"Absolutely. By the way, Paula's making an early dinner for us at the inn, at my request. Want to join us? She always makes plenty, and it's always delicious."

"Thanks, but I'll need to be at the park making sure everything's in shape. I'll probably grab something from Brian's concession stand."

"That'll be good, too. See you tonight!"

After disconnecting, Callie thought for a minute, then pressed in the number for *Stitches Thru Time*. She needed to get the relationship between George, Dorothy, and Jane straight, and the best way was to go right to the horse's mouth. The phone rang at the shop, and she readied her questions. But instead of Jane picking up, Callie heard Dorothy's voice in the prerecorded message stating that the shop was closed.

"Please leave a message," she asked, "and your phone number after the beep."

Callie didn't wait for the beep but called the number at Dorothy's cottage instead. Perhaps they'd given up on waiting for customers, or it might be a brief closure. She drummed her fingers as she listened to the rings at the other end. After four, she heard Dorothy's voice say hello. She began to talk until she realized that Dorothy was still speaking. It was another recording, asking the caller to leave a message.

"Dorothy, it's Callie. Would you call me, please?" She recited her number and hung up, unsure what was going on. It could be something or nothing. All Callie could do for the moment was wait for Dorothy to call her back.

❧

By six o'clock, Callie had been kept busy enough between customers and ongoing calls about the book event that thoughts of Dorothy had flown. It was time for her to put *House of Melody* in Tabitha's capable hands and head over to the park. Tabitha had long ago agreed to stay late, leaving Callie free to oversee whatever needed overseeing. One load, at least, had been lifted from her shoulders when the book store called.

"They're here!" the store's manager had announced, referring, of course, to Lyssa's books. "There's boxes and boxes of them. We'll be loading them up soon." The two women had laughed with relief, with Callie very happy to cross that problem off her list.

Keepsake Cove looked wonderfully festive as she drove down the street, her banners and decorations glowing brightly in the setting sun. Soon it would be dark, and the street lights would take over. The weather was cool but dry, and only a light breeze rustled the fallen leaves. It was a perfect night for an outdoor Halloween-themed book event, weather-wise. All that remained was for a few dozen other things to fall into place as planned, but she wasn't going to let that stress her. One step at a time had become her mantra.

After parking and walking the short distance to the park, Callie was delighted to spy a new wagon in place, filled with hay, a scarecrow, and carved jack-o'-lanterns. Del Hodges hadn't exaggerated about locals pulling together. That, of course, included the people on her decorating committee, who must have scrambled to find replacements for the burned items. She continued down the wide paved path that cut through dense trees and soon reached the cleared gazebo and tent area. Annie hailed her from the concessions tent.

"Is she here?" she called.

"Lyssa's going to make her grand entrance at the last minute," Callie said, then paused for dramatic effect. "In a hearse."

Annie squealed. "The crowd's going to totally love that."

Callie glanced around at the empty tent. "Assuming there *is* a crowd. Shouldn't people be arriving?"

"This is the Eastern Shore, Callie. Things are more leisurely here. Don't worry. They have another thirty-five minutes to show up. Want a sandwich? I've got a bunch, and Brian's bringing more."

"My stomach's full of butterflies. Got anything hot to drink?"

"Not yet, sorry. How about a chilled green tea?"

"I'll take it."

Callie turned to examine the area. All looked pristine and ready, the folding chairs neatly in place and ghostly decorations hanging from every possible location. Annie was holding out the bottled tea when an ear-piercing screech nearly made her drop it.

"That's Jerry Moore," she said, once she could speak. "Or rather, his sound system. He's been testing it—and damaging my eardrums—since I've been here. Jerry!" she shouted into the air. "Cut it out!"

In response, they heard maniacal laughter coming through a speaker, followed by creepy organ music.

"Where is he?" Callie asked. She took a swig of her tea and wiped a stray drop from her lips.

"Somewhere out there." Annie waved vaguely toward the shrubbery behind the gazebo. "He's been setting up speakers all over. When it's not screeching, it sounds pretty good."

"Great. Did Renata come with him?"

"I haven't seen her. I suppose she might come later on her own. Why, did you need to talk with her?"

"Well, mostly keep an eye on her. Jerry warned me that she and Dorothy have had words recently. Harsh ones. He hoped they wouldn't run into each other tonight."

"Think that's likely? I mean, I thought Dorothy was keeping a low profile lately."

"She is, but after letting out her anger toward Renata, she might also decide enough is enough and show up. She certainly deserves to be here after all the work she did with us early on. I tried to reach her this afternoon but got no answer."

"That's odd," Annie said. "But maybe she was resting."

Callie nodded. That was the most likely explanation. She wished, though, that she'd thought of stopping by *Stitches Thru Time* on her way, just to check. Should she call Dorothy again? She started to reach for her phone but then saw a small van approaching. As it closed in, she read the logo on its side: *Mapleton Mysteries and More*. The books had come!

She set down her tea and hurried over to lend a hand as a man and woman popped out from the front seat and slid open the side door. While Callie helped lift out boxes to stack on the dolly, Brian's Impala pulled up. Annie and Brian were soon unloading cartons of food and drink from the trunk and carrying them to the concession stand, weaving between the book people.

Laurie Hart had spread an orange-and-black tablecloth over the signing table in the gazebo, and she shook out a second one to cover the book table. Callie, who'd followed the loaded dolly with one of the final boxes, deposited it on the floor next to the table at the direction of the bookstore people. "We'll spread out a selection of the titles on the tabletop and replenish as needed."

Seeing that they had things well in hand, Callie went back to concessions. "Need any help?"

Annie was unpacking cartons as Brian plugged electricity into his various heating elements. "We're good, thanks," he said. "Should have coffee ready in a few minutes."

"Great! Hey, people are coming."

"I'll move my car out of the way in a minute."

"Want me to do it for you?" Callie asked, and was rewarded with a *you must be joking* look from Annie. "Hey," Callie protested. "He let Lyssa drive it."

"Got a Corvette on hand to trade with me?" Brian asked with a laugh. "It's okay. I plan to park it some distance away, for safety's sake. I can jog back quicker than you."

"Howard, you can't do that." Callie turned as Delia's exasperated voice carried from a short distance away. Delia was facing Howard Graham, who held a large box and looked defiant. Callie hurried over to see Christmas-y items from his shop filling the box.

"But the whole purpose of this event was to sell our stuff," he argued.

"Not here," Delia said, obviously striving for patience.

"What's up?" Callie asked.

"Howard wants to spread out his things to sell."

"I have my own table," he said defensively. "That was the idea, wasn't it? That we have our things lined up and ready in the gazebo for when she signs her books?"

"Howard," Delia asked, "do you know how many shops there are in Keepsake Cove? How do you think we could fit everyone in that gazebo?"

"She's right, Howard," Callie said. "I'm sorry you misunderstood. The plan was that all the shops stay open late tonight for shoppers to visit after they leave here."

"But—"

"Let me help you get these things back," Delia said, guiding the frustrated-looking man away from the tents. "I'll ask Lyssa to mention your Christmas shop as she signs, how does that sound?" As they left, she shot Callie a wide-eyed *can you believe it?* look over her shoulder, and Callie returned a grateful one for her deft handling of the situation.

As people started arriving on foot and filling the seats, Callie saw a black Lexus drive up to the area recently vacated by Brian's Impala and the bookstore van. She watched to see who would step out, hoping not to have to inform them they couldn't leave their car there. She didn't have to worry. The driver got out to open the back passenger doors for two men, then hopped back in, ready to pull away. Curious, Callie moved closer and saw Pearl Poepelman greeting the two. Pearl turned and, spotting her, waved her over.

"Callie, have you met our mayor, Tyler Elliott?" The vintage jewelry shop owner was clearly pleased as she introduced Callie to the taller of the two men, explaining that *House of Melody*'s new owner had also headed the book event committee.

The silver-haired man shook Callie's hand, then turned to his companion. "I'd like you both to meet this gentleman." He placed a friendly hand on the shoulder of the man next to him as he said his name. "Vernon Parks."

Callie automatically held out her hand but was momentarily tongue-tied as she realized who she faced: the man Dorothy had described as despicable.

Nineteen

*V*ernon Parks, shorter and more rotund than the mayor, smothered Callie's hand in a pinky-ringed clasp, apparently not picking up on her stiff reaction.

"Wonderful event you've arranged here. The best of everything, eh? Books, food, and lovely ladies." He pumped her hand vigorously, a wide though plastic smile splitting his jowly face. Both men wore suits, which Callie might have expected for the mayor at a large community gathering. But Parks? She sincerely hoped he wasn't planning to run for a local office.

"We've reserved seats for you up front," Pearl said after shaking Parks's hand. She led them both away, much to Callie's relief, though she recognized that she was perhaps being unfair. But from Dorothy's tale, which she trusted, along with the bad vibes that she'd instantly felt at meeting the man, she didn't think so.

What was Parks doing there? What if Dorothy showed up? Callie scanned the crowd worriedly without spotting her, but she did see

Renata, who was making her way toward the mayor and Parks. Joining forces to devastate Dorothy? Callie chided herself. She had no reason to think so. Besides, Dorothy hadn't shown up so far, and the likelihood was that she wouldn't. If, in fact, she did, Callie would be sure to warn her.

The crowd filled in, to the point of standing room only, nicely dispelling the lesser of her worries, and she heard her cell phone ping with a new text. It was from Lyssa.

Hearse and I are here. Signal when ready.

Callie's stomach did a little flip. Show time! She looked around for Krystal Cobb and found her near the gazebo. She was talking with two other women and not hard to spot in one of her sparkle-studded jackets. Krystal clearly enjoyed dressing up to her name. Callie hurried over.

"Lyssa's ready to be introduced," she said. She'd already alerted Krystal to the author's method of arrival.

"Okay!" Krystal smoothed her skirt, squared her shoulders, and cleared her throat. "Here we go!" She climbed the two stairs of the gazebo and tapped the microphone that had been set up in front of the throne. "Are we on? Yes? Great. Ladies and Gentlemen, welcome to Keepsake Cove!"

Callie texted Lyssa to start inching in.

The crowd quieted as Krystal first introduced the mayor, who stood up and waved, managing to look surprised but pleased at the honor. She then spoke about how exciting it was to have a world-famous author with them that evening, especially one who wrote such chill-producing stories, and particularly at Halloween. "Who doesn't like to be scared?" she asked as the crowd chuckled agreement. She gave a brief overview of Lyssa's writing career, picking out her most popular books and mentioning some of their more macabre subjects, finally saying, "Ladies and gentleman, please join me in welcoming Lyssa Hammond!"

The lights flickered as Jerry Moore's speakers sent out ominous-sounding music. Those in their seats looked around, puzzled, until the ones nearest the back cried out in astonishment and laughter. Others rose to see for themselves and joined in the merriment as Lyssa's hearse slowly approached. When she stepped out, her spiked red hair glowing above flowing black chiffon, the crowd cheered.

Lyssa's grand entrance, to Callie's delight, was a success. The author was even wearing pale, corpse-like makeup to go along with the theme.

Except … as Callie stepped closer to help clear a path, she saw that Lyssa's ghostly pallor was genuine.

"Are you okay?" she whispered.

"Sick to death—no pun intended. But I'll make it through. Don't worry. Got any water?"

Callie scrambled to grab a bottle for her as Lyssa sank into Delia's wicker chair. The author took a long drink, then beamed at her audience, picked up the microphone, and greeted them energetically. She launched into her talk, sounding for all the world as though nothing whatsoever was wrong.

Callie hovered in the shadows, watching nervously and ready to call for a doctor or 911 if needed. Seeing Lyssa in that condition was shocking after having had a lively conversation on the phone with her just hours ago. Lyssa was obviously determined to carry on and did so impressively, sharing fascinating thoughts on her story inspirations and funny anecdotes about research trips to unusual places. She then read a few pages from her brand-new book, with Jerry Moore adding perfect background music and a final, piercing scream when the victim in the story met a horrible death.

The crowd loved it, and Lyssa seemed to be drawing energy from them. When she opened things up for questions, she actually stood and began pacing a bit as she responded. By the end of the session, a bit of color had returned to her cheeks and she waved and smiled as the crowd applauded.

"That was fantastic," Callie said, hurrying up to Lyssa as a volunteer whisked the wicker chair over to the signing table. "How are you feeling?"

"Better," Lyssa said, but she held on to Callie as they walked. "I don't know what came over me. One minute I was fine and lying in the hearse—which is quite comfortable, by the way—and the next minute everything started spinning. Luckily there was a plastic bag handy 'cause I lost my dinner just as you gave the signal to move."

"Right here, Ms. Hammond," a young man said as he pulled the chair out for her. "There's pens and water. Would you like anything to eat?"

Lyssa's face turned a pale shade of green at mention of food, but she smiled and shook her head. She settled in her chair and waited for the line to get organized. A bookstore employee was asking that everyone clearly print the name they wanted Lyssa to write in their book on slips of paper being passed out. "You wouldn't believe how many different ways people can spell a simple name like Mary," the woman had explained to Callie earlier. "Merry, Mari, Mayhri. This speeds things up."

From the size of the line forming, it looked like Lyssa would be kept very busy for close to an hour. Was she up to it? The bookstore people were very helpful as the first fans approached, opening each book to the title page for Lyssa, reading the name aloud for her, and keeping the line moving. Lyssa's signature may have left something to be desired, with her hand a bit shaky. But she more than made up for it with her lively chatter as she signed. She was amazing, Callie thought, and a real pro.

Jerry Moore's spooky music continued to play in the background, maintaining the Halloween atmosphere, as did the light breeze that stirred the hanging skeletons and goblins to life. Since darkness had fallen, the only light came from the park's scattered lampposts along with the glowing jack-o'-lanterns and strings of orange lights Callie's volunteers had put up. Beyond the event area and the path leading to it, all was dark.

Seeing that Lyssa was in good hands, Callie moved over to Brian's concession stand and was glad to see him doing a brisk business. As Annie handed out hot cider and soft pretzels, she reminded customers to check out all the Keepsake Cove shops before heading home. "Lots of specials running tonight, folks," she said. People seemed to pay attention, turning in the right direction and appearing more in the mood to shop than to hurry home.

Callie remembered Dorothy and checked the crowd for any sign of her but saw neither her nor Jane. While a relief in one way, it also made her sad to think that the two had to miss out on the evening. She hoped Jane, at least, had opened up *Stitches Thru Time* to take advantage of the sales opportunities. Surely not everyone at the event that night would be aware of the connection between the shop and the murdered Clifford Ashby, or have heard Renata Moore's nasty comments.

Where was Renata, by the way? Callie didn't see her, not with Mayor Elliott or Vernon Parks, anyway, who were busy chatting with people who'd just had their books signed. In having chosen that prime spot to hang around in, Parks was acting more and more like he was in a pre-campaign mode, Callie thought. Concerned, she headed over.

After listening to the comments from the edge of their circle for a few minutes, Callie learned that she was wrong. Parks wasn't running for anything. But the mayor, whose term would be ending in a few months, was clearly looking at a state delegate position. Vernon Parks, meanwhile, sounded very much like his campaign manager.

Callie tried to blend in inconspicuously, but Parks at one point noticed her. "There's the young lady who's responsible for this fantastic evening! Wonderful job, wonderful job!"

Startled, as others turned and opened a space around her, Callie immediately disclaimed all credit, insisting it had been a group effort. "And it was Lyssa Hammond who's made it such a success."

"Yes, yes, but the diamond shines best when placed in the perfect setting."

"Well put," Mayor Elliott said, "and very true. You've shown quite a talent for event organizing, Miss Reed. We could use someone like that, eh, Vernon?"

"Absolutely, Mr. Mayor, if I hadn't already spoken to several people who—"

"I've got my hands pretty full with my shop," Callie quickly said, not having the least interest in either working on campaigns or with someone like Vernon Parks. "But thank you for the compliment." Having seen Parks's lip curl derisively at the mayor's suggestion, she turned to him. "I'm impressed that you can make the time, Mr. Parks. I understood you were interested in taking over the Foxwood Inn."

"Foxwood?" Elliot asked. "That's Cliff Ashby's place. I didn't know you were looking into it, Vernon."

"A whim," Parks said, smiling a bit too broadly. "It's an intriguing place, and Cliff was an old friend, you know. I thought it might help his widow to take it off her hands. Poor woman has her troubles right now, doesn't she? But don't worry, Mr. Mayor. If I do acquire the inn, it won't get in the way of your campaign. I'll see to that."

Callie felt her ire rising at the man's claim of concern for Dorothy. Hadn't Parks immediately pointed to Dorothy as Cliff Ashby's murderer? She couldn't let him get away with that pious pretense . "Yes, I heard you were an old friend of Cliff's," she said. "It's good of you to want to help his widow, especially since she was instrumental in that lawsuit filed against you by one of your employees for age discrimination."

"What's that?" Elliott asked, his eyebrows raised.

Parks glared silently at Callie, obviously regretting his earlier compliments. Not overly concerned, Callie added, "I wouldn't count on Dorothy being in a hurry to sell the inn. She may be under suspicion right now. But there's a lot of us working to shift that suspicion onto the proper person."

Elliott cleared his throat and looked at his watch. "I'm afraid we have to leave. My car will be picking us up."

As they walked off, Callie heard Brian's voice behind her. "Good for you," he said softly.

She turned. "I didn't know you were here."

"I came over as soon as I realized who that was. If you hadn't said something to Parks, I might have."

"I just couldn't stand hearing him talk as if he cared about Dorothy's welfare. I'll bet there's more nastiness lurking in his background than the lawsuit that the mayor didn't know about. Maybe he'll start looking for it."

Callie watched as the two men worked their way through the crowd, their progress slowed by the several townspeople who had things to say to the mayor. At one point, Parks looked back at Callie, who returned his venomous stare steadily, though she felt her knees quiver. She might have stood up for what was right. But in the process, she'd made an enemy.

Twenty

When Callie got back to *House of Melody*, she found Tabitha dealing with a shop-full of customers and plunged in to help. As expected, the smaller music boxes were flying off the shelves, but several customers showed interest in her higher-end stock.

"I never knew about this shop," more than one person said; or, "I always meant to stop at Keepsake Cove, and Lyssa Hammond's being here pushed me to finally make the trip."

This was music to Callie's ears, as it confirmed that the book event had accomplished its main purpose beyond providing a fun time for everyone involved. On her return home, she'd noticed many other shops filled with customers, and the bookstore sales had been outstanding. How Lyssa had managed to hang in there she didn't know, though the author hadn't wasted any time accepting a ride back to the inn as soon as she'd finished signing, assuring everyone that she was fine while at the same time scurrying off. Callie planned to let her rest and check on her in the morning.

By ten o'clock—well past their usual closing time—the crowd had thinned and most of the shops emptied. Callie called it a day—a very busy day—and sent Tabitha home with many thanks for her extra support.

"I think we added some new serious collectors," Tabitha said as she made her way to the door. "That man who came all the way from Arlington, Virginia, for one, and the couple who live down the road in Oxford but never knew we were here."

Callie agreed that collectors were important to connect with. She enjoyed dealing with them the most because of their greater understanding of, and appreciation for, those music boxes that might cost a little more but would enrich their lives and become family heirlooms in time.

She closed down the register, happy to see the outstanding total, locked up, and walked out the back of the shop to get home. There were many pleasures attached to living in a fairy-tale-like cottage, but on a day like this, having a commute of about ten steps ranked at the top. Within minutes, while many people might still be dealing with traffic on their drive home, Callie was climbing into her soft bed, pulling up the puffy covers and sinking into a very welcome rest.

❧

The next morning most Keepsake Cove shops, including *House of Melody*, were closed due to the late hours of the night before, although many planned to open at noon. Callie appreciated the downtime of a leisurely breakfast, then called to see how Lyssa was doing.

"One hundred percent better!" the author cried, her renewed energy coming through the phone. "A twenty-four-hour flu is all I can figure. Although I haven't heard that was going around. Maybe I was the lucky first!"

"You said you started feeling sick as you waited in the hearse. You looked like death when you first came out, but I could see you picking up during your talk."

"Yeah, the sick stomach got better pretty quick, but I was still wrung out. Is there such a thing as a one-hour flu? Whatever it was, I'm glad it's done with."

"You were a real trooper, Lyssa. Keepsake Cove and I will be forever in your debt for hanging in there."

"I couldn't let all of you down. And frankly, I adore book events. Who wouldn't love hearing people praise every word you write? I'd drag myself on a broken leg for that," Lyssa cackled.

Glad to hear her in such good spirits, Callie told her about her encounter with Vernon Parks. "Remember the guy Paula said wanted to buy the inn? Brian told me he was golfing with our police chief when Ashby was found and pointed the finger at Dorothy. I think I may have caused Mapleton's mayor to reconsider their working relationship. At least I hope so."

"He sounds like a real weasel to me."

"What about George Cole?" Callie asked. "Did you get a chance to ask him about being at Dorothy and Clifford's wedding?"

"I did, and you should have seen his eyes pop. We were at dinner—Paula fixed us amazing crab cakes—and we were talking about the inn and how old it was. Remember how Jackie, the maid, told us it was built before the Civil War? Anyway, I worked the subject around to how it probably was a great place for weddings, you know, with the gardens and all. Then, feeling extremely clever, I asked if Cliff and Dorothy's wedding had been outdoors. When he stared at me, I said, 'You *were* there, weren't you?'" Lyssa grinned. "He probably thought I was a witch for knowing that. But after a moment he babbled something about it being indoors. I pressed, asking if knowing Cliff was the reason he'd booked a room at the Foxwood Inn, and he said no, that the wedding was the only time they'd met. He claimed he'd only been there to escort his mother, who was a friend of Dorothy's mother, and that when he'd stayed at the inn before, it was under different ownership."

"Yes, he did tell me that. Did you ask why he hadn't mentioned this before?"

"He said it didn't occur to him."

"Hmm. Anything else?"

"No, Paula stepped in to offer dessert about that time, and I realized it was getting late and asked for coffee that I could take to my room while I changed. The coffee wasn't ready, but George offered to bring it up when it was. When he knocked on my door I just grabbed the mug and thanked him. My hearse was due to arrive soon."

"I didn't see George at the event last night. Was he planning to come?"

"No, he told me at dinner he doesn't enjoy big crowds. I'd already signed his book."

"How about this morning? Have you seen him? I wonder if he might have come down with whatever made you sick."

"I didn't go down to breakfast, but I did hear him leave his room a few minutes ago and then saw him head out to his car. So I guess he's fine."

"Well, I'm glad you're feeling so much better. I'd better go." Callie wished Lyssa a relaxing day, though her own would be busy. She'd start by pitching in on the clean-up at the event area.

When Callie arrived at the park, the rental staff had already taken down the tent poles and were efficiently folding up the polyethylene top. She stepped around them to get to the gazebo. The two tables from the night before had been folded and moved to the side, and she saw Missy Tate sweeping. Missy's shop sold collectible garden items such as statues and globes, which Callie enjoyed browsing through, though buying any objects for her tiny yard was out of the question. She liked Missy, finding the older woman's lively personality fun, though she'd probably find her exhausting over time. Ordinary, everyday problems tended to be crises for Missy, which, Callie guessed, might be why the woman had volunteered to clean up the day after. No pressure involved.

Missy looked up from her sweeping, saw Callie, and waved. "You wouldn't believe the amount of dirt that got tracked in." She tucked a stray strand of brown hair behind her ear. Her outfit of sweatshirt over jeans was similar to Callie's, though gray instead of navy and possibly a couple of sizes larger. "Next year let's put doormats out for people to wipe their feet." She giggled at her joke.

"I don't want to even think about next year," Callie said, stepping in to the gazebo.

"It'll be hard to top this one."

Callie turned and saw Missy's husband, Jack, on a ladder, taking down the decorations Bill Hart had put up the day before.

"Thanks, Jack. Do you have the box that those go into?"

"Right over there." He pointed to the large box several steps from his ladder.

"How about handing them down to me, and I'll pack?" Callie asked, going over.

As they began to work together, Missy said, "I loved the sound effects." As if to illustrate, she suddenly screamed, making Callie jump and Jack nearly lose his balance.

"What's wrong!" he cried, steadying his ladder.

"A mouse just ran out right at me!" Missy said. "Scared me half to death."

"You scared *me* half to death, honey." But Jack chuckled as he said it, apparently used to his wife's dramatic moments. He detached a skeleton and held it out to Callie.

"I guess Jerry packed up his equipment?" Callie asked, folding the various joints of the plastic bones.

"Last night," Jack said, reaching for a hanging black cat. "He'd just finished loading it into his car before we followed him out."

"Good." Callie heard voices and saw two more helpers arriving as the tent was bundled into its truck.

"What can we do?" one of the men asked.

Callie struggled to think of his name and gave up. "Mind picking up the litter? Either the park trash cans weren't enough or one got tipped over and blown around. There's trash bags in my tote." She pointed to where she'd dropped it near the steps.

"I'll help," Missy said. "I'm done sweeping." She found the box of trash bags and handed them out, taking one herself. The good side of Missy's overexcitability was the energy that fed it, which could be very productive.

The three of them spread out as the tent crew started carrying away the folded-up chairs, everyone working quietly until Callie was hailed by Del Hodges. "Came to take the wagon back. Anyone want to get the stuff out of it?" he asked, referring to the scarecrow and jack-o'-lanterns.

"I'll get them," one of Callie's anonymous but hardworking volunteers said and trotted off with Del.

The others continued their litter-picking, Missy moving farther into the trees to chase down several slips of paper that had been handed out for the book signing and carelessly discarded. Jack climbed down from his ladder and moved it to the other side of the gazebo, and Callie dragged the bulky but lightweight box after him. They'd just begun detaching another set of decorations when they heard Missy's piercing scream.

Jack took a deep breath. "What is it, hon?" he called out. "A dead squirrel?"

"Jack! Jack! Oh my God!" Missy cried, panic in her voice. "Come here! Hurry! It's Renata. Oh my God! I think she's dead!"

Callie and Jack both froze, staring at each other. Then Callie spun around and ran into the woods as Jack scrambled down the ladder. She found Missy backed up against a tree, one hand pressed against her mouth as she pointed a trembling finger at Renata, who was lying in a shady spot among fallen leaves, some dotting her.

From the ashen color of her skin, Callie was sure Renata was dead, but as she drew closer, there was no question. The woman's eyes stared sightlessly up at the trees, her mouth sagged open in a silent scream, and a pair of very long scissors jutted out from her chest.

Twenty-One

J ack arrived moments behind Callie. He stopped at the sight of Renata's body, then hurried over to Missy, engulfing her in a hug and shielding her from the gruesome scene.

"The scissors!" Missy cried. "Did you see the scissors? She's done it again. It must have been Dorothy!"

Callie was calling 911 and tried to shield her phone from picking up Missy's words. Her own hands were shaking and her stomach roiled as she turned away from the sight.

"Hush, honey," Jack said soothingly. "We don't know that for sure. Don't say that." He led his sobbing wife back to the gazebo as Callie reported to the operator what they'd found as calmly as she could manage. She then hurried after the pair to prevent any others from rushing in and disrupting the scene.

Disbelief, shock, and horror reigned as Callie filled everyone in, including the tent-rental team, who had been moments away from leaving. Everyone appeared to look to her for instructions, though she felt the one least capable at the moment. It was all too reminiscent of the day she'd discovered Aunt Mel's body in her shop, and many of those same emotions now flooded her. On that day, though, Callie had been the only one who'd suspected it was murder. The sight of Renata's stabbed and bloody body left no room for doubt. The only question was who had committed this horrible crime. Callie couldn't believe it was Dorothy. But Missy continued to babble about the scissors and blame the sewing shop owner.

"Please," Callie begged those gathered around her. "Don't jump to conclusions. Let the police look at the evidence. It might tell a different story." The others nodded but their faces looked doubtful. Callie could only hope it was due to shock. Thankfully, by the time they heard sirens, Jack had managed to calm Missy somewhat, though she sobbed quietly into his chest.

The first patrolmen to arrive called quickly for an investigative team and began the questioning. Callie knew from experience that they would all tell their stories multiple times. She texted Tabitha to explain why she wouldn't be able to open the shop. Tabitha immediately promised to take care of everything, which Callie was grateful for, though she privately doubted there'd be much beyond opening up to take care of. Once word spread about what had happened, all attention would be on the park and any intentions to shop would disappear.

Several minutes later, when Callie was inside the gazebo giving an account of her moment-by-moment actions to an investigating officer, she heard a commotion. Jerry Moore had rushed up the path, only to be held back by two patrolmen.

"Where is she! Where is my wife!"

"Please, sir, you can't go there."

"Who killed her? Who could do such a thing? Was it that Ashby woman?"

"Sir, we're still investigating. If you would step over here—" The officers managed to ease Jerry farther away, though Callie could still hear him.

What was happening to Dorothy in the meantime? Had she been dragged off to answer these fresh accusations? Could she *prove* she had nothing to do with Renata's death? Callie feared the worst. If the scissors she'd seen jutting out of Renata's chest proved to be Dorothy's, who would believe that Dorothy was innocent of murder?

❧

When she finally made it back to the shop, exhausted, Callie faced yet another round of questions, though from far more sympathetic individuals. The first was Tabitha, though Callie had barely stepped through the door before Brian came hurrying over.

"I tried to get to you at the park," he said, "but they've blocked it all off." He gave Callie a comforting but one-armed hug since he was holding a take-out box. "Thought you might need something to eat."

Callie smiled, pretty sure what it would be: her favorite ham and cheese with Brian's special sauce, plus a dill pickle. "I'm starved. Thank you. Does anyone know what's happened with Dorothy? *Stitches Thru Time* was closed when I passed by, and the cottage was dark."

"Keepsake Cove shopkeeper calls have been flying back and forth," Tabitha said. "Laurie Hart said she saw Dorothy and Jane being driven off in a police car."

"Not in handcuffs?"

"No," Tabitha said, though hesitantly, as though it was just a matter of time. "Were the scissors hers?" she asked.

Callie shook her head. "I don't know."

"How long do you suppose Renata was dead?" Brian asked, then added gently, "If you'd rather not talk about it, that's fine. I just wondered if and when Moore reported his wife missing."

"It's okay. I've grown numb to what I saw by now," Callie said. "My guess would be several hours. I heard Jerry say Renata was supposed to have left on a trip right after the book event for an estate sale in Pennsylvania. She had planned to stay in that area overnight to be at the sale early. He didn't know she hadn't made it until this morning. The police reached him at his brother's house in Easton," she went on. "He headed there right after taking down his system at the book event." Callie frowned. "He kept shouting that Dorothy must have killed Renata, claiming she hated her."

"That part's true, isn't it?" Tabitha asked. "I mean that Dorothy had a pretty solid problem with Renata. Renata was bad-mouthing her ever since Cliff Ashby's murder."

"And long before that," Callie said. "But I'd call that a grievance rather than hatred." Though as she said it, Callie could imagine the years of verbal abuse that Dorothy had endured churning into hatred as Renata took the first opportunity to sling more mud at her.

"However you define it," Brian said, "that bitterness between them plus the murder weapon puts Dorothy in a very bad position."

Callie flashed to the gruesome image of Renata's body with scissors jabbed into it. Could they have been wrong about their friend? "But why would Dorothy use the very tool that would point to her?" she argued. "Wouldn't she be smarter than that?"

Brian shrugged. "If we're talking about someone who's in full control and thinking logically, yes, of course. But a person who might have snapped ... ?" He left the thought unfinished, and both Callie and Tabitha grimaced as they acknowledged the possibility. Callie remembered Jerry's description of Dorothy screaming over the phone.

Movement across the street caught their attention. Customers were heading toward the café. Apparently standing watch just outside a crime scene made one hungry. "I'd better get back," Brian said.

Callie nodded.

"I'm sorry to leave you with that grim thought," he said. "I hope I'm wrong."

"I hope you are, too," Callie said. And time would tell. She'd done all she could for the moment.

Or had she? At the moment, she was tired and hungry. Maybe after Brian's sandwich and a refreshing clean-up, something would come to her. With that slim hope, she left Tabitha in charge and headed to the cottage.

❧

By midafternoon, Tabitha had taken off and Callie had answered multiple calls from other Keepsake Cove shop owners, most wanting to know what she knew. All feared for the Cove's reputation as a great place to visit. As one put it, "People will be calling us Creepsake Cove, the stabbing capital of Maryland!"

Callie understood their concerns—their livelihoods were at stake here—but she tried to keep the focus on Dorothy's predicament. "If you learn anything at all that might help her, please let me know," she begged.

She was hanging up from one such call when Delia walked in. "I've closed up for the day," she said. "Traffic has been so slow it's not worth the cost of keeping the lights on." She sighed. "Or the stress of standing around doing nothing. Who knew idleness could be stressful?"

"Pick out one of my music boxes to play," Callie said. "It'll soothe you. After all the upset people I've been dealing with, I might do the same."

Delia smiled. "Dueling music boxes?"

Callie returned the smile and was about to suggest one in particular when a woman walked into her shop. Dressed in loose denims with a floppy hat over curly brown hair, she wasn't recognizable as a regular customer, especially with half her face covered by huge sunglasses.

"Good afternoon," Callie greeted her. "What can I help you with?"

The woman whipped off her sunglasses and grinned. "Oh, about a thousand things, starting with how to start my next chapter." She slid the hat and hair off in one swoop and finger-combed her red hair back to its usual spikes.

"Lyssa!"

"Whew! That wig gets hot!" The author chuckled at Delia, whose mouth had dropped open. "It comes in handy when I need to be incognito. Today was one of those times."

"But, but..." Delia stammered. "Why?"

"Easier to mix and mingle in crowds and listen in. People tend to shut up when they recognize me, as if I were a reporter or something. Hah! Of course I do sometimes put their words in my books—disguised, naturally."

"Ah," Callie said. "So what did you manage to pick up?"

Lyssa's face fell. "Not a whole lot. I couldn't get close to the murder scene—drat! But I understand she was stabbed with scissors, just like Ashby?"

"I'm afraid so," Callie said. "And Dorothy's being questioned. She apparently came across as threatening to Renata. That, along with the scissors..."

"And the husband has an alibi?"

Callie told her about Jerry's overnight stay at his brother's.

"But you found her body fairly close to the event area, right? Could he have killed her last night while everything was going on?"

"She was in different clothes from the ones I saw her in last night. She must have gone home and changed."

"Then what was she doing back in the park?"

"I don't know."

"Hmm," Lyssa said. "I suppose the police will work out the time of death, when Jerry arrived at his brother's, and all that. What about Dorothy? Where was she?"

"All I know is I didn't see her at the book event. I wasn't able to reach her before it started, and with everything going on it slipped my mind to try again later. But I'm assuming she was home all night with Jane."

"The same alibi she had for Ashby's murder."

"Yes," said Delia. "But an alibi is an alibi."

"I agree. But it would be good if a second person other than Jane could back it up," Lyssa said. "I overheard people sharing some of the things Renata said about Dorothy, and it put her in a pretty bad light."

"Like what?"

"Like, that Dorothy had a Jekyll and Hyde personality—she was nice enough to those who went along with her but would turn on anyone who crossed her. Viciously."

"That's awful!" Delia cried.

"Agreed," Lyssa said. "And, of course, there's only Renata's word for it."

"And maybe Jerry's," Callie said. She told Lyssa about his report that Dorothy had made a screaming phone call to Renata. "He surely must have given the police Renata's version of their history."

"Still only hearsay," Lyssa said. "I'm not a lawyer, but a couple of my characters are," she said with a quick grin. Then she frowned.

"Though it might influence investigators, subconsciously ... Oh, I heard something else interesting. You know that golf tournament that Vernon Parks and the police chief were at when Cliff Ashby was found murdered? Well, Jerry Moore was there with them."

"Really? How did that come up?" Callie asked.

"Someone in the crowd threw it out during a discussion about Ashby and Renata probably being murdered by the same person—you know, because of the scissors and all. One young guy said, 'Well, that lets Jerry out. He was at a golf tournament with the chief of police when Ashby was killed. I know because I was his caddy!'"

"I'd say that's about as iron-clad as you can get," Callie said. "But it makes me wonder about Jerry's connection to Vernon Parks."

"Uh-huh." Lyssa nodded firmly.

"I did see Renata hurrying over to him last night, shortly after he'd arrived with the mayor. But I didn't hear any of the conversation."

"Pity," Lyssa said. "It might have been interesting."

Grandpa Reed's music box began to chirp, but before anyone could comment on it, the shop door opened. All three stared as Jane walked in.

Twenty-Two

J ane," Callie cried, the first to recover from her surprise. "You're
back!"

"Yes, and Dorothy is too. She went directly to the cottage to rest.
She's quite shaken. But she wanted me to come talk to you."

"So she hasn't been charged?"

"No, but I doubt she could feel any worse if she had been. It's been
devastating."

By the drawn look on her face, Jane wasn't feeling all that great
herself. Callie pulled out a chair for her. "Would you like some coffee?
Water? Something to eat?"

Jane smiled wanly. "A little water would be good."

Callie grabbed one of the bottles she kept in a cooler behind the
counter as Jane sank onto the chair. She was dressed in a hooded
sweater over jeans, more casual than what she usually wore for tending the shop. Apparently *Stitches Thru Time* had been closed that

morning, along with most of the Keepsake Cove shops. Callie wondered if it would be closed for good.

Jane accepted the bottled water, twisted off the top, and drank thirstily. After recapping it, she said, "Dorothy has been so grateful for your faith in her. She wanted me to assure you that she had nothing whatsoever to do with Renata's murder. I can verify that. I was with her all day yesterday and all night until the police hammered on our door this morning."

"The scissors, of course, are problematic," Lyssa said, leaning against a table of novelty musical boxes. She'd pushed her wig and hat out of sight, Callie noticed.

"The scissors weren't hers!" Jane said it with as much energy as she could muster. "The police showed Dorothy a photo of them. She knew immediately they didn't come from her shop, and told them so."

"How could she tell?" Callie asked.

"Because they are old, yes, but that's all. The brand name was visible. They're just common scissors. Dorothy only stocks unique collectibles. She also pointed out what looked like rust around the hinge and told the police she'd never carry something in that condition." Jane sighed. "I don't know if they totally believed her."

"But they let her go home," Callie said, "And that's good."

Jane's pinched brows showed that she worried it might be only temporary.

"She's not alone," Delia assured her. "We still believe in her."

"Thank you."

"Jane," Callie asked, "I'm sure the stress since her husband's murder has been awful for Dorothy. Is that what caused her to call Renata the day before the book event? Had she reached her breaking point?"

"What? Call Renata? What are you talking about?"

"Jerry Moore told me Dorothy had called her. He said he could hear her screaming at Renata. He was worried about what might happen if they ran into each other."

"Well, they didn't," Jane said, indignant. "Dorothy was with me the entire time the day of the book event, as I said. As far as the phone call, I can't imagine Dorothy doing that. I just can't. Dorothy didn't have a breakdown. And she gave up confronting Renata years ago after realizing it only added fuel for her. Dorothy would never have done that."

Callie nodded, but she also knew Dorothy could have made the call when Jane was out of earshot.

Jane took a final swallow of water, then stood. "I'm going to open up *Stitches Thru Time*." Seeing their surprise, she said, "I know, crazy. But Dorothy agrees, and she'll be there, too, if she can. We just can't stand the thought of leaving it closed. Even if not a single person comes in, we'll be making a statement. We haven't given up."

"Good for you," Lyssa said.

"Are you sure?" Delia asked. "You might have to deal with some unpleasantness. I hope not, but there's always someone ... "

Callie reached out and gave Jane a hug. "You'll be fine."

"Thank you. I've told my children I intend to stay here, and why, and they agree it's the right thing to do."

Callie had forgotten about Jane's family. "Two daughters and a son," she said, recalling what Dorothy had told her that day that now seemed so long ago. "Is that right?"

"Yes." Jane's eyes misted briefly, but she lifted her chin. "I miss them terribly. They're the most important people in my life since my husband's death, especially now that Emily is expecting my first grandchild. But I can't abandon Dorothy at a time like this."

She handed back her empty water bottle and bid the three women goodbye. As the door closed behind her, Callie said, "I think there's a toughness in her that's just starting to show."

"I hope so," Delia said. "She might need it."

Later that day, Callie was considering following Delia's lead and closing early when she got a call from Laurie Hart.

"Did you know Dorothy's back home?" she asked.

"I did. Jane stopped in to tell me."

"We were in our back room most of the day, polishing up our latest toy acquisitions, so we didn't notice until a little while ago that Jane's opened the shop."

"She said she intended to. It was important to both of them. I hope she didn't have any trouble."

"I don't think so. But then she might have had help heading it off."

"Oh?"

"An older gentleman left just a little while ago. From the look on Jane's face and the lingering hand clasps at the door, I'm pretty sure he wasn't a customer."

From Laurie's description, Callie recognized George Cole. What was going on there? Renata's murder had pushed the questions that had arisen about Cole to the back of her mind. She wanted the answers now. After a quick lockup of *House of Melody*, she went after them.

Stitches Thru Time was one of the few shops open, since the crime investigation at the park continued to either draw the curious or drive away potential customers. Even Howard Graham's Christmas shop was dark, unusual for Howard, who rarely gave up hope for one more sale. A peek through Dorothy's window showed Jane inside, alone, dusting the shelves. Callie went in.

"Oh!" Jane cried, surprised but not displeased. "If you came to see Dorothy, I'm afraid she's resting, though she might—"

"No, I came to see you," Callie said, noticing that Jane had changed from her sweater and jeans into a pretty blouse and skirt. The woman set down her duster and looked at Callie expectantly.

"Jane, you know we've been trying to help Dorothy in every way we can. But we need honesty." She paused. "From *both* of you."

"Both ...?"

"Yes. From you, too, Jane. You're an essential part of the picture, you see, because you're Dorothy's alibi. So it's important that we understand everything that's going on. You haven't been totally open with us, have you?" She watched as Jane flushed, just as she had on that first day when Callie had asked the reason for her sudden visit.

"What do you mean?" Jane asked.

"I mean George Cole."

"Oh!" The flush remained but a small smile appeared with it. "What about George?"

"Neither one of you mentioned to us that you knew each other. Why not? Is he the reason you came to Keepsake Cove?"

"No, I had no idea George was here. We haven't seen or heard from each other for decades. Running into one another here was a total surprise."

"But you knew George in Greenock?"

Jane blinked, apparently surprised Callie knew that. "Only briefly," she said after a moment. She picked up a wooden darning egg from a nearby shelf and looked down at it as she rubbed her fingers over its smooth surface. "We met at Dorothy's wedding," she said, glancing up briefly. "He was a little older, so we hadn't been in high school at the same time, and he went away for college afterward. We danced a few times at the reception, and I was very flattered when he asked me out. But it wasn't long before he had to leave for a new job, and I … I became involved with someone else. We lost touch—until now. It was unexpected but lovely to see him again. He seems to feel the same."

She returned the darning egg to its spot on the shelf and gazed steadily at Callie, who struggled to read her expression. Did Jane expect skepticism at the possibility of romance at her current age? Or was she challenging Callie to believe her account?

"I thought I heard voices!" Dorothy emerged from the back room. "I wondered if we actually had a customer, but this is even better. I'm so glad I cut my rest time short. It's good to see you," she said, going up to give Callie a hug.

"How are you doing?" Callie asked. Dorothy looked better than the last time she'd seen her. Surprisingly so, since Jane had described her as shaken. It appeared to Callie that a second grilling by police had somehow reinvigorated her.

"I'm good," Dorothy said. "Good and mad. I decided I'm tired of being cowed by other people's assumptions about me. They can think what they want, but I know who and what I am, and it's not a murderer. No more hiding as if I'm guilty."

"I'm glad to hear it," Callie said, though the flash in Dorothy's eyes made her uneasy. Perhaps her eagerness to take charge was natural after feeling so beaten down. "Is that what prompted you to call Renata on Monday?" she asked. Jerry's story needed to be either confirmed or denied.

Dorothy nodded firmly. "I knew what lies she'd been spreading about me lately. I'd had enough, and I told her so."

"Exactly how did you tell her? Her husband said he could hear you screaming."

Dorothy's lip curled. "I might have. I probably shouldn't have, but I've held so much back for so long that it all came rushing out. But," she hurriedly added, "I didn't threaten. And I definitely didn't kill Renata. Jane can back me up on the fact that I never left the cottage that entire day and night."

Jane nodded vigorously, though, Callie remembered, she previously hadn't been aware of Dorothy's call to Renata. "I tried to reach you, both on your shop phone and your cottage line, but only got the recording. I did leave a message."

"And I heard it. I'm sorry. I should have called you back."

"I've since learned what I wanted to ask you about," Callie said. "The man who's been staying at the Foxwood Inn, George Cole. I found out he attended your wedding."

"He did?"

"Yes, he did," Jane said quickly. "I meant to tell you, Dorothy. You probably don't remember him. But he remembered us, and he stopped in here to offer his support. He's been very kind."

Dorothy blinked but didn't ask for more explanation. Another subject concerned her more, and she turned to it. "Those scissors," she said to Callie, "were definitely not mine. They were junk, total junk! I would never have stocked anything like that, and I told the police so."

She ranted on about the murder weapon, seeming more upset to be accused of carrying bad merchandise than of killing Renata. Was that a good sign or not, Callie wondered as she let Dorothy go on. Was there a right way to react, after all Dorothy had had to deal with? Callie didn't know and decided the important thing was to concentrate on facts, not impressions.

Which was exactly what she was mulling over as she headed back home. While on the way, she heard her phone signal a call.

"Feel like hitting a few golf balls tonight?" Lyssa asked.

"Golf balls? Why? What's up?"

"Remember that caddy I overheard when I went to the park incognito? The young guy who said Jerry Moore was golfing with the police chief when Cliff Ashby was murdered? I managed to track him down. I got him to caddy for us."

Twenty-Three

"Don't you need to be a member to play at this country club?"
Callie thought to ask this only after they were already halfway
there and she'd filled Lyssa in on the latest developments. She sat in
the passenger seat of Lyssa's Corvette, having left her own car at the
Foxwood Inn, and was mostly enjoying her ride, only occasionally
grabbing onto the door during fast turns.

"It's semi-private. Luckily this isn't their peak time."

"I did tell you I've barely hit a dozen golf balls in my life, right?"

"Doesn't matter. Our story is that I'm introducing you to the
game. Just try not to hit anyone."

Lyssa had advised Callie on golf-appropriate clothing, and she'd
found a white polo shirt in decent shape to top a pair of khaki cutoffs.
She'd added a light sweater to ward off the chill. Lyssa had dressed much
more colorfully—no surprise to Callie, who'd already picked up on the
author's more eye-catching preferences, except when going incognito.

"So," Callie said, "Parks, Moore, and the police chief were playing
in a golf tournament the day Cliff Ashby was murdered."

"I'm not sure if they were *in* the tournament," Lyssa said. "They might have been there as spectators but got in a round themselves."

"With our soon-to-be-caddy."

"Right."

"And what do we hope to learn from him?" Callie asked.

"Beats me. You're the detective. I'm just going for the golf." Lyssa glanced over at Callie and grinned.

"I'm going to assume you're joking, since I'll need a lot of help, in more ways than one. For instance, are caddies likely to talk about what they overhear from their clients?"

"It's in their best interests to be discreet. But this guy seemed like a talker, so it might not be hard to get him started."

"Good."

"And a little flirting might help."

"From who?" Callie asked.

"You, of course. I'll be concentrating on my game." Lyssa grinned again, though Callie wasn't sure she was entirely joking this time. She sighed, wondering what she'd agreed to. Best case, they'd learn something important about both Vernon Parks and Jerry Moore. Worst? They'd end up with nothing, she'd look like an idiot on the golf course, and a pimply-faced teenaged caddy would call her twice a day for the next six months.

❧

The Abbotsville Country Club was impressive, beautifully landscaped with not a single autumn leaf to be seen on its manicured lawns. Lyssa drove through its open wrought-iron gate toward the Tara-like clubhouse, passing tennis courts and a swimming pool that was closed for the season. Callie gazed longingly at the tennis courts, which she at least knew her way around enough to play a decent game. But they disappeared in the side mirror as Lyssa continued on to the pro shop.

"I didn't bring my clubs with me to the B&B," Lyssa said. "Didn't expect to need them. So I'll rent a set we can both use. We're about the same height, right? We can rent shoes, too."

"And share those, too?" Callie asked wryly.

"Ha-ha. Save your jokes for Travis."

"Who?"

"Our caddy. Travis Campbell. He'll probably laugh at all our jokes, good or bad."

"But not our game, I presume."

"Not if he knows what's good for him." Lyssa parked and led the way into the shop, winding her way between racks of golf apparel. "Hi," she said to the man standing behind the counter. "Tracy Hamilton. I called for a five o'clock tee time?"

Tracy Hamilton? Lyssa hadn't mentioned being incognito again, but Callie, though surprised, rolled with it, sure that there must be times that Lyssa just didn't want to be asked about her books.

The fifty-something man with thinning hair ran a finger down the page of his scheduling book. "Yes, Ms. Hamilton. Oh, but I see we have a small problem."

"We?"

"Well, our mistake but your problem, I'm afraid, depending on how important it is for Travis to caddy for you."

Uh-oh. Callie winced. Had they come all that way for nothing?

"Travis is very important," Lyssa said. "I was told he was available."

"I'm extremely sorry. It's our fault entirely. Somehow he was double-booked. He's out on the links right now with another group."

"When will he be done?" Callie asked.

The desk attendant did some quick calculation and estimated twenty to thirty minutes. "We do have another excellent caddy available if you'd like—"

"No," Lyssa declared. "That won't do." She turned to Callie. "How about we go to the driving range instead?" She explained to the desk man, "My friend is learning the game. Perhaps Travis could come over when he's back and give her a quick lesson?"

"Absolutely!" The man's face brightened, and he penciled that in. "A large bucket of balls?"

"And two drivers."

They worked out the sizes of the clubs and picked up their balls. Lyssa paid in cash, waving away Callie's effort to chip in, and they headed toward the driving range. Callie was pleased not to have to actually play a game. After Lyssa watched her hit a couple of dribbling balls and miss the next, she was probably pleased as well. She gave Callie a couple of tips, then moved over to hit a few balls herself, all of which soared beautifully.

By the time Travis Campbell showed up, Callie's swing had improved to the point where she was actually enjoying herself. Tall, red-haired, and not much older than the teenager she'd expected, Travis apologized for the mix-up and offered a knowledgeable-sounding critique of both women's swings.

"Thanks," Lyssa said. "But we're not actually here for a lesson."

"You're not?" Travis looked as surprised as Callie at this sudden switch.

"No. We've been asked to look into the activities of a couple of people." Lyssa's voice had turned *no-nonsense investigator*. "Vernon Parks and Jerry Moore. You've caddied for them in the last week or so, right?"

"Uh, yeah! Hey, Moore's the guy whose wife was just murdered. What, is he a suspect or something?" Travis's eyes were wide with excitement. Luckily for them, he was young and naïve enough not to think of asking for credentials, though Callie wondered how much trouble Lyssa could be getting them into.

"Just standard procedure," Lyssa assured him. "Have to check on everyone, you understand."

"Yeah, sure, so what do you want to know?"

"Dates and times they were here."

"Uh ... " Travis pulled a notebook from his back pocket and thumbed through it. "The day of the tournament, I was here on the driving range with them. Vernon Parks with Jerry Moore and Ben Sommers."

"Our chief," Callie said. "We know about that one. When else?"

He read off two more dates from the past week. "Just Parks and Moore, these times."

Callie tapped the information into her phone, hoping it looked official enough to Travis. "What did they talk about?"

Travis thought hard. "Uh, lots of stuff, I guess."

"Just what you think might be important," Callie prompted. "Did Cliff Ashby's name come up?"

"Oh, yeah! But they were both here when he was murdered."

"The day of the tournament, yes," Callie said. "And the chief got the call the next morning. We're aware of that."

"Right. They all left quickly, and their tee time that day was canceled. So Ashby's name never came up then." Callie was drawing a breath when Travis added, "But it came up a lot during the times Parks and Moore were here after that."

"Go on," Lyssa said.

Travis's eyes turned skyward as he searched his memory, which Callie hoped was a good one. "Something about buying Ashby's B&B together."

Wow. Callie was glad the caddy was looking at Lyssa, who, unlike her, managed to stay stone-faced.

"Details," Lyssa said.

"Uh, I don't remember all that much. Business talk mostly goes right over my head." Travis cleared his throat. "But I do remember Parks going on about what a fantastic opportunity it was, and that they could get it for a song when the widow got charged."

"Uh-hum." Lyssa managed to sound matter-of-fact as Callie's blood started to boil. "What did Moore have to say to that?"

"He seemed to be holding back, which I guess was why Parks kept at him about it. Maybe he didn't have the money? I dunno."

"Anything else?" Callie asked.

"Uh, this isn't going to get me in trouble with them, is it? I mean, I need the jobs."

"Totally confidential," Lyssa promised.

"Okay, then. Uh, Vernon Parks talked a lot about how tight he was with the mayor, the police chief, and other higher-ups at the state-house. He said his connections would guarantee they'd have a full house at the B&B, and that they'd be looking to expand the place within a year."

"Big plans, huh?"

"Sure sounded like it."

"Are you sure Vernon Parks left with the chief that morning?" Callie asked. "Could he have left the night before?" As she said it, she hoped it wouldn't occur to Travis that they should know this if they were who they pretended to be. The chief, unfortunately, hadn't confided in either

Lyssa or her. With the negative opinion she had of Parks, though, Callie needed to be reassured that he hadn't had the opportunity to kill Cliff Ashby.

"Pretty sure," Travis said. "They all arrived in one car. A sweet one!" He rhapsodized for a while about the Lincoln Navigator that the chief had driven up in, with its twin turbo-charged engine and other features. "'Course, you can always grab a ride with Uber."

Yes! There were several ways Parks could have made it to Keepsake Cove and back to murder Ashby while maintaining his alibi.

Travis's cell phone signaled a text. "Hey, got another job waiting for me. I gotta go." He looked up with a worried face. "Is that okay?"

"Fine," Lyssa said. "Keep all this to yourself, of course. And if you think of anything else … " She searched through her purse. "Damn. Where's my cards?" She scribbled on the back of the receipt for the golf balls and drivers and handed it to him. "You can reach me direct with that number. Don't lose it."

Travis nodded solemnly and tucked the paper into his notebook. He walked off, and they picked up their clubs and ball bucket.

"You know he's going to talk about this," Callie said, once Travis was out of earshot. "Will we get into trouble?"

"We who? Tracy Hamilton? That's the only name they have. And we never claimed to be police, did we? Or flashed phony credentials."

"The cell phone number you gave him?"

"A burner phone," she said, grinning. "I haven't written all those books without picking up a few things. It's a slim chance our Travis will call with anything new he's remembered. But I'll check it every so often. You never know."

Yes, you never know, Callie thought as they dropped off their clubs and "Tracy Hamilton" chatted charmingly with the thin-haired man still behind the counter. She hadn't known how good Lyssa could be at pretense. A successful author, of course, had to be good at making up characters and putting words into their mouths. So it shouldn't be surprising that she could so easily become a character herself.

But it still kind of was.

Twenty-Four

On the ride back, Lyssa asked, "Do you really think Parks had an Uber driver take him back to Keepsake Cove that night?"

"No. There'd be a record of that somewhere, and he'd know that," Callie said. "But he could have managed it some other way."

"You want him to be the murderer."

"It'd be nice," Callie admitted. "Especially after he did his best to put Dorothy in that spot. But I don't know if wanting to get the Foxwood Inn at a bargain price is enough of a motive."

"He'd have to be pretty greedy," Lyssa agreed. "And for all we know, he is. But maybe there's other things involved. Hey, want to stop in at the B&B when we get back? I could call ahead and ask Paula if she can rustle up some dinner—nothing fancy—and maybe George will be around. He's been making himself scarce lately."

"I wouldn't mind a chat with him," Callie said. "Will Paula mind?"

"Let's find out." Lyssa placed the call through her Bluetooth system as she drove, and Callie heard Paula offer a salad with a version of Eggs Benedict on her homemade brown bread.

"It's all I have on hand," she said.

Callie quickly agreed that it sounded great.

"We'll be there in twenty minutes," Lyssa told Paula. "And thanks!"

Callie grabbed onto her seat as the Corvette picked up speed.

⮐

Paula's simple meal tasted amazing. After the long, stress-filled day, comfort food was welcome.

Of course, Paula had questions about Renata Moore's murder. Lyssa invited her to join them for a cup of coffee in the Victorian dining room, and as they ate, Callie filled her in on the basics of how the body had been discovered and the murder weapon.

"Scissors again! I heard that but didn't believe it. Were they Mrs. Ashby's?"

"Dorothy told me the scissors were absolutely not hers," Callie assured her, seeing that Paula was distressed. The sewing shop owner, after all, was Paula's de facto boss, and her ability to remain so affected Paula's livelihood. "And Dorothy's cousin vouches for the fact that she was at home all that night."

"Then ... then, who's doing this? What did Renata Moore have to do with Clifford Ashby?"

Callie wished she had an answer. All she could offer was, "We're working on that."

"Which is what made us so late for dinner," Lyssa said, reaching for a second slice of brown bread from the basket Paula had set before them. "What can you tell us about Vernon Parks?"

Paula looked puzzled for a moment before it clicked. "Oh! The man who wants to buy the inn."

"Right. We know he and Cliff Ashby knew each other from their years in Annapolis. We also know that Ashby had started pressuring

Keepsake Cove shopkeepers in a way that would make him extra money. Would Vernon Parks have been a part of that scheme?"

"I … I didn't know about that." Paula looked honestly surprised. She shook her head. "It sounds just like Mr. Ashby. But if I knew anything about it, or whether Parks was involved, that would mean I was involved, too, wouldn't it?" Her expression darkened. "I wasn't."

"No, no, Paula," Lyssa assured her. "I just wondered if you might have overheard things—phone conversations or anything."

"I didn't." She stood after that flat statement, obviously not liking where the discussion had gone, and carried her cup into the kitchen.

"Sorry," Lyssa muttered to Callie.

"It's okay," Callie answered as quietly. "I doubt she had anything to tell us."

They worked silently on their dinners until they heard the front door open and footsteps head to the kitchen.

"Ah, Paula, you're here." Callie recognized George Cole's voice. "May I possibly have a cup of coffee to take to my room?"

Lyssa recognized the voice, too, and called out, "Bring it in here, George, and join us."

George Cole leaned through the doorway of the dining room. "What a pleasant surprise. You're having a late dinner. And Ms. Reed is here, too."

"At Lyssa's invitation. And Paula was kind enough to fix us something in a hurry. Do join us."

"I believe I will, thank you. That is, if this won't inconvenience Paula?" He turned questioningly toward the kitchen.

"I need to clean things up," Paula tersely replied. "It's late."

"Yes, you're right," Lyssa said, picking up her now-empty plate. "Let us help you, and perhaps we could take our coffee into the living room? I promise to rinse out the cups when we're done."

Callie followed with her own plate and the bread basket and saw Paula pouring out George's coffee. She then silently lined up two more mugs, apparently for Callie and Lyssa, and then elbowed them out of her way to do the rest on her own. The three meekly carried their mugs away and into the dimmed living room, heading for the velvet-covered sofas that Callie had last sat on with Cliff Ashby perched across from her.

Lyssa switched on an additional lamp. "There. Now we can see each other. So, George," she said, settling down, "what've you been up to?"

"Oh, this and that." He took a sip of his coffee and turned to Callie. "Any word on the music box I ordered?"

"For your daughter? I'm expecting it soon."

George nodded, and Lyssa said, "Oh come on, George. We know about you and Jane."

George's eyebrows rose, but he turned to set his mug carefully down on the table next to him. Finally he said, "And what is it you know?"

"Only that you forgot to mention that you knew each other," Lyssa said, her voice full of exasperation. "Like you forgot to mention that you went to Dorothy and Cliff's wedding."

"I did explain how that came about," he said.

"Right, you took your mother to it. But not a word about Jane until Callie got the story from her."

"You spoke to Jane?" he asked Callie. "And she told you about us?"

"She did."

"Well, then it's all right. I wasn't sure how much she'd want anyone to know. We've just been slowly reconnecting. That's how our generation does things, you know. Plus, there's our children to think about. Even though they're adults, they'll have feelings about the situation to consider."

A small lightbulb went off in Callie's head. "The music box isn't for your daughter, is it?"

George smiled. "A little white lie. I hope you'll forgive me. I took Jane to see a performance of *Oklahoma* on our first date. I thought she would enjoy that little reminder. What I said about my late wife being a good singer, on the other hand, was perfectly true. But neither she nor my daughter saw *Oklahoma* with me."

Callie nodded. It did sound sweet and sentimental. But she also remembered the smoothness of George's explanation (which he now admitted was false) when he placed the order for the music box.

"Jane must have made a strong impression on you," she said. "Yet, you didn't keep in touch when you left for your job."

George frowned. "It was my first job after college. I was so eager to prove myself and succeed that I set my personal life on hold. When I finally tried to reach her, she'd obviously been hurt by my silence and moved on. It was my mistake, completely."

"All very well and good," Lyssa said. "But why didn't you tell us it was Jane you saw talking to Cliff that afternoon before he was killed?"

"Because I simply didn't recognize her at first." George smiled. "Oddly enough, she's changed a bit in the forty-some years since I last saw her. I had to identify myself to her too, of course, though happily my name brought a smile to her face."

"Oh, George." Lyssa sighed. "Sorry for the grilling. But under the circumstances I hope you can understand. We have to be sure about everybody. Secrets only make us suspicious."

George acknowledged this with a dip of his head. "It should have occurred to me that my discretion, particularly given Jane's proximity to her cousin, might be misconstrued." He paused. "I really didn't recognize her from my window. And when I came down to get a cup of coffee shortly after, I asked Paula if she was a new guest at the inn, which she wasn't, of course. It wasn't until her name was mentioned later, along with Dorothy Ashby's, that it clicked." George drained his mug. "Speaking of guests," he said, "we've been joined by at least four new ones. Did you know?"

"No," Lyssa said. "When did they arrive?"

"Late this afternoon. Two couples. I happened to see them as I was on my way out but haven't met them. I suppose we'll get to do that at breakfast. I'm only concerned because Paula's staff seems to have dwindled."

"The housekeeper, Jackie?"

"No, Jackie's still here. But the younger one, Kelsey, has apparently quit. Paula's going to have her hands full."

"That's right. Jackie did mention that. And we added to her work with our last-minute dinner," Lyssa said. "Now I wish she'd just told us no." She glanced toward the kitchen. "Is she still staying here overnight?"

"I believe so. One of the smaller rooms. We should probably keep her workload in mind if our rooms aren't kept completely up to snuff." He rose and picked up his mug.

"Have you heard any more of those creaking noises behind the wall?" Callie asked, getting up as well.

"No, I haven't." George paused. "Which is interesting, though I don't know what it means."

They carried their mugs to the kitchen, which Paula had left sparkling clean, and washed and dried their own things as promised. Then they bid each other a good night and went their separate ways.

Callie, fighting off a yawn, envied the other two their much shorter trips to their beds as she made her way to her car. Although she was sure all the things she had to mull over during her drive home would keep her alert.

She followed the two-lane country road that led to Keepsake Cove. Traffic was light at this time of night, as most people in the area were already home and winding down for a good night's sleep before their next day's early start. As she navigated a curve, her headlights picked up two small white crosses. Callie remembered hearing about a deadly accident that had occurred in the spot some weeks ago and shivered. She checked her speedometer, which showed she was just under the forty-five mile-per-hour limit.

She was on a straight stretch of road alone, about halfway home, when she saw headlights in the distance coming toward her. As she watched, they seemed to approach much faster than she would have expected at the speed limit. Still, it was on the opposite side, and they could pass each other safely.

She didn't start to tense until the other car began to weave. Within moments it pulled into her lane and headed straight for her. Callie wrenched her wheel to the right as the oncoming headlights nearly blinded her. At the last second the other car corrected. But it was too late for Callie, who'd steered off the road, plowed through a bush, and slid into a watery ditch.

Twenty-Five

Callie sat, stunned. Her airbag hadn't deployed, so the bush must have slowed her car down enough to avoid triggering it. She was lucky. Her headlights illuminated a stand of solid-looking trees several feet ahead.

She assessed herself. No head bumps or blood, only a rapidly beating heart, which long, deep breaths helped to ease. She glanced around and saw no other vehicle nearby. Whoever had run her off the road had driven on, which maybe was a good thing. But no other vehicles were coming by either. She was on her own.

She turned her motor off, leaving the lights on, and unbuckled and opened her door. She stretched out one leg to clear the ditch, then pulled the rest of herself out with some effort. Once on level land, she could see that driving her car out of the ditch was not going to happen. At least not by her. The good thing was that no steam rose from under her hood. The bad? Her right wheels were sunk in inches-deep mud.

After a few minutes of thought, she pulled her phone out and pressed a number.

"Brian?" she asked in a voice that was much cheerier and calmer than she felt. "Hi. Got a minute?"

⚜

The formerly dark and lonely road was flooded with light: yellow ones from the tow truck that Brian had contacted, and red and blue flashes from a police car she'd summoned herself. After wondering briefly if her accident was worth reporting, since she could state nothing about the vehicle that had caused her crash, she realized it needed to be on record, for insurance purposes if nothing else. She could definitely narrow down the oncoming vehicle to a car, rather than a truck, but other than it having very bright headlights, that was it.

After relating her story to the responding officer, she joined Brian at the side of the road to watch her mud-caked Camry get pulled, inch by inch, up the ramp to the tow truck bed. It was a grim sight but could have been much grimmer, she knew, if she'd made contact with the trees instead of a bush. Brian put an arm around her shoulders and squeezed in sympathy.

"I was halfway afraid I'd have to talk to the same officer who showed up at the park this morning about Renata," she said. "That one's shift is probably over, but I had the feeling this guy recognized my name. It's probably getting familiar among local law enforcement."

Brian squeezed again. "Not for anything bad you've done."

"Thank you for coming out," Callie said. "I really only needed the number of a garage."

Brian looked at her incredulously. "Do you really think I'd leave you to deal with this all alone? What if you'd been hurt but hadn't registered that?"

"I'm fine." She didn't mention the delayed reaction of tremors she'd suffered after placing her calls. Thankfully, she'd gotten them under control by the time anyone showed up.

"But you at least need a ride home, and I can provide that."

"I appreciate that."

Brian paused. "You could have been badly hurt, you know. Or even killed. It's possible whoever caused this did it on purpose."

Callie nodded. She'd thought of that. "But there's no way to know for sure since I have no idea who was driving the other car. It could have simply been someone drunk or falling asleep."

"Will you do me a favor and not drive on these lonely roads alone for a while? Particularly after dark?"

"Since my car is sitting on a flatbed, about to be hauled away, there's no worries about me driving anywhere for a while," she said with a smile. But she knew she'd be watching her back. Whatever the reason for her accident, it would have some lasting effects on her.

Once the tow truck took off, followed by the police car, Callie climbed into Brian's Impala and buckled up. He drove for a while, then said, "I have some amazing chocolate cake at the café. Want to stop in for a piece?"

"Hmm. Chocolate cake. Is that the recommended treatment for accident recovery?"

"It is."

"Well, in that case I'd better have some. With coffee?"

"Of course."

Callie smiled.

∞

It felt odd sitting in the Keepsake Café at eleven o'clock at night, but it was also very cozy. The front window shades were pulled down, and only one low light had been turned on. Brian refused Callie's offer of help and carried out two plates of chocolate cake to the table where she sat, then went back for the coffee. She waited for his return before picking up her fork, though resisting a quick taste of the dark and gooey chocolaty goodness before her was difficult.

"Black, right?" he said, setting a mug before her.

"Yup." She grabbed her fork then and dug in, savoring every molecule for several seconds. "Amazing was the right word for it. Did you make it?"

"Uh-uh. I've been trying various bakeries for café desserts. I think this'll be the one." He got to work on his own slice. By the time they had scraped the final crumbs and were sipping their coffee, Callie felt the bulk of her tension had gone. She told Brian all she'd been up to that afternoon and evening.

"You've been busy."

"Yes, but so far everything I learn only brings up more questions. And trails that might lead to who killed Cliff Ashby peter out before taking me anywhere."

"And now the second murder. Are they connected?"

"The only connection I see would be Dorothy, which doesn't make sense to me." Callie sank her head into her hands. "Am I wrong and just fooling myself about her?"

Brian shook his head. "I think you're a pretty good judge of character." He added with a grin, "After all, you chose to sit here alone with me late at night. And I've got a drawer full of knives back there."

"You also had chocolate cake."

"But you have common sense. Don't sell yourself short."

Callie smiled. Hank used to compliment her looks, but she liked what Brian said better. Though she doubted she could have always claimed that quality, she was proud of the recent changes she'd made in her life and the good people she'd surrounded herself with. But that hadn't solved all the latest problems before her.

She sighed. "Sometimes I just wish I could read what's going on inside people's heads."

Brian grimaced. "I doubt you'd really want that. Sounds like more of a curse than a blessing, to me. But," he added with a slight lip twitch, "it *could* come in handy, once in a while."

❦

The next morning Callie heard from the garage, who said they might be able to have the damage fixed and her car ready by the following day. "Need a loaner in the meantime?" they asked.

"No, I can manage as a pedestrian for that length of time," she told them. There were definite advantages to living close to your job, as she'd already realized. On top of that encouraging news, customers had reappeared in Keepsake Cove, and she relished her return to the soothing calm and quiet of the music box world.

"What's the story behind this one?" a woman wrapped in a red sweater-coat asked after Callie had hung up the phone.

"Ah, I love that one," Callie said, walking over. "It's a Reuge, made in the 1960s. Charles Reuge began making music boxes in Sainte-Croix back in the 1860s, and the family has carried on the business. Their music boxes are very well regarded. My aunt, who established *House of Melody*, found this one at an estate sale. It had been brought back from Paris by the seller's grandfather when he was in the army."

"I was attracted by the painting on its lid. The young girl surrounded by hills reminds me of my daughter."

"It's lovely, isn't it? According to my aunt's notes, the music is from a French opera. But I'm afraid she didn't name it." Callie opened the lid of the small jewelry box to play the tune.

The woman smiled. "I'll take it. A good friend of mine teaches music. I'm sure she'll be able to track it down."

Callie carried the little music box to her counter to pack and ring up. Shortly after her satisfied customer left, Tabitha arrived, dressed in a navy blue shirt and trousers that, with her hair pulled severely into a bun, had the look of an official uniform. Callie saw she'd added a few medal-like pins to the shirt's chest pocket which looked impressive until a closer look identified a couple of them: Girl Scouts of America and Animal Planet K9 Cop. Callie lifted an eyebrow inquiringly.

"I didn't have a lot of choices," Tabitha said, shrugging. "But after last night I've been feeling like an Honorary Junior Policewoman."

"Oh?"

"Yeah, I was doing an in-home show of my jewelry last night. I love doing those. You meet all sorts of cool people that way. One of them—I picked this up when everyone was chatting—has worked at the Foxwood Inn."

"Really? Who was that?"

"Her name's Kelsey Jones."

"Kelsey? One of the maids?"

"Right. She said she took the job to earn tuition for beauty school. But she didn't stay long. I only managed to talk to her for a minute, but I think she might have a story to tell. I asked her to come here today to talk to you. She doesn't live that far from here and hasn't found a new job yet, so she has free time."

"I can't wait to meet her." As Callie watched Tabitha stash away her purse, grateful that her assistant hadn't added a holster and fake gun to her outfit, she told her about the accident.

"Ohmygosh! Are you okay?"

"I'm fine. My car, unfortunately, had to be towed."

"And the other car never stopped? Wow, that's scary. I mean, what if it'd hit you head on?"

"I try not to picture that. But it didn't, so that's all that matters."

"You know, I had a feeling…"

Uh-oh. Tabitha hadn't mentioned her Tarot cards in a long time, not since the days following Aunt Mel's murder. Callie had almost forgotten about her assistant's more esoteric interest. She tried to divert the subject.

"I sold that pretty Reuge music box just before you came."

"Great." But Tabitha wasn't to be distracted. "I've been checking on things, especially after the second murder. The cards weren't giving me specific warnings about you, but there's been a few ominous hints."

Callie was touched at Tabitha's concern and never wanted to make light of her assistant's trust in her cards. She might put a little more credence in them herself if the hints were spelled out a lot more clearly. As it was—

She was spared any need to comment when a young woman entered the shop.

Twenty-Six

K elsey!" Tabitha cried. "Great! You made it."

Kelsey, a slim young woman who looked to be in her late teens, smiled at Tabitha. "Hi!" She pushed aside a loose curl of shining blonde hair whose striking style managed to look effortless, as though she'd simply run her fingers casually through it that morning. Callie was sure it had resulted from meticulous work and that Kelsey had a good future ahead of her in cosmetology.

"Kelsey, this is Callie Reed," Tabitha said. "I told her about how you used to work at the Foxwood Inn."

"Hi, Kelsey," Callie said. "Thanks for coming by. Can I get you something to drink?"

"No, thanks. I'm good." The girl glanced around at the shop. "Wow. Neat place. Did you make all of these?"

"No, I just sell them." Callie thought Kelsey looked a little nervous, so she showed her around, raising a few lids to play tunes and talking about music boxes in general.

"Today we have iPods, but a few centuries ago the only way people could hear music was when it was performed live. The invention of the music box brought it into people's homes."

Kelsey smiled. "But then records came."

"Right. That came much later, and it changed things tremendously. But music boxes not only survived, they took their place as their own art form."

"These are pretty special," Kelsey agreed.

"So," Tabitha said, having lingered quietly in the background, "did you want to tell Callie about your time at the B&B?"

"Sure. That's what I came for. Tabitha said you've been looking into Mr. Ashby's murder?"

"I have."

"Well, I can't help you with that, but I can tell you what a creep he was."

"We've been getting that impression," Callie said. "What's been your experience?"

Tabitha had pulled out the stools from behind the counter, and she waved Kelsey toward one. All three sat down. Callie glanced at her front windows but saw no one approaching to interrupt. She would have loved to turn her lock and pull the shades but thought that might be too unsettling for Kelsey. Best to keep things low-key.

"I started working at the Foxwood Inn in August. The family I was kid-sitting for went away for a long vacation, and they wouldn't need me after school started. So I saw the ad for a housekeeper at the inn and thought, I could do that. I'm hoping to start at the Azalea Beauty Academy in January and need tuition money."

Callie nodded encouragingly, and Kelsey went on.

"Everything was fine at first. Jackie showed me the ropes, and pretty soon I was doing rooms on my own. It wasn't bad. Change sheets, vacuum and dust, and clean the bathrooms, stuff like that.

Most people's rooms didn't need much work. Once in a while, though ..." She rolled her eyes. "You wouldn't believe the slobs some people are. And then they step out looking like Princess Di or something. Anyway, it was mostly okay, until Mr. Ashby started getting friendly."

"He hit on you?" Tabitha asked.

"Yeah." Kelsey wrinkled her nose. "He wasn't so bad at first. Just a little too talkative. Well, a lot too talkative. It was holding me up from getting my work done, and I could see Paula was getting annoyed. But I didn't know what to do! He was my boss, and I couldn't just walk away, could I?"

"And I bet his chats were getting more and more personal, right?" Tabitha asked.

"Uh-huh. First it was just telling me about the inn and stuff. Then he said he hoped the work wasn't too hard for me, which I thought was nice of him until he mentioned my slim legs and how they must get tired from going up and down the stairs a lot. I didn't like that or the look in his eyes when he said it, so I started making excuses not to stop when he was around and just avoided him as much as I could. But one day I was cleaning the Wye—"

"The Wye?" Tabitha interrupted.

"All the rooms have Eastern Shore river names instead of numbers," Kelsey explained. "Wye is the corner back one."

That was George's room, Callie remembered.

"Anyway, I was scrubbing the sink when I suddenly hear this voice behind me saying, 'Those pretty little hands should have better things to do,' in a creepy kind of way, you know? And the look on his face? Scared the bejeezus out of me. I didn't hear him come in. It was like he'd popped up out of nowhere. My first thought was, I'm trapped!"

"Geez!" Tabitha cried.

"But my next one was, he's gonna get a faceful of this cleaning spray if he comes any closer."

"And did he?" Callie asked.

Kelsey shook her head. "Paula called from downstairs. She didn't know where he was. She was just trying to find him because there was some kind of important phone call. He turned around and left, and I ran over and locked the door as soon as he was out. I finished up that room double fast, believe me."

"So you quit because of that?" Callie asked, and Kelsey nodded.

"It wasn't easy. I needed the money. But I didn't want to face that kind of thing again. Then the day after I quit, I heard he was murdered. It was weird. Scary, but weird."

She looked at Callie for a moment. "I was shocked, 'cause that kind of thing just doesn't happen to people you know. But I didn't feel bad. That makes me feel kind of guilty, like I should feel sorry for him. But all I can feel is sorry for the person who did it. I keep wondering what Ashby did that made someone do that to him." She paused, then added quietly, "I'm just glad I got out of there before it was me."

❧

"Whoo!" Tabitha said after Kelsey had left. "Strong stuff."

"Yes." Callie had taken Kelsey's contact info in case she had more questions. But she also intended to keep her eyes open for any job possibilities for the girl. "I wish she could have helped us with clues to Ashby's murderer, but at least we know more about the man himself."

"Despicable. If we didn't need to clear Dorothy, I'd almost be glad to let his murderer get away with it."

"Not a good idea," Callie said, though she knew Tabitha was simply reacting to Kelsey's story. "And Dorothy absolutely has to be cleared. She can't go on like this, knowing that she's being thought of as a murderer." She'd barely finished speaking when her phone rang. It was Laurie Hart.

"There's some trouble at *Stitches Thru Time.*"

"What's happening?" Callie asked, fearing the worst.

"Two people, a man and a woman, have been shouting outside the shop, calling Dorothy awful names and demanding that she get out of Keepsake Cove. Bill's gone over to try to stop it, and I've called the police."

"Oh, gosh. Are they anyone you know?"

"What? What's happening?" Tabitha asked, and Callie held up her hand to say *hold on.*

"I never saw them before," Laurie said. "I don't know why they feel in charge of deciding who belongs in Keepsake Cove! Uh-oh. Now they're turning on Bill. Wait! I see a patrol car coming."

"That should end it. I hope they get arrested," Callie said, though she was pretty sure the horrid couple would just be moved along.

"Oh, dear," Laurie said.

"What?"

"Jerry Moore just showed up."

Callie winced. "What's he doing?"

"Talking to the patrolman. Not shouting, at least. But he looks mad, and he's gesturing toward Dorothy's shop."

Callie's stomach sank. "Any sign of Dorothy?"

"No. Wait. There she is! She's coming out."

No, don't, Callie said silently, wishing she were there to stop her.

"She looks calm," Laurie said. "Angry, but calm. And she's talking to the patrolman. I think she's asking him to take care of this situation, or, as I would have phrased it, get these idiots out of here!"

Callie waited as Laurie watched through her window, debating if she should head over or not. Would it help or just add to the problem? When Laurie said that others had started gathering and arguing, she decided to stay away.

"The patrolman just got Dorothy back into her shop," Laurie said. "She's pulled down her shades and probably locked up. Good. Now Bill's coming back, and others are leaving."

"What about Jerry?"

"Looks like he's still arguing. No, he's leaving, but he looks pretty steamed." Laurie paused as Callie heard her husband saying something. "Bill just said the loudest ones were threatened with citations for disturbing the peace. That quieted them down in a hurry. Ah! The two that started it all are leaving, too."

"I'd like to know who they are," Callie said, "and why they decided to do this." A grim addition to her statement occurred to her after she'd hung up the phone: *How many more will there be?*

Twenty-Seven

*D*elia came into *House of Melody* about an hour later, her fore-
head creased with concern. "I've heard from a few people that
Jerry is taking Renata's death very hard."

"That's unfortunate if it's true," Callie said. "But the day I went to
The Collectible Cook, I saw two sides to the couple: an ingratiating public side and a nasty, bickering private side. I didn't pick up much love
between them."

"Sometimes loss makes you appreciate a person." Delia seemed
determined to be sympathetic.

"From what Dorothy and Jane have told us, there wasn't a lot to
appreciate in Renata," Callie said. "I'll grant you that Jerry might be
sincerely grieving. But from what happened earlier today, he seemed
more angry than sad." She told Delia about the scene that occurred in
front of *Stitches Thru Time.*

"Oh! I hadn't heard about that."

"He's been calling for Dorothy's arrest," Tabitha said. "Like he's out for revenge or something."

"Well, that makes me feel differently," Delia said. "And poor Dorothy!"

"Yes, she'd just decided to brave it out and keep her shop open," Callie said. "To show that others' opinions didn't matter to her as much as the facts. I don't know what she'll do now."

"Maybe it's just a one-time thing," Delia said, though she looked more hopeful than convinced.

"Mob mentality has a way of spreading," Callie said. "I think Dorothy might be in serious danger if it escalates."

"She should leave Keepsake Cove," Delia said. "For her own safety. And Jane's, too. I'll call and strongly urge that."

"I don't know that she'll listen, but you can try," Callie said.

"She won't," Tabitha agreed. "Would you? Wouldn't it feel like it's admitting guilt to run away?"

"Not necessarily," Delia said, though weakly. She looked determined to do something helpful for Dorothy, so Callie didn't discourage her. But she knew what she intended to do. Work harder to uncover the facts of Ashby's and Renata's murders. With that in mind, she started working out her next plan.

❦

"Like to see a little more of the Eastern Shore tonight?" Callie asked when Lyssa picked up her call.

"What do you have in mind?"

"Easton, a nice town, from what I hear. And that's where Jerry Moore's brother lives."

"Ah, the brother-slash-alibi. What did you find out about him?"

"He has a real estate office there. You've been thinking of buying a house there, haven't you?"

"As a matter of fact," Lyssa agreed, laughing, "it's been on my bucket list. This would be a perfect time to look into it."

"I thought so," Callie said with a smile. "I made an appointment for you at six thirty. Can you pick me up? I don't have a car at the moment." She told Lyssa about the accident.

"Holy crap! Why didn't you call me when it happened?"

"You were probably in bed by then. Brian helped me out. And I reported it, though it won't accomplish anything. The other car was out of there in a flash, which is about all I saw."

"I know that place you described. I've seen those small crosses when I've driven by. I'm glad there wasn't a reason to add a third one farther down the road."

Me too, Callie thought. *Me too*. "So," she said, getting back to business, "can you be here by six?"

"Absolutely. Am I Lyssa Hammond, by the way, or Tracy Hamilton?"

"You're Lyssa. I didn't see any need not to be. Is that okay?"

"Sure. And who knows, I might actually buy a house. Not tonight, of course, but sometime. Tracy Hamilton would have a little trouble getting a loan. See you soon."

❧

On the drive to Easton, Callie caught Lyssa up with what had happened in front of Dorothy's shop, including Jerry Moore's ongoing accusations.

"Who were the people who started the fuss?" Lyssa asked.

"Laurie Hart didn't know them, and she probably knows everybody in and around the Cove."

"Hmm. Maybe paid rabble rousers?"

"I thought of that, too. Do you think Vernon Parks might have been involved?"

"It's a possibility. Probably no way to find out now. If something happens again, one of us should get right on it." Lyssa negotiated a curve at a noticeably slower speed than usual, and Callie wondered if it was in consideration of her recent scare. She appreciated not having the urge to push the imaginary brake on her side of the car.

They passed a sign for Easton. "Ah," Lyssa said, "we're close. What's it like? Anything like Mapleton and the Cove?"

"All I know is what I've skimmed through on the internet. It's bigger than Mapleton and older, dating back to 1711. A few Maryland governors are buried there. And it claims to be the eighth-best small town in America."

"Good for them. If they have a good bookstore or two, I'll be sold on it. Okay, here we are," Lyssa said, driving into the town and glancing around. "Pretty."

"It is," Callie agreed. "That must be the courthouse." She pointed toward an impressive Georgian-style building. "Lots of these buildings look historic. I'd love to come back for a tour sometime."

Lyssa's GPS told her to turn left in a quarter mile, which would eventually take them to the realty office of Douglas Moore. After that, she made a right turn, then pulled up in front of a red brick-fronted building. It housed several businesses, and one multi-paned window on the ground floor announced *Moore Realty* on an Old English-styled, black-lettered sign.

"Found it!" Lyssa announced, and Callie unbuckled and climbed out.

They entered the realty office to see three desks spread about, but only one woman seated at any of them.

"Welcome to Moore Realty," she said, setting aside a thick folder. "What can I do for you?"

"Hi," Callie said. "We have an appointment with Doug Moore." She gave Lyssa's name and looked around. "Is he here?"

The fiftyish woman, who wore a gray jacket and skirt, frowned a little worriedly. "Not at the moment. But let me find him. Please have a seat." She indicated two chairs next to a rack of brochures near the front, then got up from her desk with her cell phone and walked toward the back. Though she kept her voice low, Callie picked up that Douglas Moore had forgotten about their appointment but would hurry on over.

"I'm so sorry," the woman said. "Mr. Moore had a small emergency to attend to. But he'll be here shortly. In the meantime, I'll be happy to get you started, if that's all right. I'm Gayle Hawkins."

"Lyssa Hammond," Lyssa said, extending her hand. "And my friend, Callie Reed. "I hope we aren't pulling Mr. Moore away from something terribly important. But he was recommended to me by a friend."

"Oh, no," Ms. Hawkins protested. "It wasn't anything major. It just, um, needed to be seen to. Mr. Moore will be most happy to work with you, as soon as he gets here. Now, what exactly are you looking for?" She waved them over to her desk and pulled chairs over in front of it for them.

"Well," Lyssa began, then launched into a broad description of her ideal house, starting with a slate, or perhaps cedar, roof and working its way through multiple bedrooms, or maybe one very large master suite with a single guest room, on down to open-plan living areas or possibly a cozier closed-off-style huge kitchen, sun room (or not), and finished basement.

"I see," Ms. Hawkins said, looking very much like she didn't. "And your price range?"

Lyssa threw out numbers that seemed reasonable to Callie, at least for a house somewhere in the middle of Lyssa's supposed wish list. Maybe with a smaller kitchen. Ms. Hawkins asked about location preferences and discussed the pros and cons of a few with Lyssa. Waterfront? Close to shopping and restaurants? Wooded property? She had just started pulling up listings on her computer when the door burst open and a heavyset man with a fringe of gray hair edging his otherwise bald head hurried in while pulling on a tweed jacket.

"Oh, good, you're here!" Ms. Hawkins said, standing up. She introduced a flustered and red-faced Douglas Moore to Lyssa and Callie, adding that Lyssa was the prospective client.

"Please accept my apologies," he said, shaking their hands. "One of those days," he explained vaguely.

Callie could see a resemblance to Jerry Moore, though Douglas looked several years older. His manner was milder, at least at the moment. He thanked Gayle Hawkins nicely for stepping in for him, and she looked happy to have done so, which showed a good working relationship between them.

Moore looked over his colleague's notes and asked a couple of questions as he settled himself in, seeming to quickly catch up on things to that point. But then he turned to Callie and asked, "Were you hoping to move to Easton soon, Ms. Hammond?"

"No, Doug, this is Ms. Hammond." Ms. Hawkins, who had lingered nearby, gestured toward Lyssa.

"Right," Lyssa said. "And please call me Lyssa. I'm in no hurry to move, but I'm open to buying if there's something available that I can't resist. If not, I'm okay with waiting."

"I see. And, uh, I also see you have a fairly wide range of preferences on your wish list."

Which was putting it mildly, Callie thought.

"I'm not really picky," Lyssa said. "I like a lot of styles and sizes. I'll know the right house when I see it, but I didn't want to miss it by narrowing things down too much."

"Okaaay," Moore said. "Well, we can start by showing you what's on the market right now." He continued what Gayle Hawkins had started, pulling up listings on the computer, then turned the monitor toward Lyssa. His discussion of each property showed a sharp understanding of real estate, especially once they got into the finances. In addition, he explained points about loans and mortgages so clearly that Callie, who'd never gotten into that because of her good fortune of inheriting from Aunt Mel, was able to easily follow.

At one point, when Moore offered coffee and got up to make it on the nearby office Keurig, Lyssa brought up Keepsake Cove. "I've been visiting there. A nice place, normally, but a lot's been going on lately."

"Keepsake Cove? Yes, my brother has a place there." Doug frowned as he made a second coffee. "It was his wife who was recently killed. You may have heard about it."

"Oh, gosh! Moore!" Lyssa said. "I should have connected the name. I'm so sorry."

He shook his head. "Moore is a common name. He was with me when they told him about it," he said quietly.

"That was yesterday morning, after it happened?" Callie asked.

"Yes," he said, setting the mugs before each of them. "Tuesday morning."

"I think you mean Wednesday, right?" Callie said.

Moore looked confused for a moment, then gave a slight laugh. "Wednesday, yes. So much has been happening. Hard to keep the days straight. Well, I didn't mean to bring that all up." He rubbed his hands briskly. "Shall we get back to work?"

He discussed more properties with Lyssa, who continued to show appreciation of everything but particular interest in nothing, though to Moore's credit he seemed perfectly understanding and fine with that. They finally ended with Lyssa thanking him profusely for the great overview he'd given of available properties and apologizing for not picking any to look into further.

"Not at all, not at all," he assured her. "No need to rush into this, especially since you're in no hurry to buy. Think over what you've seen tonight." He gave her the link to study them online herself. "You can get back to me if you have any questions or if you'd like to go see a few. I'll be here all day tomorrow and Saturday—"

"Not Saturday," Gayle Hawkins called from another desk. "Remember the open house?"

"Open house?" Moore pulled up a calendar and peered at it. "That's this Saturday? Oh, dear. Well," he said to Lyssa, "I'll be here tomorrow and next week. You can always leave a message, of course ... "

"Of course." Lyssa stood, along with Callie, and they all three shook hands, Lyssa thanking him again.

When they were back in her car, Lyssa said, "I noticed a restaurant a couple of blocks back. Want to grab something to eat?"

Callie agreed and Lyssa made a U-turn to get to a cozy-looking café with electric candles in the window. Hunger-stirring aromas greeted them as they entered. A friendly hostess seated them, asking as she handed them menus, "Visiting our area?"

"Yes," Lyssa said. "With a look to possibly buying and settling in."

"Oh, lovely," the woman said. "If you're looking for a realtor, Doug Moore's office is just down the street. Good at his job and a super nice person to deal with. As a matter of fact," she said, stepping back, "he dined with us tonight, though he left in a hurry without really finishing. Something must have come up." She smiled indulgently. "He can be just a bit forgetful."

Twenty-Eight

So, what did you think of Jerry Moore's alibi?" Lyssa asked as she drove them back to Keepsake Cove. They'd avoided the subject during dinner in the small, quiet restaurant where conversations could easily be overheard.

"Shaky," Callie said. "As shaky as Douglas Moore's memory. He might have been fuzzy about exactly when his brother showed up and been convinced by Jerry that it was earlier in the evening than it actually was by the time police arrived."

"'Might,'" Lyssa said. "The operative word, unfortunately. Do we know Renata Moore's time of death?"

"Brian got it from his police deputy friend that it was between ten o'clock and midnight, Tuesday night."

"So my book event was over and most everyone had cleared out of the park at least by nine, right? Renata had gone home to change clothes for her planned trip to the estate sale."

"Jack Tate, one of the volunteers, saw Jerry leaving after packing up his sound system." Callie said. "And the next morning at the park, I heard Jerry tell police he had driven directly to his brother's, since he believed Renata was on her way to Pennsylvania."

"So, Easton is about half an hour's drive from Keepsake Cove. If he went directly, he has an alibi for the time of the murder."

"If Douglas was aware of and accurately remembered the time of Jerry's arrival."

Lyssa nodded. "Nice man, Douglas. I feel a little bad about dragging him away from his dinner for nothing. I know one or two people to recommend him to as a realtor, but I'll warn them to confirm any appointments more than once." She negotiated a turn. "Getting back to the murders—Dorothy, you know, could have slipped out of her cottage once her cousin Jane was asleep, killed Renata, and been back within minutes."

"But would she?" Callie asked. "The timing works, but do you see Dorothy Ashby stabbing anyone with an old pair of scissors? I really don't. Plus, how would she have lured Renata to the park?"

"Yes, that's a sticking point. Why would Renata go alone to meet up with Dorothy, who she knows has a grudge against her? As far as Dorothy stabbing anyone, I'm sorry, but I don't put it past anyone if they're angry enough. Dorothy may look frail, but you'd be surprised what adrenaline can do for a person. That's not to say I believe she did. I'm just saying that's how the police likely are looking at it. Besides, she has that connection to both Cliff Ashby and Renata. She'd gain control of a valuable inn and get rid of a difficult husband, and with Renata she'd finally strike back against a lifelong enemy."

Callie fell silent, unable to refute Lyssa's points, though she wasn't happy with them. She stayed that way, mulling over things, until Lyssa reached Keepsake Cove. As they traveled down the street and neared *Stitches Thru Time*, Callie turned to look at the darkened shop. "Stop!"

Lyssa slammed on her brakes, fortunately with no one behind her. "What?"

"Look at Dorothy's window," Callie said. "Somebody's thrown eggs against it."

"Oh, crap!"

Just what Callie felt like. The mob reaction she'd feared was starting to take hold. What next? Torch-bearing, rock-hurling crowds?

They moved on, and as Lyssa pulled up in front of *House of Melody*, Callie half expected to see eggs on her windows as well, or worse. She, after all, had been outspoken about her belief in Dorothy's innocence. Who knew how far blind retaliation would reach? She thanked Lyssa for driving to Easton and glumly bid her good night

"Don't worry about the egg-tossing idiots," Lyssa said. "They'll be the ones with egg on their face once this is over."

Callie smiled. "Hope so."

"And it might just be kids, you know."

That didn't cheer Callie. "If so, it would be kids who picked up the attitude from the adults around them." She climbed out of the car with a weak farewell gesture and headed down the side path to her cottage. When her motion sensor lights flicked on, she heard Lyssa's Corvette drive off.

As she slipped her key into the lock, something white at the base of the door caught Callie's eye. She bent down to pick up a white envelope with *Callie Reed* hand-printed on the front. Nothing else. She frowned. That method of delivery, whatever the envelope contained, was immediately worrisome. Friends didn't communicate in this digital age by leaving notes at doors. They texted, emailed, or called. She stared at the piece for several moments before opening her door and stepping in. The envelope was sealed, but just barely at the tip of its flap. Setting down her keys and purse, Callie tore it open, then pulled out a single sheet of paper that bore a brief, hand-printed message:

Lyssa Hammond isn't who she says she is. She's Alissa Hanson—MURDERER! Cliff Ashby knew and he died. Who else?

It wasn't signed, of course. Callie's first impulse was to crumple it up and throw it away. Anonymous letters were evil attempts to stir up trouble and nothing else. They couldn't be believed.

But the message had wormed its way into her head.

As she hung up her jacket and gave Jagger a treat, the words repeated themselves in a continuous loop. *Alissa Hanson. Murderer. Who else?* Finally she went up to the guest room and woke up the laptop sitting on the small desk there. She typed in *Alissa Hanson,* which pulled up several pages. She clicked on a few listings that took her to Facebook pages. These Alissa Hansons were obviously not Lyssa, from their photos. She ruled out those who had a cat or flower for their profile photos if their locations or other information didn't work. An Alissa Hanson posing with multiple grandkids was an instant no. Checking her search list again, Callie saw that nothing had popped up that connected any Alissa Hanson to a murder, so she gave up.

She was ready to discard the letter a second time until she remembered the cookout at Annie's and Mike's. Annie, interested in Lyssa's writing career, had asked about her earlier life, curious if she'd found instant writing success or if she'd had to earn a living in other ways while scribbling late at night. Lyssa's evasiveness had nudged Callie to do an internet search on her, but it had turned up little beyond the author's public persona. At the time, she'd thought nothing of it, attributing it to an understandable need for privacy. But now it could be taken as a need for secrecy. Callie shook her head. If she expected answers, the only thing left was to ask Lyssa herself. Unsure if she wanted to do that, she logged off and closed the laptop. She decided to sleep on it. If she could, in fact, sleep.

∞

The next morning, Callie still hadn't made up her mind. She dealt with her few customers in a distracted way, her thoughts on the lingering dilemma. Delia had stopped in, upset over the egg-throwing incident at Dorothy's shop, which Callie had nearly forgotten, so absorbed had she been in her latest problem. She needed to dredge up the horror she'd felt at the sight of the windows, which was still there but had been pushed back by that disturbing anonymous letter.

The decision about whether or not to confront Lyssa finally came to a head when Lyssa herself showed up at the shop.

"I'm on my way out of town. Have to run back to my house," she announced brightly as she came in. "Another renovation problem to discuss. By the way, I saw a couple of people cleaning off Dorothy's windows for her as I drove by."

"Good to hear," Callie said.

"Anyway, I should be back sometime tomorrow, by the latest. But call me if something comes up, okay?"

Callie paused. "Actually, something did come up."

"Oh?'

Callie walked back to her counter and reached to the lower shelf where she'd tucked the note. "I found this on my doorstep last night." She handed it to Lyssa and watched as she read it. When the author's face blanched, Callie had her answer.

"Who ... who wrote this?"

"I don't know. Is it true? I mean about you being Alissa Hanson?"

"It is." Lyssa's answer was barely above a whisper.

"But it calls you a murderer."

"That's not true." Lyssa had tears in her eyes. "Some people thought it was. It was a long time ago. I'd rather not go into it." She said the last part firmly, lifting her chin slightly with glistening eyes.

Callie saw that she meant it. But she had to ask. "The note said that Cliff Ashby knew. Is that right?"

Lyssa looked Callie in the eye. "He wasn't blackmailing me, if that's what you're wondering. Maybe he knew and maybe he was planning to, but I promise you it wouldn't have worked. What happened is not something I talk about, and I choose to write as Lyssa Hammond partly to keep that horrible incident from coming up over and over. But if it had, I would have admitted it. It might have lost me some readers, but I could live with that. I never would have caved to blackmail. Never."

Or killed to prevent it? Callie didn't say it, and she didn't think she believed it, but the question was there. And Lyssa knew it.

"I have to go now." Lyssa was out the door before Callie could say anything, and within moments the red Corvette raced down the street.

Callie stared after it, struggling with what she'd just heard.

Twenty-Nine

House of Melody was quiet for a while, for which Callie was grateful. It gave her a chance to think. Did she believe what Lyssa claimed, that she wouldn't care if it came out that she was Alissa Hanson, a woman some considered a murderer? She'd cared enough to let Alissa Hanson virtually disappear as Lyssa Hammond was created. If in fact Cliff Ashby had threatened blackmail, could she have stood up to that?

Lyssa had denied the accusation of murder, and Callie wanted to believe her. But what was the truth? Without getting more facts, she had only Lyssa's word for it. She'd found nothing on the internet. As far as she could determine, Alissa Hanson had never been charged. But did that mean she was innocent? The two things didn't always go together. There could have been insufficient evidence to bring charges even if there was guilt. Which was it?

Callie had come to like the author, and trust her. She'd believed that Lyssa chose to work with her to clear Dorothy of suspicion. But had she really? Lyssa's comments about Dorothy during their drive back from Easton had bothered Callie—Lyssa had pointed out how Dorothy could in fact have committed both murders. Was she protecting herself with misdirection while only pretending to search for the truth? That was a terrible thought, one that jarred Callie to the bone. It meant she might have totally misjudged the woman, and that someone she'd grown close to might actually be a murderer.

Might, she reminded herself. It was by no means an established fact. But she was glad that Lyssa would be away from Keepsake Cove for a while. She needed that time and space, and decided to look into a couple of things on her own without Lyssa's input. This included talking with Dorothy again. With that goal, as soon as Tabitha arrived, Callie headed over to *Stitches Thru Time*.

The two men who'd cleaned Dorothy's windows of the egg splatter were just packing up their buckets and squeegees. Callie recognized one as Jack Tate. He greeted her and introduced the second man as his brother-in-law, Mark Lyons.

"Mark had the window-washing equipment," Jack explained. "He didn't just lend it to me but came along to pitch in."

"That was great of both of you," Callie said, sincerely. "Have you heard anything about who the culprits might be?"

"'Fraid not," Mark said. "Jerks and idiots, whoever they are."

Callie agreed, then excused herself after spotting Dorothy inside the shop and went in.

"Are they done?" Dorothy asked. When Callie said they were, she asked, "Just give me a minute?" and hurried out to thank the two men effusively. As Callie watched, Jane emerged from the back of the shop.

"That means the world to Dorothy," Jane said, nodding toward the activity outside. "She needed that show of support. The name-calling yesterday and then the egg mess have really tested her resolve to tough it out."

"While she's outside," Callie said, "I'd like to ask you something. Have you told her about what's going on now with George?" When Jane looked surprised, she added, "I got the definite impression, when it came up, that Dorothy had no clue about your relationship."

Jane glanced toward the front window. Laurie Hart had crossed over from *Kids At Heart* and was speaking with Dorothy, keeping her longer. "I don't know if I'd call it a relationship at this point," Jane said. "We're getting to know each other again. A lot of years have gone by, you know. But yes, I did talk to her about it. She was surprised, of course, since she'd never heard about George. She and Cliff were off on their honeymoon when George and I began seeing each other. After that they settled in the place they'd bought in Annapolis. By the time we saw each other again, George had moved on. I was too hurt, then, to want to talk about it."

Dorothy came back in, a smile on her face after talking with her window washers and Laurie. "Such good people. Things have been such a roller-coaster of ups and downs over the last two weeks that I'm going to savor this particular up while it lasts."

"The people who know you well have always been in your corner," Callie said. "I hope you'll always remember that."

"I do, and I appreciate it so much. It's just hard to take the kind of viciousness that's shown up from others. I try to tell myself that those people might be coming from their own dark places that have little to do with me. But it's difficult." She waved away a frown. "But enough of that," she said brightly. "It's good to see you. Would you like a cup of tea?"

"No, thank you. I can't stay too long. But there's something I wanted to check with you. Yesterday, I spoke with a young woman who'd worked until very recently at the Foxwood Inn as a maid. She told me she quit when she felt threatened by Cliff."

"Threatened!" Dorothy said. Jane's hand flew to her mouth. "Do you mean ... ?" Dorothy began.

"Sexually harassed," Callie said. "It had escalated enough to cause this woman to quit a job she needed. At least, that's her side of it. I need to know if it sounds plausible."

"How could I know? Cliff and I were separated."

"You weren't there, of course. But you knew him probably better than anyone. Had something of that sort ever happened before? Was he capable of it?"

"Cliff and I had grown very far apart. I don't pretend to know everything about the man by any means. There were things he hid from me and things about him I didn't like. But they were mostly about his spending habits or his choice of friends, such as that odious Vernon Parks. I never saw or heard about any such kind of harassment." Dorothy sighed. "Did this young woman report it to anyone?"

"She didn't say."

"Then maybe she made it all up. Who knows? Maybe she just wants money and plans to sue the estate."

"Don't say that," Jane begged. "It's very difficult for a young woman in that kind of situation to speak up at all. There's never any witnesses, but just because nobody else can confirm it doesn't mean she's lying."

"You're right, of course," Dorothy said, shaking her head. "That was very wrong of me. I'm just not thinking straight what with all that's been happening. But being unfairly accused myself should have made me more sympathetic, not less. I wish I could help you, Callie, but I'm afraid I can't." She hesitated. "The harassment... What, that is, to what extent...?"

"Verbal, only, from what she said. At one point it might have gone farther except for an interruption."

"Thank goodness. And this was recently, you said?"

"The final incident was the day of his murder. And before you ask, no, I don't suspect her of Cliff's murder. The worst this girl would have done is spray cleaning solution in his face. The threat ended when she quit."

Dorothy and Jane were silent for several moments, apparently dealing with this new revelation about Cliff Ashby's character.

"In fact," Callie said, turning to Jane, "it might have happened shortly before you were there to get the papers from Cliff. Perhaps you noticed him being a bit off?"

"Papers?" Dorothy asked.

"The ones you asked Jane to pick up for you."

Dorothy stared at Callie, uncomprehending, then turned to look at her cousin, whose face had flushed a deep red. "Jane?" she asked.

Jane shook her head, apparently from embarrassment. "That's what I told Callie," she said softly.

"But... why? Why would you go there without telling me? And make up a story about some papers?"

Jane drew in a deep breath. "I was hoping to see George."

"Oh!" Dorothy continued to look puzzled, and Callie waited.

"It was one of the reasons I came here," Jane said. "I wanted to see you, too, Dorothy. Absolutely! But this strange coincidence came up back home." She paused, twisting her fingers awkwardly. "I met someone who knew George. It came up so unexpectedly I could hardly believe it. I happened to mention Mapleton and Keepsake Cove because of you, and this woman said she knew a man who had always stayed at the Foxwood Inn near there with his late wife. She said it became an annual thing and that he'd continued it after she died. It was very likely that he'd be there again around this time of year. Then she said his name."

Jane stopped the finger twisting and pushed her hands into her pockets. "I've been lonely, Dorothy, ever since Richard died. I ... I'd been thinking of George a bit, and wondering about him. I know it was foolish of me, but I just thought if I could run into him again, maybe ... "

Dorothy took hold of Jane's shoulders. "It's not foolish at all," she said, shaking her affectionately. "I'm just surprised you didn't tell me right away." She stepped back. "But didn't you say you saw George for the first time when he came here to my shop?"

"That's true. I never saw him at the inn. I was waylaid by Cliff. It got so unpleasant that I never asked about George and didn't see him."

"But he saw you," Callie said. "From his window, as you were talking to Cliff, though he didn't recognize you at the time."

"Oh! I didn't realize that."

"Well, you found each other, anyway," Dorothy said. "I'm just sorry Cliff got in the way."

Jane turned to Callie. "You asked if I picked up anything a bit off with Cliff when I spoke to him. I'm afraid I was too flustered. I regretted the whole thing and just wanted to get out of there."

"Understandable," Dorothy said, patting her cousin on the hand.

"Well, thank you both," Callie said. "I'd better get back."

"Thank you," Dorothy said as she walked Callie to the door, "for your efforts on my part. And Lyssa Hammond's, too. Please thank her for me when you see her."

Callie nodded but said nothing. She was happy to see a text on her phone from Tabitha saying that she was needed at the shop. She said her goodbyes and hurried off, trying to focus on Tabitha's message instead of Lyssa … or Alissa.

Thirty

Once again Callie went through the motions of tending to her shop and its customers. Even Tabitha's outfit of the day, a medieval-looking dress topped with a furry shawl, couldn't pull her fully out of her thoughts. A woman customer asking "Is she Sansa Stark?" had Callie reacting with a "Huh?" until she realized she was referring to Tabitha's *Game of Thrones*-inspired ensemble.

"You got it!" Tabitha answered happily. She tossed her braid over her shoulder and stroked the shawl fondly. "This is fake, of course. Sansa would have had a wolf skin or something. But that was a different time."

The customer and Tabitha launched into a discussion of the latest episodes of the popular HBO series, which Callie tuned out, only returning to the present when her customer held up the music box she'd been looking at.

"Ma'am? I'll take this."

"Oh! Sorry. I was somewhere else for a minute."

The woman laughed. "I do that all the time. New boyfriend?"

Tabitha grinned as Callie managed a smile while shaking her head. "Just something I need to work out."

Later in the day, the garage called to say her car was ready. Delia had offered to drive her to pick it up, so Callie arranged to be there shortly after six. Not long after that a delivery arrived. As Callie watched Tabitha unpack it, she recognized the music box she'd ordered for George. She'd almost forgotten about it.

"This is pretty," Tabitha said as she held up the rosewood box.

"It's for George Cole. He wanted a specific tune: *The Surrey with the Fringe on Top*. He said it would mean something to his daughter, whose birthday is coming up."

"That's sweet. Shall I call him to say it's here?"

Callie thought a moment. "I'll do it."

A customer walked in, and Callie let Tabitha deal with him. She went to her office and put in the number for George's cell, explaining, when he answered, that his music box had arrived.

"Great. I'll come by a little later to pick it up."

"I was thinking I'd bring it," Callie said. "This evening, if that works for you. There's a few things I'd like to talk to you about."

"Sure, that's fine. You know Lyssa's not here right now, don't you?"

"I do. I'll be there around seven. Okay?'

"See you then."

Callie disconnected and sat at her desk. She could hear Tabitha's voice and the lower tones of her male customer's, but it was white noise as far as Callie was concerned. Things about Ashby's murder had started to come together, but there were several missing pieces. She needed to find them to fill in the holes. Hopefully tonight would bring her closer to doing that.

Callie grabbed a quick sandwich after checking with Delia about the ride to the garage, turning down her suggestion of dinner out. Any other time it would have been great. But she had too much on her mind to be much of a dinner companion that night. Once at the garage she settled her bill, glad to have her own transportation back, and then leaned out of the office door and waved to Delia that all was okay. She saw her friend wave back and drive off.

Callie took a different route to the Foxwood Inn, one that avoided the area of her near head-on collision. But she was aware that her hands gripped the steering wheel more tightly, especially when oncoming headlights approached. She expected she would feel the tension even more on the way back, when the roads would likely be quieter, but she'd have to deal with it. Some things were more important than catering to her nerves.

When she pulled up the driveway to the B&B, she saw only two cars parked at the top of it. She didn't know what George drove, but assumed one of the two vehicles was his. As she parked nearby, a gray Ford backed out, and she thought she recognized Jackie at the wheel. So the black sedan must be George's, though it did look older and more worn than she would have expected.

Callie grabbed the packed-up music box and climbed out. On reaching the front door of the inn, she stepped right in as she had on her first visit, then rang the small brass bell that sat on the hall table. Though she'd half expected George to be waiting near the entrance, she wasn't particularly surprised not to see him.

"Hi Paula," she said when the woman appeared from the kitchen. "The parking lot looked pretty empty. Didn't you get new guests recently?"

"They only stayed one night. We were a stop-over for them on their way to Florida."

"I see. Well, I brought something for George. Is he upstairs?"

"Mr. Cole isn't here."

"Oh! He knew I was coming. Did he say when he'd be back?"

"He didn't know. He got a call from his daughter about some kind of emergency. One of the grandkids is in the hospital."

"I'm sorry to hear that. But he didn't check out?"

Paula shook her head. "He kept his room. He said he'd let me know what his plans are."

"Well," Callie said, "I brought this music box he ordered. Can I leave it with you?"

Paula nodded. "I'll put it in his room right now." She took it before Callie could assure her there was no hurry and dashed up the stairs.

Callie waited until Paula returned, then said, "I'd like to take another look at Ashby's office while I'm here. If you'll just unlock it for me, I won't bother you anymore."

Paula looked less than pleased at that, but she didn't protest. Dorothy had already given full approval for Callie to look around as much as she needed. Paula turned and led the way through the kitchen and to the office, grabbing the keys as she went. After unlocking the door, she stepped aside for Callie, who walked in not sure exactly what she expected to find that she'd missed the last time.

Paula lingered at the doorway, watching as Callie opened the top drawer of the file cabinet that Lyssa had already looked through. Lyssa had declared nothing of interest to be in it at the time, but Callie wanted to see for herself. As she fingered her way through the file tabs, she said, "If you want to get busy on your own things, Paula, I promise not to take anything away without running it by you."

"I can wait," Paula said.

Callie nodded and pulled out a couple of files. She looked through them rapidly, then replaced them and closed the drawer. She paused before opening the next one. "There's something I need to check with you, since you're here," she said, looking over at Paula. "About the day Cliff was murdered. Did you tell Lyssa it was your afternoon off?"

Lyssa had said exactly that when she'd explained about George spotting Jane on the grounds of the inn. Callie thought she'd better verify Lyssa's report.

"I must have, since it *was* my afternoon off."

"But I'm confused, because George later told me that he spoke with you in the kitchen a minute or so after he saw Dorothy's cousin, Jane, from his window. It was that same afternoon."

For Callie, it was simply a matter of placing everyone correctly. But to her surprise, Paula's face darkened. "Are you checking on me now? Do you think I'm lying?"

"No! I just want to get it all straight. I didn't mean—"

"Maybe it's George Cole who's lying! But of course you look at me right away. 'Paula, huh? All she does is cook and answer the phone. No real education, so of course you can't trust her.' Isn't that how it goes?"

"Paula, I was just—"

But Paula had turned on her heel and rushed off. Callie stared at the empty doorway, not sure what to make of that or what to do. She knew this reaction wasn't normal. Clearly she'd hit a nerve. But of what? Why would Paula's being, or not being, at the inn that afternoon matter?

She heard rattling noises coming from the kitchen and had just decided to go speak to the woman soothingly, to try to get to the bottom of her agitation, when Paula reappeared.

"I *was* here," she said, "if you have to know. You have to know everything, don't you? Well, here's some information for you. I saw Cliff and Jane talking outside. And I opened the window so I could hear them. You don't know what they said, do you? I'll bet Jane never told you. Well, she was begging Cliff to keep her secret!"

"Secret?" Callie didn't like the dark look in Paula's eyes. Or the raised pitch of her voice. She was also blocking the only way out of the office as she talked.

"Yes, secret!" Paula spat the word. "And I heard enough to figure out what it was. Cliff had been up to his ways with her some time ago."

"Up to his ways. You mean as with—"

"He used her. Probably against her will, because that's the kind of beast he was! I knew that when I took this job, but I *needed* it. Badly. I told myself what happened was a long time ago, and I should get over it."

"So, the same thing had happened to you? Paula, I'm so sorry—"

"He didn't remember me," Paula said, waving away Callie's interruption. "I could see that right away, and I wasn't young and pretty anymore, so it wouldn't happen again. He was old, I told myself, and not the same person anymore. So I took the job. And it was okay. I cooked. I got paid. And I could pay my rent and keep my old car. But then I saw he hadn't changed. Oh, not with me. It was the maid, Kelsey. I saw him watch her. And I heard him stop her to talk, over and over, and I knew where it was leading."

"Paula, can we talk about this in the kitch—" Callie began. Then she saw the knife. Paula had been holding it behind her back, but now she let it show.

"I couldn't let it happen again. He had to be stopped."

"Do you mean you … ?"

"He told Dorothy's cousin to meet him in the park. He said he couldn't talk here. That they could come to an agreement. There was a child involved! Did you know that? That woman had a child she had to give up. And he expected money to keep her secret from her family. When it was his fault!"

Callie was beginning to see it now. How had she missed it? "So you went to the park that night?"

"I followed him. I waited on the side of the road a short ways down from here. When he drove by, I slipped in behind. I lost him for a while after I parked. But then I heard their voices. She was pleading with him to leave her alone. He'd contacted her after her husband died. Said he was sure she didn't want her children to know about their 'love child.' That's what he called it. I wanted to throw up. She said she didn't have as much money as he thought. That her husband's medical bills had gobbled up a lot. He laughed and said she'd have to get it some other way. That's when she pulled out the scissors."

Callie gasped. "So *Jane* stabbed him?"

"No!" Paula looked confused for a moment. "She didn't stab him! He took the scissors away from her like they were nothing and tossed them aside. Then she ran off."

"What did you do after that?"

"I had this with me." Paula held up the long knife she'd probably used countless times in the kitchen. "I brought it for protection. I had to, didn't I? I didn't know what might happen. But when I heard the things he said and how he laughed..." Her eyes hardened. "I knew what I had to do. He was an evil man. He had to be stopped." She paused, holding the knife in front of her now with both hands. "He didn't know I was there. When I rushed at him there was nothing he could do."

Callie remembered that day she'd first met Paula. She'd been kneading her bread dough, a task she did almost daily and that surely had built up strength. That plus the anger coursing through her that night could have done the job. But something was wrong. "Paula, the police named the scissors as the murder weapon, not a knife."

"It was both. He deserved to die more than once, didn't he? For all the women he'd hurt. After I stabbed him with my knife, I did it again with the scissors, over and over. I did it for Jane. And for all the others."

And hadn't been concerned that Dorothy or Jane might go to prison for the murder as a result, Callie thought. But she knew the truth, now, and could keep that from happening. If only she could get out of there alive. She had to calm Paula down somehow. Could she gain her trust?

"I'm so sorry for all you've gone through, Paula. It must have been terrible having to work for a man like him, day after day, knowing what he was."

Paula cocked her head, seeming to appreciate the sympathy. Perhaps it was the first time she'd heard it. "It was," she said. "But I had an advantage, didn't I? I knew who he was, but he didn't know who I was. That made him careless. I got to see what he was doing."

"Other than stalking Kelsey, you mean?"

"Yes. He was a predator, but he was also a blackmailer. Not just with Jane. He collected things he could use against lots of people. The police never found that. He didn't keep it in the file cabinet or anywhere you could just stumble on it." She waved the knife. "He redid this office when he bought the place. You think all that fancy molding on the paneling is just for show? It's to hide a secret compartment. I'll show you."

Paula stepped closer to Callie and pointed her knife toward the corner of the wall behind the desk. "Go ahead, pull that printer table out," she said. "It's on castors. It'll move easy."

Hoping to stall until she had a chance to get away, and also genuinely curious, Callie grabbed hold of the table. It rolled out smoothly but exposed nothing more than dark paneling.

"Now, take that picture down."

Callie had thought on her first visit to the office that the large framed print of sailboats on the Chesapeake was out of proportion to the size of the room. But she'd assumed Ashby chose it for some personal reason. She took hold of each side of the frame and lifted it off its hanger, finding it awkward but manageable.

"Just lean it against the desk. Now, look close at the molding in the paneling where the picture was. Run your fingers along it. In the center."

The paneling had struck Callie as overly elaborate for an office as well, with the molding trim making large squares in the walls from floor to ceiling. But apparently it had a purpose. What had Ashby hidden behind it? She felt along the molding and found the crack. Then another, about six inches away. A section of the molding was a separate piece.

"That's it," Paula said. "Turn it down toward the floor."

Callie did. Doing so uncovered a locking bolt. Looking more closely, she also saw a faint vertical crack in the paneling that ran up at least six feet from the floor. The outline of a door?

"Now, slide the bolt open and pull," Paula instructed.

Callie hesitated, not liking how Paula had moved up close behind her.

"Go ahead!" Paula urged.

Callie slid the bolt and tugged at it. A door swung toward her, revealing a shallow room, possibly four feet deep. It was paneled the same as the office and had a row of shelves on its back wall.

"Ashby built this?"

"It must have been here to begin with. A cubby to hide runaway slaves, maybe. Nothing this fancy, of course. He discovered it and had it redone for his own use. And look! There, on the shelves. Those piles of papers are the dirt he'd been collecting on people."

Callie's eyes swept the mounds of papers along with boxes that might have held even more papers, or photos. She knew that Ashby had worked in the court system. Was all this from records he'd copied and smuggled out? How long had it been going on?

"So you knew about this?" She was thinking of the anonymous note left at her door that gave Lyssa's real name and called her a murderer. "You've gone through some of it?"

"Why shouldn't I? Was I invading his privacy? With what he was doing?"

"No, I—"

"I suppose you think I'm just as bad as he is. Because of what I did to him. You should thank me for getting rid of him!"

Paula had grown agitated again. Callie tried to step back, to face her and talk to her calmly. But Paula quickly blocked her. "See what he was doing?" she cried, pointing her knife at the secret room. "I put an end to it. But you, all you can think about is what I did. If that's what matters to you, I'll give you plenty of time to think."

Callie instinctively grabbed the edges of the door frame, but Paula was too strong for her and pushed her into the small room and against the shelves. She heard the door slam behind her and the bolt click into place. All was dark except for a sliver of light at the bottom edge of the door.

She banged her fists on the door. "Paula, don't do this. Please! Open this door! Paula!" But she heard nothing in response, and in a moment the sliver of light went out.

Thirty-One

*C*allie continued to hammer at the door, calling out to Paula. She tried throwing her weight against it, then kicking, but gradually saw it was hopeless. The door and its bolt were too strong for her, plus she could gain no leverage in the shallow room.

She slid to the floor. What could she do? Was there any hope? Her cell phone was in her purse, sitting on the office desk. The inn was currently empty of guests. George planned to return, according to Paula, but when? Perhaps never if his grandchild's emergency became too serious. Lyssa, she knew, had left her things behind and would need to return, which lifted Callie's hopes briefly until she remembered how Lyssa had sped off in tears. After being accused of murder, she might decide to send for her things and never come back. And who could blame her?

Callie knew she would be missed, but after how long? Who would think to look for her here? Paula could keep the inn to herself by turning away guests until she was sure Callie was dead. And who would know? Was this it? Was she doomed to a slow death in this secret tomb?

The thought was too much. Callie pulled herself up to pound and kick again at the door. It did nothing toward freeing her, but it burned off some of the panic that had threatened to paralyze her. She needed to rid herself of emotion and stick to rational thought.

As she calmed, still panting from her efforts, she realized that the small enclosure she was locked in hadn't grown stuffy, meaning it wasn't airtight. That was obviously a good thing. But the door she'd opened from the office had fitted snugly into the paneling. It likely wasn't allowing much air to flow in. So it must be coming in some other way. How?

Unable to see her hands in front of her face, Callie reached blindly toward the side wall to her right. With no shelves attached to it, it was at least a place to start. She leaned her face close to it as she slid her hands downward over the same paneling and molding that had covered the office walls. When she got to the floor, she felt it. A flow of air coming in where the wall didn't quite meet the floor. Could it be a way out? Callie's hopes rose—minimally.

As she pondered her next move, she caught a whiff of something else that made her freeze. Smoke. It was very faint, but she was certain it was coming from the office. She bent down to press her nose against that slit, confirming her suspicion. She tried at first to convince herself it was cigarette smoke. Or cooking smoke drifting from the kitchen. But it wasn't that kind of smell. She'd never seen a working fireplace in the inn. She was sure of that. Which left only one thing. The inn was on fire. And she was trapped and would die a much worse death than what she'd imagined!

Panic threatened to block all thought. Her impulse was to once more kick wildly to try to break through some part of the room. But that hadn't worked the first time, and it would cost her energy she couldn't afford to waste. She had to think! There must be a way.

The creaks. She thought of the creaks George had heard behind his wall and the unaccounted-for space at one end of his closet. Ashby had suddenly appeared in that room while Kelsey was cleaning its bathroom. Was there more to this runaway slave hideaway than this lone cubby? Was there a way to get to other parts of the inn from here? A way that Ashby had discovered, and in the process of restoration had hidden so cleverly that Paula never found it?

Callie ran her hands over the side wall again, growing desperate as the smell of smoke increased. Nothing, nothing … then she stopped as it came to her. The bolt in the door from the office had been hidden behind the molding. It could be the same here.

Her fingers inched their way across a row of molding that was about the same height as the office door's. She tried section after section, but none of it would turn downward. She coughed. More smoke had filled the space. She had to hurry. What if there was nothing to find? If there was no door. No escape? Just as panic threatened to rise again, a piece of the molding moved. She twisted it. There was a bolt underneath. She cried out in relief, but there was no time to celebrate. She had to get out.

The bolt slid easily. It had obviously been used often. She first pulled it toward her. When that didn't work, she pushed. The door that had been smoothly fitted into the paneling moved outward. It was just as dark on the outside, but the air was fresher. Callie took one tentative step and found a solid floor. Stretching out one arm, she felt another wall, seemingly an extension of the shelved wall of the hidden room. Had she just moved from one trap to another? But then she touched the opposite wall, the one that she guessed would parallel the inn's main staircase. There was a ladder attached to it! Where it led she didn't know, but it was at least a way to escape the coffin of a room she'd been in. She tested the lower rungs and found them solid, then set one foot on a rung, grabbed a higher one, and started to climb.

She had to assume that Paula had set fire to the inn—that it wasn't accidental. Was she trying to cover her tracks by erasing all signs of Callie having been there? There was still the problem of her car parked in the drive. What could Paula do about that?

Callie's foot slipped on one of the rungs, and she held on tight to keep from falling. Concentrate, she admonished herself. With nothing to distinguish either above or below her, she could only guess she'd gone up about five feet. She kept climbing.

What would she do if the second floor of the inn was on fire? Don't think of that, she told herself. Just climb as fast as possible without falling. She worried about finding her way out of this inner passage at the top, but urged herself to keep focused. One thing at a time.

Her head brushed something. She reached up and felt the edge of a board. Directly above was empty space. She climbed one more rung, then another. The board to the right seemed to be part of a landing. An additional rung upward and she could slide onto it. The ladder had come to an end, so it was all she could do. She did so, carefully, and as she slid over, she realized she was in an enclosed passageway of some kind. But exactly where?

She crawled forward, taking the time to feel her way as she went, both on the floor in front of her and on each side. It was slow going, and when she thought of the fire that might be spreading, she had to fight the urge to stand and run. That could be just as dangerous. Without any light to guide her, she could fall into another ladder opening. The thought was stomach-clenching.

She'd grown disoriented as to exactly where she was in relation to the rest of the inn. She hoped it was somewhere behind the upper guest rooms. If George's room had an entry into the closet, she needed to find it and soon. Her time could be running out. How would she know, though, if she'd reached it or not?

Then she heard the sound. It was so faint, at first, that she feared she was hallucinating. But as she moved forward it grew loud enough for her to believe what she was hearing. Music. A tune. *The Surrey with the Fringe on Top*. It was George's music box! And she was within inches of it. She had found George's closet!

Callie ran her hands over the wooden section on her left, looking for the same bolt-lock arrangement she'd found on the office and cubbyhole doors. Nothing. There must be a way to get in. When she and Lyssa had tapped on that wall from inside the closet, the sound was definitely hollow. She must be on the other side of it now. But how to make it open?

Then she found it. A small metal button. She pressed and heard a spring release. The door moved slightly toward her, and she could grab the edge with her fingertips and pull it farther. There was enough light on the other side for her to see the outlines of a few hanging garments. George's closet door had been left open, and moonlight from the window had made its way in. Dim as it was, it was a life-saving beacon to Callie compared to the total darkness she'd just been in.

She crawled in, her hand touching a shoe, then a fallen belt, until she made it through the closet and into the room. There, on a small table, she saw the package holding George's music box that Paula had brought up. The music box had been well-wound, she knew, having tested the mechanism herself before packing it up. But what had made it play? She had no time to wonder. She had to keep moving.

She stood, then, feeling dizzy with the relief of having made it out of the claustrophobic tunnel. But the relief was short-lived as she saw smoke curling under the closed door of George's room.

She had to get out, but when she pressed her hand against the hall door, she felt the heat. That way out was closed to her. She rushed into the bathroom and grabbed a bath towel to throw into the tub. She spun the faucet open to soak it, then rolled and jammed the towel against the base of the hallway door. That would give her a little time.

She looked around frantically for a phone but saw none. With no way to call for help, she ran over to the window. The moonlight allowed her to see the outlines of a tree, some branches stretching close to the window. Were they sturdy enough to hold her? Could she reach them?

She found the window latch and released it, then paused to look back at the hall door. The wet towel was apparently working, as she saw no smoke making its way through. But that wouldn't last. Her only way out was through the window. She threw up the sash.

The rush of cold air was bracing. But the thought of trusting her life to something that she had no way of judging for strength or condition was terrifying. She leaned out to grab the closest branch and pressed on it. It barely moved. A good sign, perhaps. But could she get her whole self onto it? Swinging from it by her hands twenty feet from the ground was terrifying. Plus she realized, as she peered downward, that she was directly over a basement window well. If she slipped and fell, there was no soft landing below.

She waited, screwing up her courage to make that first move, and had just about reached it when she heard the siren. Then she saw the flashing lights coming around a curve. A fire truck! And it was moving toward her.

"Over here, over here!" She screamed and waved, knowing they were still much too far away to see or hear her. But they were coming! And they would find her. She would be okay.

Thirty-Two

"A passing motorist saw flames coming from the inn and called it in," one of the firefighters told Callie as she perched at the back of an ambulance. Despite her protests that she was fine beyond a few scrapes and bruises, an EMT had insisted on checking her out. She was exceedingly glad not to have had to attempt a Tarzan-like escape from the inn via the tree and grateful to her rescuers, including the alert motorist.

"How bad is the damage?" she asked as the smoke-smudged firefighter took a well-earned water break. The hoses had stopped pumping and were being rolled up.

"Looks like it'll be salvageable," he said, which she was glad to hear. She didn't know what insurance would cover in a situation like this, but with luck Dorothy might have a structure to repair and then either reopen or sell. Callie had given her account to a police officer of what had happened inside the Foxwood Inn that led to the fire, and was assured by him that Paula would almost certainly be found soon.

That meant the truth of Cliff Ashby's murder would come out and Dorothy's ordeal would be over.

But then Callie thought of Renata Moore's murder. Paula had only admitted to killing Ashby. Could she have been responsible for both murders? Callie grimaced, unable to see how that was likely, and doubted the police would be able to connect Paula to it. That meant Dorothy might still be labeled a murder suspect.

❧

On her return home, Callie was fussed over first by Delia, then by Brian, and urged by both to take the next day off. Though reluctant at first, she was glad she'd agreed to it when she woke the next morning to stiff and sore muscles. Some of that, she was sure, had come from agitated dreams that had replayed her ordeal. She had just poured a mug of coffee after getting up when she heard a knock on her door and went to answer it, half expecting that Delia had come to check on her. Much to her surprise, it was Lyssa.

"Hi," Lyssa said in an uncharacteristically subdued manner. Her hair lay flat against her head instead of rising in its usual perky spikes, and she appeared to be wearing the same clothes from the previous day. She looked as though she'd spent the night in her car. "Got another one of those?" she asked, pointing to the coffee mug.

"Of course. Come in." Callie quickly led the way to the kitchen and filled a second mug. "Where have you been?" she asked, handing it over. "Didn't you go back to your house?"

Lyssa shook her head before taking a tentative sip from her mug, then turned back to the living room. "I've got a lot to say, so you might as well get comfortable."

Callie took a seat across from the author and waited.

"First of all," Lyssa said, "I heard about Paula and the B&B. Are you okay?"

"I'm fine. And at least Dorothy's off the hook for Cliff's murder."

"And maybe for Renata's, too. That's partly what I came to tell you." Lyssa took another sip, then drew a tired breath. "God, how did we miss that it was Paula?" she asked, shaking her head. "There I was, seeing her every day but apparently looking right through her."

"I don't know. Looking back, I can see signs. But we just didn't pick up on them. You said you had something to share about Renata?"

"Right. Well, after we talked yesterday morning—geesh, it seems like a month ago!—I didn't go back home. I drove around a while. I was upset. But once I got over feeling sorry for myself, I started thinking about the person who was worse off—Dorothy. She's been going through a lot of what I went through. I couldn't fix anything for myself, but I thought maybe I could do something for her. So I went back to Easton."

"Easton? To talk to Doug Moore?"

"Actually, I spoke with Gayle Hawkins."

"The woman in his office," Callie said.

"Doug was out, and she was free, so we had a good long chat. When we were there the first time, I could see that she was aware of Doug's memory problems. She was trying her best to cover for him as well as keep him on track. So I told her about how Jerry was using his brother as an alibi for his wife's murder and how someone else was the chief suspect because of that. Gayle said she'd never liked Jerry, that she'd watched him take advantage of Doug's good nature far too often. She knew about the murder, but she didn't know details like timing and such, and she didn't know Jerry had claimed Doug as an alibi."

"So what does that change?" Callie asked.

"What changes is that Gayle can attest to the fact that Jerry arrived at Doug's house much later than he said."

"Really! How?"

"She happened to be driving past Doug's house late Tuesday evening, the night of the book event and Renata's murder. She'd been out with friends, and her way home took her past Doug's house. She's been concerned about him for a while since she's been aware of his memory slips, and she automatically slowed down to glance over at his house, just to see if everything looked all right—like, that he hadn't left his front door wide open or his car running. She saw Jerry getting out of his car in the driveway and Doug coming out to greet him. Jerry had just arrived, and it was nearly eleven."

"Eleven! Renata's time of death was put as early as ten. So Jerry could have done it."

"I've reported this to the police, and they're probably talking to Jerry right now. Or maybe Gayle first, I don't know. But I think it looks pretty bad for Jerry and a lot better for Dorothy."

"Absolutely. That was terrific of you, Lyssa. If this gets Dorothy off the hook, she'll have her life back."

Lyssa made a small, tired smile, and swallowed more of her coffee. She drew a deep breath. "I think I owe you an explanation about that other thing. You know, the anonymous letter."

Callie drew in a breath. "That probably came from Paula," she said. "And I've been thinking of all the other things she must have caused—the canceled book order, the hay wagon fire, and your stomach illness. She wanted to get rid of you to stop all the probing into Ashby's murder."

"You were a target, too."

"She came after me next. After she'd taken you out of the picture. Or thought she did."

"Well, she didn't make up the stuff about me in that letter. And that's what I need to talk about."

Callie grew quiet. Did she want to hear what Lyssa was going to say? This could change a lot between them. But the door had been opened by the letter. The truth had to come out. She waited.

"It happened in my teens," Lyssa began, "one summer, near where I grew up in Eldersburg. A bunch of us were driving around one night, bored. At least, I was bored. I wanted excitement. I always did." She'd started speaking faster now as if she needed to get it all out before she lost her courage. "I talked everyone into going swimming in the reservoir. I was a good swimmer and didn't think twice about it. Justin wasn't, and I knew that. I should never have urged him to jump in that night." She hesitated. "I was the first. The others held back, but I called them chickens, over and over. Justin finally couldn't stand it anymore. He took a running jump and sank. Maybe he hit his head on something. I don't know. But he didn't come up."

Tears had sprung to her eyes. "At first I thought he was fooling around. Then the kids on the bank started screaming at me to help him. But I couldn't. I tried, I really tried, but I couldn't find him in time to save him. He drowned, and it was all my fault."

A long silence followed as Callie absorbed this. "You were in your teens?"

Lyssa nodded. "Sixteen."

"Kids that age don't think things out so well."

"His parents filed a wrongful death suit. They blamed me, and they were right. They said that I"—she looked up as though reading the words on the ceiling—"had knowingly coerced their son into extremely risky action that ended up causing his death." She paused. "It was dismissed a year later."

"So you weren't responsible."

Lyssa shook her head. "Not legally, but I knew it was my fault. And a lot of other people back home thought so, too." She wiped away her tears. "Anyway, when I started writing, I decided not to be Alissa Hanson anymore. I didn't like her very much." She shrugged. "So there you are."

Callie looked at the misery on Lyssa's face and the effort it had taken for her to talk about an incident that continued to pain her after so many years. She got up and went over to kneel in front of her. "I'm sorry this had to come out, and that I thought—just a little because of what Paula wrote—that Cliff might have been blackmailing you with it. But I think you need to forgive yourself, don't you? I believe it was truly accidental, and besides the name change, you're not the same person you were at sixteen. You're a good and responsible person. I've seen that." She reached up to hug her friend, feeling her shivering until finally Lyssa pulled back.

"Thank you," Lyssa said softly. After a few gulps of coffee she managed a weak smile. They stayed silent for a long while until Callie felt a nudge at her side. Jagger had come down from the bedroom to join them. He put his paws up on Lyssa's knees, and after a moment she scratched his head, only blocking his efforts to jump onto her lap. Lyssa was not a cat person. She did, however, smile a little more strongly.

When Callie scooped Jagger up and carried him to the sofa, Lyssa stood as well. "Hey, can I use your shower?" she asked. "And maybe run a couple of things through your washer? If any of my stuff at the inn wasn't burned up, it's probably either smoky or melted." She ran her fingers through her hair. "Oh, and got any hair gel?"

Callie smiled and led her up the stairs. Her friend was back. She was happy to lend her anything she needed.

❧

Later, when Lyssa had left, Callie had a second visitor. It was Dorothy, and she'd arrived holding a casserole.

"I know it's nothing compared to what you did," Dorothy said, looking down at the foil-covered dish, "but it's the most I could manage on short notice. Besides, it's what I do when I'm excited."

Callie happily accepted the dish as well as a long hug from Dorothy. "I'm just so glad your ordeal is over," she said, waving Dorothy in.

"Except for Renata," Dorothy said, stepping into the cottage. "From what I understand, Paula had nothing to do with *her* murder."

"She didn't, but I think there's a good possibility you'll be cleared on that one very soon." Callie went to the kitchen and slipped Dorothy's casserole into the refrigerator. "Coffee? Tea?"

"Just water, please, with ice if you have it." Dorothy took a seat on the sofa. "What do you mean?"

Callie ran a tall glass under the tap and added several ice cubes. "I mean that Jerry's alibi has been blown, and the police are looking more closely at him now." She brought the glass to Dorothy and took the nearby chair. "We will probably hear more before too long."

"Oh, it will be such a relief to have it all washed away. Of course, it won't be, not totally. Such terrible crimes don't go away without leaving their mark." She took a tiny sip of her water, then said, "Jane has told me all."

Callie nodded and waited to learn what sort of mark that might have left on Dorothy.

"I wish she'd told me long ago about what happened with Cliff. It was a painful secret for her to keep for so long. She said she felt she'd betrayed me and couldn't bear to hurt me further by telling me. And then there were her children, who never knew about their older sibling." Dorothy shook her head. "You may find it all hard to understand, hiding such things, but it was a different time. Plus, after a person has buried something deep inside for years, it becomes nearly impossible to speak of it."

"Cliff must have counted on that," Callie said.

"I blame myself for bringing Cliff into both our lives," Dorothy said, her eyes downcast.

"The blame, I think, is his," Callie said.

"If you're right, he was more than punished." Dorothy drew a long breath. "Jane told me she took the scissors with her at the last minute that night for her own defense. She was, after all, going out alone in the middle of the night. She didn't know what she was thinking when she actually pulled them out. She was so upset and frightened. When he took them from her, she ran off. She said she was horrified when they said the scissors were what killed him, and she couldn't understand it. But she felt too paralyzed to say anything. If she admitted she'd left the scissors there, she'd most likely be charged with a murder she didn't commit. She said it was tearing her up inside. And as things grew worse and worse for me, she was on the verge of going to the police. But then Renata Moore was murdered, and with another pair of scissors! She couldn't believe it and thought she was going crazy."

Dorothy paused to take a deep breath. "I truly believe she would have spoken up very soon if you hadn't brought things to a head as you did. You have to understand how difficult this was for Jane. She's never been a strong person, and Richard's death was a blow that left her floundering. She'd relied on him for so much. Oh, her children stepped in to help where they could, but it isn't the same as a husband, is it?"

Dorothy appeared to be excusing Jane's inaction and ready to forgive it. Callie wasn't sure she could be as generous, but it was Dorothy's choice, not hers. She knew the two had grown up more like sisters than cousins, which meant a lot. Dorothy might also have sympathized with Jane's struggle because of the paralysis she herself had felt during much of her married life before she finally found the strength to leave Cliff.

"I don't know where things will lead with her and George Cole," Dorothy said, "but I have my hopes up. He could be just what Jane needs."

"Has she heard from him?"

"She has. His granddaughter is better, and he intends to drive back in a day or so. They'll probably have a lot to work out," she admitted.

Callie nodded agreement. But she remembered the care with which George had chosen his music box gift for Jane, and the years that Jane's memory had apparently lingered in his heart. She had a feeling things would come together for them.

Thinking of the music box reminded her of the part it had played when she was struggling to find her way out of the dark, smoky passageway at the inn. She'd set all thought of it aside in the heat of the moment but since then had mulled it over. This didn't mean she'd come to any conclusion. Far from it. But Grandpa Reed's music box had seemed to send her messages and warnings ever since Aunt Mel died, and now George's new music box had led her out of a very tight spot by its playing. Coincidence? Or had her "guardian angel," whoever that might be, taken to music box hopping?

The image made her smile, and she realized she'd likely never know. Or know for sure. Best not to overthink some things and just be grateful. Getting a little help now and then, however it comes, isn't such a bad thing.

⚮

"Trick-or-treat!" The three-foot-tall astronaut waddled through *House of Melody*'s doorway in his moon boots and bubble helmet, stiffly holding out his plastic pumpkin as a diminutive Wonder Woman followed behind.

"Wow, neat costumes," Tabitha cried. Though it wasn't her usual time to be at the shop, no way was she going to miss being a part of the biggest dress-up day of the year. She had taken one of Callie's musical globes for children as inspiration and transformed herself into Mary Poppins, complete with umbrella and flower-trimmed hat, which earned her open-mouthed stares from the younger trick-or-treaters. Callie had decided to keep it simple and dress only as a shop owner and official candy dispenser.

Halloween night was the high point of Keepsake Cove's fall celebration, which had officially begun with Lyssa's book event, and it had drawn scores of families with their costumed little ones to wander streets filled with live music and shop. Things had started to wind down, with these latest two trick-or-treaters looking to be their last, and Tabitha had started to eye the packaged M&Ms and Milk Duds that remained.

"Help yourself," Callie encouraged her, grateful to have had Tabitha's help on that busy night. She'd already opened a box of Gummy Bears for herself, a treat she hadn't had since she was a kid, and soon remembered why as the rubbery candies quickly stuck to her teeth.

Brian wandered over from his café, which she saw he'd closed up. "I'm done," he announced, and within a minute Delia joined them as well.

"A successful night!" she exclaimed. "Looks like Keepsake Cove has managed to hold on to its reputation as a family destination, thank goodness."

"It's because Jerry's arrest for Renata's murder was overshadowed two days later by that major earthquake in Mexico," Brian said. "That's all people have heard or thought about since. It's amazing how quickly something can become old news."

"So they traced the scissors that were used to kill Renata to him, huh?" Tabitha asked.

Brian nodded. "He bought them at a place that called itself an antique shop but mostly carried a lot of junk. He apparently thought anything old would look like it came from *Stitches Thru Time*. He paid cash, but there was a security camera that caught him making the transaction."

"Lucky, especially for Dorothy," Delia said. "Horrible man. And he did it to get at Renata's money, from what I heard."

"That's what's been coming out," Callie said. "Renata had a sizeable inheritance from her father, but she was holding on to it tightly. Jerry wanted to get his hands on it, maybe to take advantage of the investment opportunity Vernon Parks was dangling in front of him, which could happen if Dorothy needed to sell the Foxwood Inn in a hurry. Or maybe just to have money without Renata pulling all the strings.

They were not a happy couple, despite the jolly front they put on for their customers. I think he already had incentives to get rid of her."

"Did he kill her in the park because that's where Cliff Ashby had been killed?" Tabitha asked.

"Probably," Brian said. "It was a copycat murder from the start, using scissors and the same location."

"Except, thanks to Callie, we now know that it was really Paula's knife that killed Ashby," Tabitha pointed out.

"And her multiple jabs with the scissors apparently covered up the knife wounds as far as the forensics were concerned," Callie said. "But it was thanks to Lyssa's research that Jerry's alibi was destroyed."

"What a team you made," Tabitha said. "Who knew, when you invited Lyssa to come and talk about her books, what you'd both be getting into."

Yes, Callie thought, who knew? It had turned out all right, all things considered. But she still had occasional nightmares about her harrowing crawl through that hidden passageway that Ashby had used to gather information on unwitting guests or creep up on an attractive young maid. And would Lyssa have accepted her invitation if she'd had the least inkling that a painful part of her past would be revealed?

Callie hadn't seen Lyssa since she'd left the cottage the day after the fire, though she'd received a couple of brief texts. She assumed Lyssa had gone back to her home in DC, where the renovations might be done, perhaps happy to wipe all thoughts of Keepsake Cove from her memory. Callie was just about to say to the others that it had been great knowing Lyssa but that she'd probably moved on when a flash of red pulled up in front of the shop, followed by two sharp honks. A familiar, roundish figure clothed in a khaki trench coat, her red hair once again spiked jauntily, jumped out of the Corvette and burst into *House of Melody.*

"Congratulate me," Lyssa said. "I just bought myself a nice little house not very far outside of Keepsake Cove. Woo-hoo!"

As a chorus of congratulations rose up, she added, "It's waterfront, so I might get myself a boat of some kind. Or maybe a kayak! I've always wanted to try kayaking. But it has a cute little den overlooking the water, that I can use to write. And guess what? I have a great idea for a murder mystery."

She held up her hands to frame the words of her projected title as the others waited with uneasy expressions. *"Murder in Keep*... Hah! Just kidding!" she cried, laughing as the shopkeepers exhaled. "We've had enough real excitement around here, haven't we? Maybe I'll write a nice romance instead, just for a change."

"You're really moving here?" Callie asked, not sure if that part was a joke as well, though she hoped it wasn't.

"For at least part of the time," Lyssa said. "I still need my city living. But this'll be great for getaways."

"That's terrific," Callie said, and the others agreed. "But I admit it's the last thing I expected."

"I've got wine at the café," Brian said. "How about we head there for a welcome toast?"

"Yes!" four voices said at once, and Callie scrambled to close her shop as the others went ahead. It was wonderful to have something to celebrate that wasn't related to police activities. And Lyssa was going to be close now! How great that was going to be. Or was it?

Callie paused in the act of closing up her register. After all, it was Lyssa, she remembered, who'd insisted she get involved in solving Clifford Ashby's murder. And that tan trench coat she'd arrived in looked suspiciously close to being a *Lyssa Hammond, Private Eye* outfit.

Callie laughed. No way. Lyssa had surely had enough of murder and mayhem, just as she had. She most certainly was looking forward to nothing more than quiet, possibly even boring, times. Besides, Keepsake Cove had surely met its quota for major crime. She grabbed her keys and flicked off the lights. Nothing worse than jaywalking or littering was likely to happen around here now.

A car filled with boisterous teens dressed for Halloween drove noisily by as Callie pulled the door closed behind her, so she didn't hear the tune playing softly inside her shop. If she had, she might have had a second thought.

The tune, after all, was coming from Grandpa Reed's music box.

The End

Acknowledgments

Many thanks, once again, to the patient and supportive members of my critique group: Shaun Taylor Bevins, Becky Hutchison, Debbi Mack, Sherriel Mattingly, Bonnie Settle, Beth Schmelzer, and Marcia Talley, for keeping me on track, on schedule, and quite often in stitches.

I'm very grateful for the efforts of Terri Bischoff, Sandy Sullivan, and the entire Midnight Ink team, who saw that my story made it into print at its best, and to Kim Lionetti, who got the ball rolling.

Top thanks go, as always, to my husband, Terry, who listens to my often tangled ideas and helps straighten them out as well as willingly pitches in to find ways around the dreaded blank wall when it appears. This might have been a very different book without him.

© Angela Powell Woulfe

About the Author

Mary Ellen Hughes is the bestselling author of the Pickled and Preserved Mysteries (Penguin), the Craft Corner Mysteries (Penguin), and the Maggie Olenski Mysteries (Avalon), along with several short stories. *A Vintage Death* continues her Keepsake Cove mystery series with Midnight Ink, which began with *A Fatal Collection*. A Wisconsin native, she has lived most of her adult life in Maryland, where she's set many of her stories. Visit her online at www.MaryEllenHughes.com.